# NOT FOOLING ANYONE

## LESSONS LEARNED BOOK #2

### ALLIE WINTERS

WWW.SMARTYPANTSROMANCE.COM

# COPYRIGHT

# CONTENT WARNING

Please be aware that this story contains mature themes including mentions of attempted assault and parents with substance abuse issues.

# CHAPTER ONE

## LEXIE

"DON'T FORGET rent's due tomorrow."

Shit. Is it the end of the month already?

I keep applying my winged eyeliner, not looking at Travis. "Thanks, I'll get it to you."

He lingers in the doorway of my room, shuffling his feet, until I have no choice but to look over.

"And you still owe me for last month's electric and water bills," he hedges, clearly uncomfortable.

Damn it, I know. It's been the only thing on my mind for the past two weeks.

I stand and grab my phone off my dresser. "Oh my God, I totally forgot. I'll send it to you right now."

Well, looks like it'll be ramen for breakfast, lunch, and dinner with my empty bank account. I won't start out on the wrong foot living with my best friend. I'm already so lucky he agreed to let me move in after his roommate graduated and left.

I can't mess this up. There's nowhere else to go.

"Thanks." His relief is obvious, but along with it comes a kernel of guilt that wedges its way into the pit of my stomach. He shouldn't have to ask me for the money I owe him.

He walks behind me, fingering a long strand of my dark auburn hair in its high ponytail. "How about you come out with me and Isaac tonight for dinner? My treat."

God, he's too good to me. I don't want to intrude on his time with his boyfriend, though. "I'd love to, but I'm working."

"Rain check, then?"

"Definitely."

He leaves, the room seeming to dim without him, and I finish applying my makeup in silence, then open the bifold doors of the closet to find my faux leather bustier. I swear I make better tips when I wear it, so I've pretty much made it my bartending uniform along with low-cut jeans that show off my midriff.

I head outside, wincing at the screech of my car door as I open it. Maybe I should buy some WD-40 for it. Heaven knows the whole thing's only running on duct tape and sheer luck.

I hate the longer commute it takes to get to Element, the club I bartend at, but it's more upscale compared to my last dive. And that means better tips. Now if only I can get them to give me more shifts.

One of the other bartenders gives me a head nod as I enter through the back door. "I didn't know you were working tonight."

I pause, sliding my bag off my shoulder. "I was the last time I checked."

"Oh, I think Sarah changed the schedule."

I stow my stuff in an empty locker, then head out to the bar, pasting on a smile as I see our shift leader. "Hey, I'm here. What do you need help with?" It kills me to play nice with her, but I'm never going to get the lucrative Friday and Saturday night shifts if I don't.

"Oh, Lexie," she simpers. "I meant to text you. You're not needed tonight."

I grit my teeth, keeping the smile on my face. "Well, I was on the schedule when I last checked."

"Yeah, I had to switch some things around since then. But it's up to you to check the latest version of the schedule."

Is this lady for real? If she changes it and doesn't tell me, how the hell am I supposed to know? "So I should call every night to see if I'm actually working?"

Her gaze sharpens. "You don't have to be snotty about it."

I firm my jaw even more to contain the expletive that wants to come out. "Well, since I'm already here, can I still work? I'll run drinks or clean tables. Whatever you need help with."

"We're covered, thanks," she says, blatantly dismissing me before turning around.

My fists ball at my sides, but what am I going to do? Fight her?

I return to the back, glancing at the schedule hanging on the bulletin board, and lo and behold, I have no shifts again till next Monday night. Enough to keep me on without actually firing me. Why'd they hire me if they don't want to put me to work?

I take a little too much pleasure in slamming my locker door as I retrieve my bag and stalk back out to the parking lot. The whole reason I quit my last bar was to make more money here, not work one crappy shift a week.

I check my phone before I start my car, seeing a text from Dad.

**Dad**: *Can you stop by the gym? I have a business opportunity for you.*

What's he on about now?

Well, I've got nowhere else to be. I'm not admitting to Travis I'm not getting shifts at work. Then he'll know I can't afford rent. I literally have just enough in my account to pay my half tomorrow.

**Me**: *Be there in ten.*

I head over to Marty's Boxing Gym where Dad works, holding onto the handrail as I descend the outside steps to the basement level. Why people willingly work out in this dank place, I'll never understand.

As I'm about to open the door, I happen to glance down and catch myself, remembering the bustier. Oops. I run back to my car and slip on my hoodie, using the end of the sleeve to cover my nose as I enter the gym. It's like they've never heard of actually cleaning the equipment. Or showering.

A few guys look in my direction, but most are focused on hitting speed bags, skipping rope, or punching heavy bags. Over to the left is the big ring, with a burly guy in the center calling out commands. That'd be Dad. With him are two others, one on the offensive and one guarding.

I wander over to the edge of the ring, sighing at the needless brutality of it all.

"You interested in training?"

I glance over, cut biceps the first thing I notice. Ugh, save me from boxers. Every time I come in here, at least one of them has the bright idea to hit on me.

"No." I keep my gaze straight ahead, waiting for Dad to finish up.

"Lawrence is the best trainer at this gym. If you were interested, he'd be your guy."

Is he trying to make small talk or something? "Look, I'm not interested, okay?" In training or him.

He continues to stand next to me and I finally take a peek, finding a guy my age with vivid green eyes and an amused smile on his face. His teeth are almost startlingly white against the dark of his beard.

That's weird. These guys don't usually smile. They're too focused on their bloodlust.

"No problem," he says easily, turning his attention back to the ring.

I stand there, slightly unnerved. That's the first time a guy hasn't gotten defensive or slunk away when I make it clear I'm not receptive to whatever they're offering. Is this a mind game or something he's playing?

4

Dad finally turns my way, noticing me, and takes a moment to set the guys he's coaching up with training drills, telling them he'll be back in a few.

"Lex." He slips through the ringside ropes and hops down, pulling me into a sweaty hug.

"Ew, Dad. You're all gross." I push him away and he wipes his face off with a random towel laying across the ropes. God, I hope that was his.

"I see you met Ethan. He's not like the other meatheads around here."

"Who you calling a meathead?" one guy in the ring calls out good-naturedly.

Dad turns to trade insults with the guy, and I glance over again at the dark-bearded man. Ethan. I highly doubt he's all that different from the other brainless idiots getting their heads punched willingly.

"All right, sit tight and I'll go tell Marty you're here."

"For what? You didn't say whatever this business opportunity is."

"Marty needs a bookkeeper. I told him you could do it."

"Me?" I clear my throat to get rid of the squeakiness. "I'm not certified to do that."

"Yeah, but you know how, right? You took a class on it or something?"

"I mean, I'm an accounting major. I understand theoretically how to do it. But I've never actually done it for a business."

He waves his hand to dismiss my concerns. "You'll learn on the job. And I already talked you up to Marty."

Of course he did. This is just like him to assume everything will work out fine without thinking through the details. "Dad, I'm not dressed for an interview." I point to my face. "I've got my slutty makeup on to get tips at the bar." Not to mention I'm wearing a bustier, for Christ's sake. Thank God I had stowed my hoodie in my car earlier.

"And how's that working out for you? Are you at the bar now making tips?"

I complained to him last week about how I wasn't getting enough shifts there when he asked. He knows I need the money.

"You said you wanted a side hustle, so here it is."

I resist the urge to roll my eyes. It's actually kind of sweet of him to look out for me like this. "Fine, I'll talk to Marty."

He nods, walking across the gym to an office door and knocking.

"Bookkeeping, huh? Sounds exciting."

I glance over at Ethan, who, for some reason, is still hanging around. "Sure, I guess."

"Do you like your major?"

I turn to face him. "Look, no offense, but I don't date boxers." Or anyone, actually. But no need to go into that. "So you don't have to make conversation or anything."

His gaze dances with mirth as he angles his big body toward me, completely unexpected from how I thought he'd recoil. "I don't recall asking you out. But it's interesting how your mind went straight there." He grins, his eyes crinkling at the corners.

"So what are you doing, then?"

He crosses his arms over his chest, but if he thinks I'm intimidated by all those muscles, he's forgotten who my dad is. "It's called being polite." He doesn't say it with censure, but the implication is there all the same.

Heat crawls up my neck, but I pretend like it's not happening. I'm in too deep now. "Well, you don't have to be. We don't know each other."

"Yeah, but maybe we will. You'll be around here more often if you get this bookkeeping gig."

"I won't be out on the floor with the meatheads."

"Ouch." He smiles as he says it, clearly not taking me seriously. "I thought Lawrence gave me a pass."

My lips quirk, though I didn't tell them to. "You're all meatheads."

He laughs, the sound rich and full of warmth.

"Lex." Dad waves to get my attention. "He's ready for you."

"Well, it was nice to *meat* you, Lex," Ethan says, still grinning.

I blink up at him. "Did you make a pun?"

"Yep." He beams, way too pleased with himself.

Seriously, who is this guy? "It's Lexie," I tell him. "Only my dad calls me Lex." Just Dad and… Nope. Not thinking about her.

"All right, Lexie." There's friendliness in his gaze, but in my experience, it rarely stops there. Guys always want more.

"I have to go," I blurt out, heading across the gym. I don't need some random boxer getting in my head. I apparently have an interview to see about.

I cautiously move past Dad into Marty's office, eyeing the gruff man behind the desk. I've never actually met him, only heard about him from Dad, but he looks exactly how I pictured with his grizzled face and military-style haircut.

"It's nice to meet you," I tell him, sticking out my hand for a handshake, but all I can think about is Ethan saying the same stupid thing. Ugh.

"Let's get to it," he says, returning my handshake before motioning for me to take a seat across from his desk. A man with little time for pleasantries. Finally, someone with their priorities straight.

He opens a filing cabinet and pulls out an honest-to-God ledger. I didn't know people still used those. "My eyes are getting tired looking at all these columns and rows, and I'm doing well enough now to outsource it. Lawrence said you're good at this stuff."

I take the ledger from him and flip through it, trying to decipher his chicken scratch handwriting. "I am. But I'll be honest, I've never actually used a physical one of these. Everything is online now."

"Online," he mutters. "Call me a Luddite, but doing it on paper works fine."

I hide my smile. "I agree. It does work fine. But you can reduce errors and save time by letting the computer do the math for you."

He grumbles something under his breath but concedes my point. "Tell me about your qualifications."

7

I rack my brain, wishing I could have rehearsed, and list for him the classes I've taken for my major, including a small project I worked on last semester that involved some bookkeeping exercises. "I will say," I admit, "I wasn't exactly prepared for this today. Dad sprang it on me when I got here. If I had more time, I could have brought in a resume."

His mouth briefly forms a smile. "He's a little trigger happy, isn't he?"

Yeah, that definitely describes him.

"So tell me what you'd recommend to use online."

"Well, Quickbooks is kind of the standard for small businesses, but I don't know the exact pricing off the top of my head."

"So I have to pay a bookkeeper and for online stuff? Doesn't seem right."

"There's free software out there that gets the job done, too. Especially if you don't need anything complicated."

"And what would you be doing?"

"I'd record transactions, check for accuracies, and reconcile discrepancies, to name a few things. Just differently than you're used to doing. But before all that, this needs to be digitized." I motion to the ledger, still unable to believe he's been using that relic all this time.

He strokes his chin, eyeing me carefully. "How about fifty bucks a week for a few hours of work?"

"It's going to take me longer than that to record everything from that ledger. Call it seventy-five and we have a deal."

Please let my gamble pay off.

He lets out a rusty laugh. "I like a girl who can haggle. Shows you've got a spine. I'm not looking to hire a yes-man."

"Um, thank you." I'm not sure how else to respond.

"Okay, I'll give you a trial run where you digitize whatever you need to, explain the bookkeeping system you decide on to me, and if I like how it sounds, we'll make it permanent. Deal?"

I stand and shake his hand. "Deal." I can do some unpaid work to get something better. Lord knows I'm not busy at the bar.

"This doesn't leave my office, though. Got it?" He points to the ledger. "I'm already trusting you enough with my finances. You do the work you need to here."

"Understood."

We set up a time for me to come in later in the week to start transferring records from this mess of a ledger and I exit the office, giving Dad a thumbs-up on my way out as he spars with someone in the ring.

The guy with him turns, and I realize it's Ethan. The tee he had on earlier is off now, his defined muscles glistening with sweat as he punches at the mitts on Dad's hands, bobbing and weaving expertly, fierce concentration on his face. It's a one-eighty from the affable, goofy guy from before, and I pause for a moment, caught off guard.

He stops when he realizes Dad's attention has strayed, his gaze meeting mine briefly from across the room, flaring in recognition.

I hightail it out of there, not wanting to get trapped in another conversation with him. Not that it matters if I talk to him. It doesn't.

Obviously.

I don't have time to talk. I have a new bookkeeping job to prepare for. Dad's text turned out better than I thought. Extra money and something applicable to accounting to put on my resume for the future. More than bartending anyway.

And if I see Ethan again at the gym, I'll simply avoid him. No one's that friendly for no good reason.

Not with me, at least.

---

"Remember, check your syllabus before you ask me any questions. If you waste my time because you couldn't bother to read something, prepare for me to deduct points from your grade."

I roll my lips between my teeth to hide my smile. It's only the second week of classes, but I'm already loving Dr. Clark, my Intro to Psychology professor.

"And come see me after class if you're interested in participating in my department's new study. It pays twenty bucks. Dismissed."

My head perks up. Twenty dollars is twenty dollars. I desperately need to refill my bank account after wiping it clean paying for utilities and rent.

But everyone else has the same idea as students rush to form a line in front of Dr. Clark's podium. This is the problem with introductory level classes. There are too many damn people.

I find a place in line, resisting the urge to tap my toes since it's going to be a bit of a wait.

"Lexie," a deep voice from behind me says. "I thought that was you."

I whip around, craning my neck up to spy none other than Ethan, the man my brain kept turning back to when trying to sleep last night. "What are you doing, following me?" I raise my brows, eyeing him, and he grins in response, sticking his hands in his pockets. Why doesn't he ever act the way I expect him to?

"I'm in this class. And apparently, so are you."

My lips twist. It would have been easy enough to miss him. There are probably close to two hundred students in here.

"So Marty said he's giving you a trial run," he continues when I don't reply. "Congratulations."

"Thanks," I mutter, hitching my backpack up higher on my shoulder as the line moves forward. "Were you checking up on me?"

"You know, your dad's a pretty sociable guy. Those genes didn't pass on to you, did they?"

I roll my eyes, not letting my lips tilt up again like they want to.

"That's okay. I can talk for both of us. I've got middle child syndrome. You have to talk a lot to be heard."

You mean there are others like him? "No kidding."

"Yep. Four brothers."

There are five Ethans out there? Good Lord.

The line moves again, but not fast enough for my liking.

"Do you have something against making new friends?"

Friends? I can count the number of friends I have on one hand. One finger, really. And I don't need any more. "Is that what you're doing? Trying to be my friend?"

"Yeah."

I give him a once over, taking in his muscular build and good looks. I'll admit, he's an attractive guy. Which is all the more reason to stay away. I'd bet anything he was some popular jock in high school. "Guys like you aren't friends with girls like me." I already learned that lesson the hard way.

He blinks at me, taken aback for the first time. "What's that supposed to mean?"

"Forget it." I turn back around, wishing I'd kept my mouth shut.

He touches the edge of my shoulder softly. "I'd be your friend, Lexie."

I shut my eyes, swallowing past the sudden hot lump in my throat. Maybe he's being genuine. Maybe he really does want to be my friend.

Yeah, and maybe pigs fly. Meatheads only have two things on their mind—fighting and fucking. And I'm not interested in either.

He's silent after that, so quiet I can't even be sure he's still behind me as the line inches forward, except for that sixth sense on the back of my neck that prickles the hairs there.

Dr. Clark's face is weary as I finally reach her, and she holds up a hand before I can open my mouth. "I'm sorry, the guy in front of you filled the last slot. I had no idea so many of you would be interested."

My stomach drops. Not that twenty bucks is a great loss, but I need money if my next shift at Element isn't till Monday and Marty isn't paying me yet.

"Are there any more studies? Maybe in a different department or something?"

She tilts her head thoughtfully, blonde ponytail swinging. "You know, we do have one other study. But it's a lot more involved. You're required to report once a week for six weeks, and it pays two thousand dollars."

Holy crap. Sign me up.

"Well, a thousand for each partner," she clarifies.

"Partner?"

"It's a study on love. You and your significant other will take part in a series of scans, tests, and self-reports as they measure levels of hormones, neurotransmitters, and brain activity. Are you in a relationship?"

Definitely not. "I, um, yes. I am," I blurt out. Wait, I am?

"Great. The sooner you can get your partner here, the sooner I'll sign you up before the spots in the study fill up. I'll offer it to everyone else still waiting in line, too."

Oh God. That money would help so much. Besides food, if one more thing goes wrong with my car, I don't know how I'll pay for it. "He's, um... he's here with me now." I turn around and grab onto Ethan's arm like it's a lifeline. "This is my boyfriend."

Please let him go along with it. Not that I deserve it at all. I've been nothing but rude to him.

He looks down at me, amusement flickering in his eyes as his mouth stretches in a wide grin. I bet he's loving this.

"Boyfriend?" he asks, the moments afterward seeming to extend endlessly. My stomach sinks as my chance for extra money slips through my fingers. "Only boyfriend? I thought I was the love of your life."

The tension in me loosens as relief pours through me. He's a real comedian, all right.

What the hell have I gotten myself into?

# CHAPTER TWO

## ETHAN

"WE NEED TO TALK."

Wow, just what every guy wants to hear five minutes into his new fake relationship. "Are you breaking up with me? And just when I thought we were having a real breakthrough."

Those full lips of hers twitch, even as she rolls her eyes, but she stays silent as she steers me over to the corner of the lecture hall, her arm still linked with mine, and waits until we're out of earshot of others to whisper, "We have to come up with a game plan."

"I think what you meant to say was *thank you, Ethan. You're my hero.*"

She blinks up at me and lets go of my arm, crossing her arms over her chest. She's got this shapeless black hoodie on, the same as last night, but her face is clear of the heavy makeup today, her hazel eyes filled with annoyance.

"Thank you," she mutters. I don't doubt her sincerity, but I still can't help teasing her a little all the same.

"Was that painful? You looked like you were in pain saying that."

Her mouth tilts up at the corners for the briefest moment before she stops herself. "I'm being serious here. I really am grateful. I just don't... I don't like being in anyone's debt." She looks down, the smallest bit of vulnerability seeping through before she clears her throat, looking back up at me. "How about I tutor you so we're even?"

Tutor me? She honestly thinks I'm a meathead. I shrug, inwardly grinning. I can't wait to see the look on her face when she finds out the truth. "Sure. I never turn down free help."

"So how do you want to play this?"

"For being your fake boyfriend during the study?"

She nods, gaze darting about.

"Do you not trust me to keep my mouth shut around others?" I ask.

She releases a sigh. "I'm just double-checking."

"Why'd you pick me?"

She blinks up at me, caught off guard. "You were right there."

Fair enough. "So you don't have anyone else you'd rather do this with?"

Her gaze narrows slightly. "If you're trying to ask if I'm seeing anyone, the answer is no."

Guess that was kind of obvious. "And you need the money because you're not making enough tips at the bar?"

"How do you—" She cuts herself off. "Oh, my Dad." She drums her fingers against her arm. "Yeah. Listen, I get that I put you in a tough spot. I'm..." She looks down at her crossed arms. "I'm sorry. If you don't want to go through with it, I understand."

My fingers twitch to reach out to her, but she'd probably karate chop my hands away. "I said I'd be the love of your life, didn't I?"

The small smile she gives in response is worth continuing with... whatever this is we're doing.

"So, what's this game plan of yours?" I ask, shoving my fists in my pockets.

She blows out a breath, uncrossing her arms to run a hand through her hair. "Maybe a list of facts about each other? Making up a story about how we met?"

"Well, we met at the boxing gym. You took one look at me and fell madly in love, obviously."

"Obviously," she replies drily. "I'm sure Dr. Clark will completely buy that. Especially considering I didn't even know your last name when we signed up just now."

I wave my hand. "Details. Who needs last names when you're soul mates?"

"I do. I don't want to get tripped up if they ask me something about you that I should know. How about we meet up tonight to go over stuff? We only have until tomorrow afternoon to get our stories straight."

Dr. Clark signed us up to go into the lab at three on Wednesdays since we're both available then. "How about now? I'm done with classes for the day."

"I've got one more after this. Will you be at the gym tonight? We can meet up then."

I wasn't planning on going, but I can train an extra night this week for her. "Yeah, I'll be there."

"Good. Let me get your number in case I need to text you before then."

"Desperate for my number, huh?"

The look she gives me is so unimpressed, I can't help but grin. She's so easy to rile.

"For the study," she clarifies, rolling her eyes.

She texts me after I recite it to her, and I add her to my contacts.

"What'd you label me as?" she asks, glimpsing my screen.

I angle it toward her, relishing her second eye roll.

"Girlfriend?" she deadpans. "Really?"

"I'm a method actor. I need to totally immerse myself in this role."

"You're crazy." She readjusts her backpack straps, turning from me, but she can't fully hide the amused twitch to her lips. "I'll see you at Marty's. I should be finished with the books by eight."

"See you."

I watch her walk away, her ass glorious in those tight jeans. I'm allowed to look, right? She's my fake girlfriend, after all.

A smile creeps over my face imagining how fun the next six weeks will be.

---

"Earth to Ethan."

I swivel my head back where it belongs. Namely, away from Marty's office. "Sorry, man."

Tyler grunts. "You said you wanted to box tonight, but all you're doing is staring at that girl in there."

Of course he'd notice that. The man's too observant for his own good. Then again, he's my closest friend and roommate. If anyone would notice, it'd be him.

I rub at the back of my neck, the tape on my hand scratchy. "Actually, she's kind of my fake girlfriend."

He blinks at me uncomprehendingly, so I tell him what happened during class earlier, his head shaking slowly by the end.

"You're the only person I know who gets himself in situations like this. How do you do it?"

"Pssh." I wave off his statement. "If you weren't so busy brooding and keeping to yourself all the time, you'd know this kind of thing is totally normal. Happens to everyone."

His brows raise slightly, but he doesn't call me on my bullshit. "And agreeing to this is completely altruistic on your part?"

I glance over at Marty's office again, Lexie's auburn hair like a beacon, her head bent low as she studies something on the desk. "Of course."

"Yeah, okay."

My gaze cuts back to Tyler, his sarcasm thick enough to cut with a knife. "What? I can't be nice? She's Lawrence's daughter. Maybe it'll give me an in so he'll train me more." Since Marty doesn't do work in the ring anymore,

Lawrence is the most popular trainer, with decades of fighting experience under his belt. The serious boxers get first dibs at him, which leaves guys like me who haven't fought in a match yet with slim pickings.

"Wait. She's Lawrence's daughter? What the hell are you thinking getting tangled up with that? He could eat you alive."

Yeah, he can be scary when he wants to, but that's with the guys who don't take him seriously. I do. "It'll be fine. He loves me."

"That's what you think now," he grumbles. "So, are you training or not?"

"Yeah, let's go."

Forty-five minutes later, I'm dripping sweat, wiping at my eyes with my now-soaked shirt I stripped off long ago. "Give me a sec." I grab my gallon jug of water, taking a huge swig. I've been so thirsty lately.

Out of the corner of my eye, there's movement from Marty's office, Lexie standing and placing something on the desk.

"Your girlfriend ready for you?" Tyler asks, his tone conveying how ridiculous he finds the whole thing.

"You jealous?" I tease. "Afraid I won't have enough time for you anymore? I promise there's room for both of you in my life."

"Get the fuck out of here," he says good-naturedly. "And take a shower before she smells you."

I do a sniff test, wincing. Yep, he's right.

I jog over to the office door, rapping on the glass before opening it. "I'm going to grab a quick shower before we meet up, okay?"

Her gaze travels over me, something about the action heating my blood. I doubt there's anything sexual about it on her part, though. She practically screamed *not interested* at me yesterday, but I like her eyes on me all the same.

She nods, looking away as she stows her notebook in her backpack.

"You hungry?" I ask. "There's a diner across the street we could talk at."

"Sure."

I take a closer look at her. "You all right?"

She pinches the bridge of her nose. "Just tired. Trying to decipher Marty's handwriting is no joke."

"We could—"

"Ethan, I can't take you seriously when you're shirtless. Can you put something on?"

I glance down at myself. "Does the sight of my bare torso offend you?"

Her lips twitch. How is it that I've known her for only twenty-four hours and I'm already living for the barest signs of her amusement?

"Go take your shower. I'll be in the parking lot." She brushes past me, careful not to touch my sweat.

All right, message received. Guess she really is not interested.

I clean up and meet her outside, both of us driving to Kate's Kitchen around the corner.

"Think there's actually a Kate?" I whisper as the hostess guides us to a booth near the back of the diner.

Lexie glances at me. "What?"

"The name of the place. Did they choose it because it was alliterative or because someone named Kate founded it?"

She waits till we're seated and alone before she responds. "Is this what I have to look forward to? You don't have to voice everything your brain comes up with."

I grin at her. "But it's more fun that way."

She sets her menu aside. Did I imagine the lip twitch this time?

"You know what you're getting? I'm thinking the country special. The bacon is *Canadian*," I stage whisper. "Very fancy."

Okay, definitely a twitch that time. "I don't need anything."

"Already ate?"

She nods, looking out the window. Unfortunately, her stomach chooses that moment to let out a loud grumble, protesting her statement.

"I won't think less of you if you have a second dinner. It works for hobbits."

"That's second breakfast," she says, her cheeks pinkening. "And I'm fine."

"You guys ready to order?" a waitress interrupts, apparently with little time for pleasantries. Looking at her nametag, I'm disappointed it's not the infamous Kate.

Another waitress walks behind her holding two platters filled with greasy breakfast goodness, the aroma of fried hash browns and crispy bacon wafting over us. Oh yes, come to Papa.

Lexie stares longingly after her, stomach grumbling once more.

"I'll have two country specials," I tell the woman. "One with sausage, home fries, and pancakes, the other with Canadian bacon, hash browns, and waffles. Scrambled eggs with both and orange juice to drink."

The server doesn't bat an eye, turning to Lexie next. "And you?"

"Nothing, thanks," she says, handing her the menus. She waits till we're alone to ask me, "Are you seriously going to eat all that?"

I stroke my beard, appearing to think it over. "Yeah, guess I got a little carried away. You'll help me eat it, right?"

Her lips twist as she unrolls the wrapped silverware in front of her. "You're real slick, you know that?"

I make a noncommittal noise, silently savoring my victory. "How about we do some fact quizzing? You said you wanted facts about me, right?"

She reaches in her bag to pull out a blue notebook. "I actually made a list for us to fill out the basics. Family info, likes and dislikes, things like that."

She rips out a few sheets, sliding them across the table, and I look them over.

These are the basics? There have to be at least a hundred questions on here. They're front and back, for crying out loud.

"You can fill it out here," she continues, "and I'll study your answers before we meet at the lab."

I set them aside. "You're one of those Type A people, aren't you?"

She gives an exasperated sigh. "We need to be prepared. There's a thousand each at stake."

"All right, all right." I hold up my hands in a *don't shoot* gesture. "But really, I doubt they'll ask about—" I glance down at the top sheet. "Our childhood pets."

"It could come up. You never know."

"Well, Skittles, may he rest in peace, is wagging his tail in doggy heaven knowing we're talking about him."

The pained look she gives me is laughable. "You named your dog Skittles?"

I shrug. "It was the only thing me and my brothers could agree on. My vote was for Groucho Barks."

She groans in response. "Oh my God, I didn't think it could get worse."

"You know, that pun was pretty clever for an eight-year-old."

"I guess," she concedes.

"Any childhood pets on your end?"

"No."

"What? I can totally see Lawrence with some big pitbull or something. The kind that looks all mean but is the biggest softy when you pet them."

She glances up as the waitress returns with my orange juice, setting a glass of water in front of Lexie too, even though she didn't order it. "Thanks." She takes a sip, delaying her response, but I wait her out, curious as to what she'll say. "Dad didn't stick around in one place long enough to have a dog," she finally tells me. "He was always competing in different invitationals. Had to travel a lot."

"Your mom didn't want one?"

Her mouth tightens. "No."

So the mom is a sore spot. Duly noted. "See? I'm learning way more talking to you about this stuff than by filling out a bunch of one-word responses. Why don't we pretend like this is a date so we can get to know each other better?"

There's still that firmness to her mouth. "This isn't a date."

"Yeah, but if we *were* dating, which we're telling Dr. Clark we are, we would have gone on a first date at some point. It's part of our cover story. You asked me out to Kate's Kitchen, we laughed and wondered if there was a real Kate, yada, yada, yada. So, what would you talk about if it was a real date?"

She shifts in her seat, the vinyl booth squeaking. "I don't know."

"What do you normally do on a date?"

She's silent, looking everywhere but at me. Tough crowd.

"I mean, you've been on a date, right?" I joke. She's gorgeous. She must get asked out all the time.

Her cheeks redden and she slides out of the booth, grabbing her bag. "Just text me your answers to the list, okay?"

"Whoa, whoa." I'm out of my seat before I fully register what I'm doing, hands on her shoulders steering her back as my brain finally puts two and two together. The insistence this isn't a date. Telling me right off the bat yesterday she doesn't date boxers. Has she been on a date with anyone? "We don't have to talk about dates. They're overrated, anyway."

She reluctantly sits back down, draining half her glass of water to avoid responding.

"Our new story is that we didn't have a first date," I continue. "We locked eyes across that crowded boxing gym floor and our souls merged together as one. We were inseparable from that day on."

She rolls her eyes, quickly setting her glass down as she covers her mouth. "You almost made me spit that water everywhere."

"Because you liked the idea so much?"

She shakes her head softly. "No, your first story was better. We went out to eat and wondered about the restaurant's name. Like the beginning of some dumb rom-com. You know, if it comes up during the study."

"In our version, we could even meet the real Kate."

She shrugs, but I can tell she likes the idea from the slight curve of her lips. "Sure. Why not?"

The tension in my shoulders finally releases. Hopefully she won't make a break for it again.

"Hope you're hungry," our waitress says as she returns with my ridiculous amount of food.

Lexie's eyes go wide at the platters in front of me. They don't skimp on portion sizes here.

"Take anything you want," I tell her, digging in. I had dinner earlier but I'm still starving. Must be all the time at the gym. "And we can go over your questions." I push the sheets of paper back toward her. "Fire away."

"Don't you need to write my answers?"

I tap my temple. "It's all up here."

She sighs, comfortable enough at least to pick up her fork and spear a few home fries. "All right. Favorite color."

We go through the likes and dislikes, some of her answers surprising me. Whose favorite ice cream is actually mint chocolate chip?

"That would literally be my last choice," I tell her, finishing up the hash browns.

"Guess there's more ice cream for me, then." She smiles smugly at me, pouring syrup over a waffle.

"You can have it." I shudder dramatically, relishing the way those full lips of hers widen. "You ready to move onto family stuff?"

Her grin drops. "Yeah, I guess."

Shit. Should have made up more likes and dislikes. "You want to start or should I?"

She pokes at the waffle with her fork. "I will. You know my dad already."

She's silent after that, and I wait a few moments longer, wondering if that was the end of her statement. "And your mom?" I prompt.

"She's not important. I'm not saying anything else about it."

Guess I was right about that being a touchy subject.

"Dad's parents are dead and he has an older brother that lives out in California. I met him when I was little, but I don't remember it. And I don't know any of my mom's family." Her tone is almost robotic, stilted in the way she delivers it. "No siblings."

She leans back in her booth and crosses her arms, glaring at me like she's daring me to say something. Does she think I'd make fun of her?

"Only child? Sounds amazing. Try fighting with four brothers for everything."

"That's right, the four brothers." She loses her hard edge, picking up her pen to scribble something down. "Give me details."

I stroke my beard reflexively. "Let's see. Scott is the oldest."

"How much older?"

"Uh…" I do some mental math. "Six years older. Then there's Brian. He's three years older. And Jacob and Jordan are the babies. They're twins and two years younger."

"Fraternal or identical?" she asks, noting everything on her list.

Is that important? "Fraternal. But they get mistaken for identical a lot." Strangers sometimes lump me in with them too, thinking we're triplets.

"Parents?"

"Gayle and Terry Hudson. Married twenty-eight years. Pretty much the most boring, suburban family in America."

She taps her pen against the table. "Is that why you started boxing? For some excitement?"

"My roommate got me into it. But yeah, I do like the excitement. The adrenaline."

"Do you like hurting people?" she asks softly.

The pancake I'm chewing turns dry in my mouth. "I'd say that's a side effect. Not the reason I do it." Did someone hurt her? A boxer?

Was it her dad?

No, she seemed fairly close to him yesterday at the gym. At least that was the vibe I got.

Maybe an ex?

No, she doesn't date.

She picks at her food again. "Some guys, you know, they get off on that kind of stuff."

I set my fork down carefully. "Have you met guys like that?"

She shrugs unconvincingly. "Forget I said anything."

"You keep saying that a lot."

Her jaw sets.

Shit. I should have kept my mouth shut. Mom always says I don't know when to quit.

"Yeah, I do." Her fork clatters next to her unfinished waffle. "I appreciate you helping me out, but I don't have to spill all my secrets to you. We just met."

Time to retreat. "You're right. Sorry."

"I think we have enough to get through tomorrow," she says, opening her bag to pull out her wallet.

"You don't owe anything for dinner."

"But I ate—"

"I asked you to meet up here. I ordered the food. It's on me."

She stares at me for a beat longer before stuffing her wallet back in. Sliding out of her side of the booth, she shoulders her bag but doesn't leave right away. "The study's at three," she finally says.

I nod, afraid to set her off again.

"Thanks… Thanks for taking this seriously. A lot of people wouldn't." She turns, speed walking toward the exit before I can respond.

Well, that could have gone worse. Could have gone better too, but I'll take what I can get.

She said earlier today guys like me aren't friends with girls like her, whatever that means. But I bet by the end of this, I'll have her opening up to me.

And if I'm lucky, maybe more.

# CHAPTER THREE

## LEXIE

"COME IN, COME IN," Dr. Clark says, waving me forward into the room. "It's Ethan and Alexandra, right?"

"I prefer Lexie," I tell her, staring at all the equipment in here. I thought she was a psychologist, not a scientist.

"And I prefer Ethan," he jokes from behind me. Ugh, when does he ever stop cracking jokes?

She smiles at him and directs us to a row of empty chairs along one wall, handing us clipboards and pens. "We just need this paperwork filled out."

She leaves us be as she greets another couple coming in, and Ethan leans in, whispering, "You never told me your name is Alexandra."

Does he have cologne on or something? It smells… amazing. Have I been this close to him before?

No, no. Wrong thing to focus on. "I hate my name. It's so formal."

"It sounds regal. How about that be the name only I call you? Like a special boyfriend thing?"

"No."

"Okay, how about Pookie Bear?"

I glance over at him. "Try it."

Based on the gleam in his eye, that was the wrong response.

"Hey, Ethan," the guy who just entered says, walking over toward us. "You're in this study too?"

Oh, God. He knows people?

"Christian." Ethan stands, giving the man one of those weird bro handshake hugs. "How'd you hear about this?"

"Dr. Clark's Psych class yesterday. We figured it'd be easy money. This is my girl, Amber."

A pretty girl with dark, curly hair gives us a wave, her light brown skin complementing her boyfriend's golden tan and blond hair. Great, now we have to compete with some gorgeous couple who are actually in love?

"The two o'clock class?" Ethan asks. "We're in that one too." He motions to me. "This is my girlfriend, Lexie."

I give a head nod to the two of them, silent. At least he didn't call me Pookie Bear.

"Good to see you know each other," Dr. Clark says. "It was easier for us to schedule two couples at a time in here. Once you've finished filling out your forms, I'll start with Lexie and Ethan in the next room."

I stare at my clipboard, concentrating on filling out the papers rather than the fact that this lie is already spiraling out of control. Ethan knows this Christian guy and he's in our class. That means we'll have to act like a couple outside of the study too. It would be weird if we didn't acknowledge each other in class and they saw. They might report us or something.

"You freaking out?" Ethan whispers in my ear.

"No."

"Yes, you are."

I catch myself before I roll my eyes. I realized too late yesterday he likes it when I do that. "Finish your forms," I grit out.

He leans back, grinning widely, and picks up his pen again.

Despite me starting earlier, we're somehow done at the same time, turning in our clipboards to Dr. Clark in the adjoining room.

"Good," she comments, glancing over our paperwork. "We'll do a lot of preliminary stuff today. Getting info about you as a couple, taking baselines —that kind of thing. And I'm sure you read the informed consent form, but each week we'll be looking at physical markers in the body of what we consider to be love. It's more invasive than anything we've done in this lab before, so I'm excited to see how it plays out."

Invasive? What's she going to do to us?

She motions us toward two chairs next to her, crossing one knee over the other. "Let me get to know you two a little. How long have you been together?"

"Two months." I clear my throat, hating how hoarse I sound.

"Oh, good. A newbie couple. I'd love to see your results compared to some longer-term, established couples."

Great. Just what we need is for her to scrutinize our results and realize how fake we are.

"And where'd you two meet?" She directs this question to Ethan. Please let him not go off-script.

"My boxing gym. Her dad's a trainer there and she came in one day to meet him." He reaches over and intertwines his fingers with mine. "I was a goner from then on."

I squeeze his hand in warning, but he merely smiles. He better not push it.

Dr. Clark nods. "So, in your case, there was an immediate attraction you acted upon." She writes something down in the notebook on her lap. "And it was the same for you, Lexie?"

"Um, yes." What's she writing? What do our answers mean?

"Yeah, she was actually the one who asked me out," Ethan boasts. "She can't get enough of me."

I squeeze his hand harder, digging my nails in, and he subtly flinches.

Good.

"That's a first for the couples we've interviewed so far."

"When I see something I want, I go after it," I say, forced to play along.

She scribbles in her notebook again. "Love the attitude. I wish I was more like that."

He leans in, barely audible as he whispers, "See? She loves it. And damn, I liked hearing you say that, too."

I elbow him while she's still only half paying attention and jotting down notes, shooting daggers out of the corner of my eye toward him. He's going to get us busted.

She asks us a few more questions about our living situations, how often we see each other, and what we like to do together. Our answers must be satisfactory because she smiles at the end and directs us back to the first room, introducing us to Justin, the fifth-year grad student who is her second-in-command for the study. He raises a hand in greeting, his brown hair flopping over his forehead, and hands us questionnaires to fill out as Christian and Amber follow Dr. Clark to the other room.

"What would you say is your level of happiness with your partner?" Ethan asks, reading from the page. "Definitely a ten. Am I right?"

"I'm marking down a one," I hiss, careful to make sure we're not overheard. "I can't believe you said I asked you out. I thought you were joking about that yesterday."

"What? It's not like it's a bad thing. I'd find it incredibly hot if you asked me out."

I snort. Like that would ever happen.

"I mean, I know you're secretly dying to, so you might as well get it over with and ask me out for real already." He sighs dramatically, and I have to fight the urge to roll my eyes again.

"Stop messing around and fill out the questionnaire."

What must he be like in class if he can't ever concentrate? Tutoring him is going to be a bitch.

"I don't have to look at the questions. You get a ten in everything."

"Put other numbers too. It needs to be realistic. No one's perfect."

"My Pookie Bear is."

I take a deep breath, letting it out slowly. He's one of those people who loves riling others up. I just have to not react. "Hurry up so we can get out of here. I need to read the first hundred pages of a book before class tomorrow."

"What book?"

"*War and Peace.*"

"Oh, God. That one's so long."

I set my pen down, staring at him. "Have you read it?" There's no way. It's too dense. *I* can barely get through it.

"Uh…" He scratches at the back of his neck. "I watched the movie."

Yeah, that sounds more his speed.

Justin approaches us, holding a digital camera. "You guys almost finished? I have to take your pictures. And if you have any water, I'd start chugging it now because I need a urine sample from both of you later."

Um, what now?

"Why do you need our pee?" Ethan asks him. God, does he have to be so crass?

"We're getting a baseline of your neurotransmitter levels."

I exchange a glance with Ethan, who shrugs. "Okay." To be honest, I'm not completely sure what neurotransmitters are. Something about chemicals in the brain?

We finish up and turn in our questionnaires, then stand against a white backdrop as Justin takes our pictures individually.

As he leads us through our next tasks, I see why he needed the pictures. We're outfitted with special goggles that track our eye movements as images of strangers interspersed with our partner come in rapid succession, the muscles in my upper back tense as I search for Ethan's image. Am I seeking

31

him out fast enough? Would a person in love be able to recognize their partner quicker? I only met him two days ago. I don't have his features memorized yet.

Oh, God. We're going to fail this.

I roll out my shoulders when the test is finally over, but I don't have much of a break before there's a second eye test, this time measuring the size of our pupils as we're shown different images. This one has the picture lingering for longer, and as Ethan pops up on the screen, I concentrate on his face.

The dark slash of his brows, the straight nose, the strong jaw lurking underneath his carefully groomed beard. And looking closer, there's a flicker of laughter in those striking green eyes. A hint of mischief in his smirk.

He really is… handsome.

Objectively, obviously.

"How'd you like looking at my face all those times?" he asks when we're finished. "Sick of me yet?"

He's grinning, laugh lines prominent around the corners of his eyes. The sudden urge to trace them strikes me, my hand almost reaching up before I remember myself.

What the hell am I thinking? He doesn't need his ego fed any.

"They could have at least used a few different pictures to make it more interesting," I tell him.

Somehow, his grin spreads even wider. "I mean, if you want pictures, I'll send you pictures."

I tilt my head. "And what kind would those be?"

Devilry curves over his lips. "Whatever kind you want."

"You're incorrigible. Don't you take anything seriously?"

"Not if I can help it."

"Come on. We have to go pee in a cup."

Justin hands us each a specimen collection cup, directing us down the hall where the restrooms are. As fancy as the lab is, I guess they couldn't get their own bathroom.

Ethan gives me a little salute as he goes into the men's room, and I roll my eyes once he's out of sight. There's a distinct possibility I might strangle him before the study is over.

I go to open the handle of the women's restroom and it swings outward on its own, the girl from earlier, Amber, looking startled as she sees me there.

Something in her hand wobbles, and we both look down at it, her filled specimen cup almost falling.

"Oh, shit," she exclaims, clutching it tighter. "Well, this is awkward."

"No," I assure her. "I've got my own." I hold up my empty cup.

"It's Lexie, right? Christian was telling me stories about Ethan. He sounds like a fun guy."

"Yeah, he's… great," I reply awkwardly. This is too weird to pretend I'm dating him. "How do they know each other again?"

"They had a class together last semester. Calculus, I think."

She must be misremembering. I highly doubt he took that advanced of a course.

"You should sit with us tomorrow in Psych," she continues.

I blink, taken aback. She doesn't even know me. What's her angle? "I, um… I'll ask Ethan," I tell her, not wanting to offend her right off the bat. She might get suspicious about us then.

But if we sit with her and Christian in class, it'll be harder to keep up the ruse. They'll see right through us. God, this is a nightmare.

"Great. See you tomorrow." The smile she gives me seems innocent enough, but four years of high school hell taught me you can't trust anyone.

I do my business and turn my cup in at the lab, Ethan already waiting for me in there.

"You're free to go," Justin says. "Same time, same place next week."

I nod, grabbing my backpack, but Ethan takes it from me before I can put it on.

"Boyfriends carry things for their girlfriends," he whispers when I give him a *what the hell* look.

I paste on a saccharine smile. "Thanks, Snookums."

His eyes light up with glee. "Anything for my Pookie Bear."

Justin gives us a strange look as we exit, which I don't blame him for.

"Snookums," Ethan exclaims once we're down the hall. "That's perfect. You have to call me that all the time."

I scrunch my eyes shut for a moment, rubbing my temples. Is he insane? "Aren't you embarrassed? That's the most ridiculous pet name ever."

"Come on. If we have to do this, we might as well have fun with it."

A lead ball drops on my stomach. He said *have to* do this. Like I'm twisting his arm. And I practically did, didn't I?

"Christian's girlfriend invited us to sit with them tomorrow in class," I tell him, pushing aside the guilt. "Do you think it's a good idea or is it too risky?"

He pushes the door to the stairwell open for me to go through first. "You act like they're out to get us. If we tell them we're a couple, they'll believe us."

"Yeah, but it's an extra chance to slip up. We hardly know each other."

"Think of it as an extra chance to practice being a couple, then. It'll show Dr. Clark we're real if she sees us in class together."

Ugh. How is he always so positive?

"Fine. We'll sit with them tomorrow. But if they're mean at all, I'm out of there."

He waits till we're down the stairs and on the sidewalk outside to quietly ask, "Why would they be mean?"

I shrug, not liking the way he's looking at me. "Some people just are."

"Have people been mean to you?"

I ignore his question, saying instead, "I have to get to work." One of the other bartenders happily gave me her shift tonight so she could go out with her boyfriend, and it's Sarah's night off so she can't say anything about it.

"It's a bar. They don't open till late." He's right. My shift doesn't start until seven. "Why won't you answer my question? You criticize me for not being serious, but when I ask you serious questions, you get all prickly and leave."

I squint at him, crossing my arms. What is he, an armchair psychologist or something?

He's silent, waiting me out. If anyone were watching us, they'd think we're having some kind of standoff.

Which we are, I guess.

My stomach tightens uncomfortably, but it seems he's not breaking first.

"I always sit by myself in classes," I finally say, not really answering his question. "So I don't have to deal with people. I don't like... people." I stare at the sidewalk, pushing a stray leaf over to the edge with my shoe.

"Could have fooled me," he says drily.

I glance up, his characteristic grin present, and something about it sets me at ease, the knots in my belly loosening just as quickly as they appeared.

I take a deep breath, adding, "People can be cruel. They—" I swallow past the sudden lump in my throat. "They can let you down. So it's easier to just..."

"Avoid them?"

I nod.

"I'm not going to let you down, Lexie."

My heartbeat grows loud in my ears, like my whole body is pulsing with it. This got way too personal. What was I thinking telling him that? "I still have to read that book before my shift. I'll find you in class tomorrow."

I turn and head toward the parking lot before he can say anything else. I know what he's doing trying to knock down my defenses. But they're there

35

for a reason. A jock like him wouldn't understand. He might've even been one of those guys who...

No, I have to give him more credit than that. He's proved himself at least a little trustworthy.

We can get through this study as friendly acquaintances if he wants, and afterward, we'll part ways. Easy.

There's no need to divulge everything about each other. It's all fake anyway.

And that's how it's going to stay.

# CHAPTER FOUR

## ETHAN

I KEEP an eye on the main double doors of the east side of the room, waiting for Lexie to enter the lecture hall. She better sit with me after promising she would.

Then again, there's the lesser-used south entrance behind me, too. I turn around, but there's no sign of her there either, my gaze bouncing from head to head, searching for her distinctive auburn hair.

I face back front, finally spotting her as she stands at the edge of the first row, looking out over the sea of students. She has on that same black hoodie, the garment so shapeless and large, it drowns her. Now that I know her a little better, I'd say it's the perfect thing to help her escape the notice of others. Why does she want so badly for people not to see her?

She pulls out her phone, and a few seconds later, I get a text from her.

**Lexie**: *Where are you?*

I stand and shout her name, waving my arm till she spots me.

She ducks her head and ascends the steps along the side of the room until she reaches my row, scooting past others in the aisle.

"All you had to do was text me," she mutters as she sets down her backpack and takes the seat I saved for her. "Not shout so half the room looked at us."

"Who cares?" How am I supposed to describe over text where I am in a lecture hall with over two hundred people in it?

She shrugs. "Thanks for not shouting Pookie Bear, I guess."

"I can next time if you want."

Her lips twist. "As long as you don't mind me shouting back Snookums."

I grin at her. I like this Lexie who gives back as good as she gets.

"Where are Christian and Amber? Did they get cold feet?"

"He texted and said he's running late."

She unpacks her bag, setting out a notebook, a pen, a highlighter, and other various essentials until there's not an inch of space left on her desk.

"Got enough stuff there?"

She gives me a dirty look. "I like to be prepared."

I hold up my hands. "No judgment here."

"Where are your things? Don't you take notes?"

I tap my temple. "It's all up here."

She blinks and shakes her head, muttering something under her breath about dumb jocks.

I bite my lip to contain my laugh. "Did you finish your reading last night?"

She nods, opening her notebook to a fresh page, labeling the date in the upper left-hand corner.

"And are they at war or peace?"

"War, so far. I could barely keep my eyes open after work finishing it."

"Don't torture yourself. Read the Cliff's Notes or something."

"The teacher makes it sound so interesting, though. In class, everyone's talking about the book like it's the second coming, but it's as if I'm reading something entirely different."

"So Tolstoy isn't your thing. Try Pushkin or Dostoevsky."

Her head swivels, staring at me. "How do you know about those authors?"

"Oh, look. There's Christian."

He and Amber make their way down the aisle, taking the two empty seats next to Lexie. "Hey, what are you guys up to?"

"Just discussing the finer points of Russian literature," I reply.

She can't completely suppress her eye roll as she turns from me.

"Oh, have either of you taken Dr. Kroft's Russian Lit class?" Amber asks, leaning forward in her seat to address us both. "I took it last semester and absolutely loved it."

Christian groans. "Are you still going on about that? She wouldn't stop talking about this professor. She had a huge crush on him."

"I did not," she declares. She turns till she's out of his line of sight and mouths *I did*, grinning.

"I'm in his class now," Lexie says. "But I think he has a girlfriend. I saw him on campus the other day holding hands with someone."

"She look kind of like me? Same skin color and curly hair?"

"Yeah, actually."

"I've seen them too. And they're, like, disgustingly in love."

Does she sound a little disappointed?

"You should ask her for help understanding your book," I whisper to Lexie.

She waits till Amber's preoccupied getting her stuff out of her backpack to whisper back, "No way."

"Why not?"

She faces toward me, hissing under her breath, "Because I don't know her."

"She seems nice. You should make friends."

"Will you shut up?"

"Hey, Amber," I say in a louder voice. "Lexie's having some trouble understanding *War and Peace*. Did you read that one?"

Lexie's jaw firms so hard, it's a wonder she doesn't break a tooth.

"Oh, yeah. That was one of the first ones we read. I was so lost at the beginning of that class, but it gets better, I promise. If you want to talk about it, let me know."

"Thanks."

I bite my lip as Lexie presses the heel of her foot into the top of mine, smashing my toes.

"Actually," Amber continues, "we were thinking of forming a study group for Psych. I have a friend in the Monday-Wednesday class who knows some people who'd be interested. Would you want to join?"

"Oh, we'd love to," I tell her before Lexie can decline. She presses her foot down even harder in response.

"Great. We could get together tonight since our first test is next week. Do you want to chip in for a few pizzas?"

"Sure. Lexie and I will split a meat lover's."

"The one thing you remember I like," Lexie mutters, barely audible.

"Do you live in the dorms?" Amber asks. "We're on different floors in Chapman Hall."

I actually have no idea where Lexie lives. We never got around to that during dinner Tuesday night. "I rent a room in a house with three other guys not far from here."

"I'm off campus," is all Lexie supplies.

The sound of Dr. Clark's mic turning on has us quieting, the scritch of pens and pencils on paper mixed with the clacking of keys on keyboards echoing through the room. I lean back and listen as she goes over operant behavior, absorbing her words, and after about ten minutes, Lexie leans over to ask, "Are you sure you don't need to take notes?"

I stretch my arm out, resting it on the back of her chair. "Why bother when my tutor's taking notes for me?"

"You're infuriating," she whispers, not looking at me again for the rest of the class.

I won't push my luck by dropping my arm over her shoulders the way I want to. I've already pushed her far enough for now.

After class, she's silent as I make plans for us to be at Chapman Hall at six to study and walks ahead of me as we exit the lecture hall.

"Where's your next class?"

She points vaguely in front of us.

"What? You won't talk to me now?"

"Oh, am I allowed to talk? I figured my input isn't necessary since you're making plans for me and all."

"I was staying in character. A couple would accept an invite for something like that."

She stops in the middle of the path, spinning toward me. "That's the thing, though. We're not a real couple. This is totally unnecessary. You don't even know what my plans are for tonight."

"Did you have plans?"

She throws her hands up, narrowly missing a guy trying to bypass us. "That's not the point!"

I tug on her arm, pulling her to the grass so we're not blocking the way.

"Don't make decisions for me, Ethan," she says in a serious voice. "And don't try to control me."

She stares at me, flinty-eyed, nostrils flared, and it's at that moment I realize I fucked up. A dull ache spreads through my chest, settling in my stomach disconcertingly.

"I'm sorry. I didn't know…" I clear my throat hastily, hating how dry it is. "I didn't think it was that big of a deal, but I was obviously wrong. I wasn't trying to control you, I just wanted—"

To spend more time with you. To get to know you better. To crack that hard outer shell you keep so solidly around you. "I won't do it again. Promise. And I'll text Christian and tell him we can't make it after all."

The hardness gradually leaves her face, and she hugs her arms tight over her midsection, looking about five feet to the left of me. "No, you said we'd go. I don't want to raise suspicions. But this counts as your tutoring for the week."

"Of course. Can I pick you up and drive you there after your class?"

"I'll walk."

"What about after? I don't want you walking back in the dark."

"Fine, whatever. Pick me up."

She tells me what building she's in and the time her class lets out then stalks off, pulling her hood over her head so she's an anonymous, shapeless form. One more college student among thousands.

But as much as she tries to hide herself, she ends up unintentionally revealing more every time we're together. And one day soon, I'll have her figured out.

---

Leaning against the outer brick wall, I keep an eye on a set of double doors for the second time today, waiting for Lexie.

They open, a stream of students pouring out, my gaze flicking from person to person. No… no… there.

I pick up the grocery bag at my feet, dodging people walking the opposite way until I'm in front of her, watching as her gaze lifts to meet mine, recognition hitting.

"I got you something," I say before she can tell me again how much I hurt her, thrusting the bag in my hands toward her.

She takes it, brows knitting as she pulls out what's inside. "Are you serious with this?"

Shit. I thought it was the right thing to get her.

She lifts the lid off the pint of mint chocolate chip ice cream and hands it to me, then reaches back in the bag for the plastic spoon. As the frozen dessert hits her tongue, her face transforms into an expression of bliss, different from anything I've seen from her so far.

I could get used to this face.

"So… it's good? I ask, still unsure of her reception.

She sighs. "You make it impossible to stay mad at you."

That hollowness in my chest from earlier fades, lightness replacing it. Thank God.

I take the last swig from the water bottle I bought at the gas station and toss it in a nearby trash can, then tug at the top loop of her backpack, encouraging her to take it off. "I'll carry that for you."

"There's no one we know around. You don't have to."

"I want to. Method acting, remember?"

"Knock yourself out, then." She shrugs it off, focusing on devouring her ice cream, and we walk in comfortable silence toward the nearby student parking lot where my SUV is.

"This is nice," she comments as I open the passenger door for her. "It's okay if I eat in here?"

"You think I'd buy that for you and make you throw it away before you get in?"

She rolls her eyes. "Okay, jeez."

I cross around to the driver's side and get in, wincing as I spot her glancing in the backseat.

She makes eye contact with me, raising her brows. "I take it back. This is a pigsty. What'd you do? Take all the junk in the front seat and toss it back there real quick before I got in?"

That's exactly what I'd done. "Don't worry about it," I tell her.

"You must single-handedly keep every fast food place in a five-mile radius in business." She reaches back, fisting a handful of food wrappers.

"All right, enough of that. Eat your ice cream."

She shakes her head and faces forward, buckling her seat belt as she scoops another mound of mint chocolate chip into her mouth.

I glance over, nearly three quarters of the pint gone. "I didn't think you'd actually eat all of it. We're about to have pizza." I check behind me and reverse out of the space, heading toward Chapman Hall.

"I skipped lunch," she mumbles between bites.

She hadn't had dinner before we'd gone to the diner either. She's not one of those girls who skips meals to diet, is she? She looks great the way she is.

Well, if she was dieting, she wouldn't have inhaled a pint of ice cream so quickly. Or eaten that greasy diner food.

So if it's not that, is she just forgetful? No, her stomach had rumbled that night and she'd still refused to order anything. She said she was short on money…

Shit. Is she really that broke? No wonder the thousand dollars from the study is so important to her.

Okay, new mission—feed Lexie. Not that I'm swimming in cash myself, but I can definitely afford to get a few extra things for her. Scott's always willing to give me more hours at the hardware store.

If I've learned anything from the past few days, it's to keep my mouth shut about this newfound knowledge, assuming I've even come to the right conclusion. No need to put her on the defensive. It'll only make her more resistant to accepting anything I offer.

When she drops her spoon in the empty carton, I take it from her, affixing the lid and tossing it in the backseat. It's trashed back there anyway.

"Feel better?"

"Yes," she says, patting her stomach happily. "I haven't had that much ice cream in… God, I don't think ever."

"Really? I could eat three of those things easy."

She looks over at me. "Where does it all go? How do you eat like such crap and still look like that?" She points to the backseat as evidence of my poor eating habits, and she's got a fair point.

I shrug, turning on the street that leads straight to the dorms. "I work out a lot." And, if anything, I've been eating more lately and actually losing weight. I don't get it.

"Yeah, but boxers are supposed to be serious about what they eat. You can't stay in your weight class, otherwise."

I stroke my beard, catching a tangle. "Yeah, I need to get better about that." If I could drop to a lower class, I'd have an advantage.

"Do you compete?"

"Not yet. I'm still training."

"Don't let it go too long. Dad complains about the guys who spend years *training*, and then miss their window to actually fight."

I nod. "Maybe you could put in a word with him to schedule more sessions with me. He's always booked up."

"Nope."

I turn sharply toward her, then remember I need to focus on the road. "What do you mean? I just bought you ice cream."

"Oh, so it was a bribe?" I catch her smirking out of the corner of my eye. At least she's relaxed enough again to joke. "If you're hellbent on boxing, that's your choice, but I'm not getting involved. It's barbaric and pointless and a waste of time."

"Don't let Marty hear you say that. You're an employee of the gym now."

"I know when to suck it up and keep my mouth shut," she says.

"Seriously, how can you hate boxing so much? It should be in your blood. Your dad fought for years. He was great."

She lets out an exasperated sigh. "I love my dad, but he's washed-up."

I suck in a breath. That was harsh, even for her.

"Okay, that sounded bad," she concedes. "But he tried for so many years and never got to the level he wanted to."

"He made a living off of it, though. That's more than a lot of people can say."

She makes a noise of dismissal. "In one place one day, three states away the next, just for a chance to compete. Every fight was going to be his big break. And it never was." She tucks her leg under her, hugging her other knee. "He was living out of his car at one point because he hadn't won enough prize money for hotels. He'd call when he could, but man, that sucked."

My grip tightens on the steering wheel. "You were with him?"

"No, he wouldn't let me." She gives a soft smile. "I begged him, but he always said the road was no place for a kid."

I take my chances and push it a bit. "Because you wanted to be with him? Or didn't want to be at home?"

She's quiet for a moment. "Both."

"Your parents weren't together?"

She picks at her thumbnail, avoiding looking at me. "They split when I was little. I guess I should feel lucky he wasn't a complete deadbeat."

Wow, what a standard.

"Don't tell Dad I told you all this." She chews at her nail, muttering, "I'm not sure why I said anything in the first place."

"I can keep a secret."

"It's only, he has a reputation at work, you know?"

"I get it."

She nods gratefully. "And he's a great coach. Better than he was as a boxer. But the guys there see him and think wow, he was living the dream. I could be like him. But that's not the reality. He must have loved it, though, if he kept at it that long."

"Maybe he didn't know any other kind of life."

"Maybe."

Chapman Hall is just ahead, but I slow the car a little, not wanting our alone time to end yet. "Have you told him?"

"What?"

"That you missed him as a kid. That you wished he was around more."

She shrugs. "What's the point? It's in the past."

"He still might want to know."

Shaking her head, she says, "Things have been okay between us since he settled down here and got this job. I'm not ruining that by whining about things we can't change."

Well, if Lawrence wasn't around much until recently and she won't even talk about her mom, what kind of support system does she have? She seems too guarded to have a lot of friends. "Where do you live? Other than off campus."

She shifts in her seat as we turn into the dorm's parking lot. "I moved into a new apartment last month."

"And before that?"

"We're here," she says, unbuckling her seatbelt.

Good timing for her.

# CHAPTER FIVE

## ETHAN

"LET me run to the bathroom real quick," Lexie says after we sign in downstairs. "I'll meet you up there."

"I can wait—"

She makes a shooing motion at me. "Go ahead."

Okay, fine. I take the stairs up to the third floor, spotting Christian and Amber surrounded by two other girls and a guy at a table in the corner of the common room area.

Christian waves me over. "Hey everyone, this is Ethan."

I hold up a hand and give a short wave, taking the only free seat in between Amber and a brunette I don't recognize.

The girl turns my way, flashing me a smile. "I'm Savannah. Are you in Clark's Monday-Wednesday class?"

"Tuesday-Thursday."

She pouts. "That's a shame. I definitely would have remembered seeing you."

I glance around the table, but everyone else is in their own conversations. "And why's that?"

"You're cute," she says bluntly, twirling a lock of hair around a manicured finger.

Wow. What would Lexie say if she heard this?

I twist in my seat and search for her, only to discover her about ten feet away, face pale and stricken.

I'm up before I know it, jogging over to her and settling my hands on her shoulders. "What is it? You all right?"

"What's she doing here?" she whispers.

"Who?"

"Savannah." There's pure loathing in her voice, catching me off guard.

Whoa. There's history there.

From behind me comes a bubblegum-sweet, "Oh my God, sexy Lexie, is that you?"

The color returns in Lexie's face, twin splotches of red on her cheeks.

There's a touch on my arm, and then Savannah is there, giving me a coy look. "That's what everyone called her in high school."

I glance between the two of them, Lexie's jaw set incredibly tight, Savannah with a smug smile on her face.

"I almost didn't recognize you at first," Savannah says to Lexie. "Your hair definitely wasn't that color before." It's clear from her tone she thinks the dye job leaves something to be desired, but Lexie's hair looks great.

"Could you give us a minute?" I ask Savannah, steering Lexie further away.

Her body is rigid, muscles tense under my hand as we move toward the stairwell. I wait for her to explain, but she's silent, still looking over my shoulder at the study group.

"You going to give me anything?" I know she's not one to broadcast details, the car ride over being an exception, but I need something to work with here.

"We went to high school together."

"Yeah, I got that. I'm guessing you weren't friends?"

"She was..." She stares down at her shoes, my normally confident girl missing in action right now. "She was one of those... people."

The ones who were mean to her?

"All right, we're out of here, then." I move past her, opening the stairwell door. "I'll text Christian later and tell him an emergency came up."

"No." She spins toward me, pressing the heels of her palms against her eyes. "If I leave, she'll know exactly why. That she ran me off."

What the hell did this girl do? Well, there's no way I'm asking why she called her sexy Lexie. That's sure to be met with a non-answer.

"We don't have to do anything you're uncomfortable with. I'm fine with quitting the study group."

"No, that's what she wants." She moves her hands away from her face, those hazel eyes flashing with fire. "And I'm not giving her that."

All right, there's the Lexie I'm used to.

"Okay, uh..." I scratch at the back of my neck, not sure how to bring this up, but it needs to be said. "Just letting you know, she kind of hit on me before you got here."

The devilish grin that spreads over her lips is unexpected. "Perfect."

It is?

"Please play along," she whispers as she grabs my hand, her fingers chilly as she intertwines them with mine.

She leads us back toward the group, an unnaturally cheerful smile on her face. "Hey, Amber. Thanks so much for inviting us."

Oh, so she *can* be sociable. She just chooses not to.

"Glad you could make it." Amber smiles at us. "Pizza should be here in about half an hour."

Savannah glances at our joined hands, then back at Lexie, her gaze narrowing slightly. "Sorry, there's no room for you, Lexie." She points to the single chair left. "There's already six of us, and you were the last one here, so..."

Lexie's fingers tighten against mine. "No problem. Ethan and I will share."

We will?

She squeezes my hand harder and I spring into action, sitting in the empty seat, hesitant as she slides on my lap. I instinctively hold her waist to help balance her as she settles in place, my hands itching to pull her closer, grip her tighter, discover the soft warmth of her right underneath that hoodie.

Pretty sure she'd slap me upside the head if I tried, though, even with trying to make Savannah jealous.

Christian chuckles at us. "Creative."

Amber points a finger between Lexie and Savannah. "You said her name. Do you guys know each other?"

"Yeah, small world," Savannah replies. "We went to high school together." She turns to face us. "I'm not sure I ever heard you talk, though. You were usually busy doing *other* things."

An awkward silence descends over the table after her weird emphasis on the word *other*. What the hell is this girl's problem?

"Like making honor roll," I pipe up. "You were salutatorian. Right, babe?"

Lexie gives a jerky nod, her body tensing. "Right."

Savannah's brows narrow again. "You were?"

"Mm-hmm. Hey, why don't we get started studying?"

Not the smoothest transition, but I help her seize on it, pulling my textbook out of my backpack and setting it down in front of her on the table.

The other girl, Heather, introduces herself, as well as the guy, Patrick, and then we get to it. Lexie doesn't contribute much to the conversation, but fishes in her bag for her notebook, taking notes of everything that goes on.

As for me, I'm limited as to what I can do due to the girl on my lap, but it's not like I'd take notes anyway. I'm an auditory learner. And while I would normally join in more, I'm too focused on the way Lexie keeps shifting atop me.

Leaning forward to write something down. Turning to face someone who's talking. Wiggling to get into a more comfortable position.

It's pure torture.

Imagining her moving on me in a different way, me pumping into her, our bodies slick with sweat, her hoarse cries...

Shit. Coupled with her repositioning herself, my dick responds to the new train of thought, eager to explore it further.

Maybe tonight alone in bed, but now's not the time or place.

My hands tighten on her waist, stopping her from scooting back. "You've got to stop moving so much," I whisper in her ear.

She glances over her shoulder, looking peeved. "I'm trying to get comfortable."

"Well, you're making me a little *too* comfortable."

I pointedly look down, her eyes widening as she catches my drift. She goes still, gaze flicking south, not that she can see anything.

She whips back around, barely moving until the pizza arrives. I offer to go downstairs and collect it from the delivery guy, using the opportunity to adjust myself so no one's the wiser.

I cede the chair to her for the remainder of our time, perfectly content to stand behind her, and avoid Savannah as we make our goodbyes an hour later, not wanting to get caught in whatever weird rivalry they have going on.

Lexie grabs my hand once more for the short trek to the stairwell, her slim fingers still chilly, and lets go as soon as we're out of sight of the others.

Once we're outside, I say, "All right, you've got to let me in on this beef the two of you have."

"I don't want to talk about it," she mutters, crossing her arms.

"You voluntarily held my hand," I point out. "Whatever it is must be serious."

She's silent, picking up her pace when we get to the parking lot.

"If I'm pretending to be your boyfriend in front of her, I need something to go off of. If this were real, wouldn't you have told me about this history between the two of you?"

"If we were really dating, I wouldn't ever tell you about the rumor she helped spread." She presses her lips tightly together and scrubs a hand over her face. "Please forget I said that," she whispers.

Rumor? Does this have anything to do with how Savannah called her sexy Lexie?

She stops at my SUV, hand on the door handle, waiting for me to unlock it.

I fiddle with the keys, needing to say something to make this right, to get her off the edge. "It's forgotten." For now, at least.

She nods, looking up at me. "I'm not saying I'll never tell you anything, but…" She wrings her hands together in front of her. "Can it be some other time? Seeing her threw me for a loop."

I'll say.

I unlock the doors, driving us back to the lot she parked in, the brief ride silent.

She doesn't immediately escape as soon as I park like I expected, though. She continues to sit there, playing with her hoodie strings.

I glance out the window at the car she indicated is hers, a nearly twenty-year-old Corolla that appears to be on its last leg based on the amount of rust on it.

"Thank you for letting me hold your hand," she finally says. "And sit on your lap. I'm sorry for… using you."

Is she seriously bothered by that? How would she react if I told her she could use me however she wanted?

"You were method acting." I shrug, overly nonchalant. "No need to apologize."

Her lips tilt up at the corners. "What made you say I was salutatorian? She could easily have called me out on that."

"Nah." I wave off her concern. "No one remembers them. Valedictorian, yes. Salutatorian, no."

"How do you know?"

"Because—" Because I was the salutatorian of my high school class. She wouldn't believe me if I told her, though. She seems convinced I'm a dumb jock. "Because trust me, that's how."

She nods, twisting her hoodie strings. "Well, thanks."

"I've got your back, don't worry."

She unbuckles her seatbelt and opens the car door, hesitating for a moment. "As far as fake boyfriends go, I guess I could've picked worse."

It's a terrible compliment, but coming from her, it's akin to throwing her arms over my shoulders and showering me with praise.

I nod, watching her go, the Corolla's door screeching painfully as she opens it. I make a mental note to grab some WD-40 at work after my shift tomorrow.

I don't follow her right away as she reverses and leaves, idling in the lot instead. It's only seven-thirty, and it's not like I've got anything special to go home to. I don't speak much to my two roommates who are a decade older and not interested in socializing, and Tyler usually spends Thursday nights over at his girlfriend's apartment.

Maybe Austin's at the gym tonight. He's always up for sparring.

I pull out my phone to text him, startling as it rings, an unknown number on the screen. Despite my surety it's a telemarketer, I answer anyway, surprised when one of the lab researchers from the study, Justin, introduces himself.

"Is there something wrong?" I ask, unsure why he's calling so late. Did I mess up my paperwork? Did he figure out from my eye test I don't really love Lexie? She's going to kill me.

"No. Well, yes. Sort of." Okay, that clears things up. "It's with your urine sample."

Uh… what?

"I was going through the results from your analysis," he continues, "and everything looked great except for one thing. Your ketone levels."

"Ketone?" Doesn't that have something to do with a diet?

"They're an energy source for the body. And yours are exceptionally high. I've never seen this level before."

"Okay, so is that good?" Energy is good, right?

"No. They're usually only present when you're on a restricted carbohydrate diet or your insulin levels are low. Even then, they shouldn't be this high."

I wipe the palm of my free hand on my jeans, suddenly sweaty. I'm not a science major, but none of what he's saying sounds good.

"Are you on an extremely low-carb diet? Or have a disease related to insulin resistance? I'm sorry to be invasive, but I felt I had a duty to report this to you if you weren't aware. You checked on your intake form that you'd never been diagnosed with anything."

"I—" I take a gulp from the extra water bottle I bought earlier to ease the dryness in my throat. "No. I don't eat low-carb or have any diseases." What's he getting at?

"If you don't mind me asking, have you had any unusual symptoms lately? Increased thirst or hunger? Blurred vision? Unexplained weight loss? Irritability? Fatigue?"

"Um..." I rub at my temple, trying to process his words. My gaze lands on the nearly empty water bottle in the cup holder, and I glance behind me to the backseat at all the fast food wrappers. "I've been thirsty and hungry more than normal, I guess. And I've been losing some weight." Even though I'm eating all the time. "But not the other things." Not any more than usual, at least.

"Okay." There's the sound of shuffling papers over the line, and he says, "Well, I'm not a medical doctor, but I think you should get tested for diabetes."

A scoffing noise escapes me involuntarily. "I don't have that. I'm in great shape." Seriously, what is he thinking?

56

"Type one diabetes," he clarifies. "It has nothing to do with lifestyle factors. Your body just doesn't produce the insulin it needs to. There's a student health clinic on campus if you don't have a primary care doctor you see regularly…"

He continues speaking but there's a momentary disconnect between his words and my ability to process them. Diabetes? There's no way. I've never had anything worse than a cold. I've been healthy my whole life.

I tune back in to what he's saying—something about taking a glucose tolerance test, whatever that is. "What'll happen if I don't go to the doctor? With these ketones?"

"If your body doesn't have the necessary insulin to process them, there are a number of things that can go wrong. Dehydration being a big one that you may already be experiencing. Worst-case scenario, the excess ketones basically poison your blood, which can be fatal."

I swallow, my throat parched. Is it really dry or only because he suggested I could be dehydrated? I guzzle down the last of the water anyway and thank him for calling, promising to make an appointment at the clinic as soon as I can.

I drop my phone in my lap and rest my head on the steering wheel. Getting tested is only a precaution. It doesn't mean I'm giving credence to his theory. He's probably just being overcautious.

But what does it mean if he's right? How will this change my life? Five minutes ago, my biggest concern was figuring out a way to get closer to Lexie. Now this?

You know what? I'm freaking out over nothing. I'll go to the doctor and they'll do whatever test they're going to do and confirm it was a freak occurrence of these ketone levels.

A shiver runs over the back of my neck and up to prickle my scalp, the sense that something's not right stealing over me.

No, no. Everything is fine.

It has to be.

# CHAPTER SIX

## LEXIE

**Ethan**: *One last study session before the test tomorrow? Just you and me—*
*no Savannah.*

I stare at Ethan's text, drumming my fingers on my desk. I did promise to
tutor him in Psych, and as much as the review on Thursday night helped, I
could use a refresher.

**Me**: *I can meet any time after five and before eight.*

**Ethan**: *Library at five-thirty?*

**Me**: *See you then.*

THAT SHOULD GIVE me enough time after class to go to the computer lab
to type up a paper, then stop home after studying for a bite before work. You
know, for my one assigned shift. Thank God someone gave me one of their
shifts Saturday night. I'd made bank. Sarah wasn't happy, but I don't care.

My Cost Accounting professor clears her throat, and I glance up, finding her
gaze narrowed on me. Shit.

I tuck my phone away and focus on the whiteboard where she's going over
cost-volume-profit analysis. I don't want her to think I'm not taking this
class seriously. She's one of the professors that help set up senior year
accounting internships. I need her to like me.

The rest of class is uneventful, as is my next one, and I head over to the library at five-thirty to meet up with Ethan.

I find him already sitting at a table in the main area on the first floor, running a hand through his dark hair till it stands on end, then flattening it down again, over and over as he stares at something on his phone. He doesn't notice as I approach, fixated on whatever's on his screen, and as I get closer, the dark circles under his eyes are apparent.

"Rough weekend?" I ask, dropping my backpack on the table.

He startles, swiftly turning over his phone so it's facedown. Could he be more obvious?

"Something like that," he mutters.

"Party too hard?" It's nearly evening, though. Any lingering effects from his weekend antics should be long gone by now.

"I'm not much of a partier."

Really? With as social as he is?

He's uncharacteristically silent as I unpack my textbook and notebook, sitting there glumly as I spread my things out on the table. What's going on with him?

I can't believe I'm initiating this, but I ask, "Are you okay?" Usually, I can't get him to shut up. And after the way he helped me out last week, I should make more of an effort to be nicer to him.

He runs a hand over his beard, tugging at the ends. "Yeah, fine. I, uh…" He stands, rounding the table. "I'm actually going to grab a coffee." He motions toward the small coffee shop attached to the library. "You want anything?"

"No, I'm fine."

He nods, still seeming distracted, and walks off, leaving me alone. What the hell was that about? Well, if he wants to waste his tutoring time, that's on him.

I review my notes from Thursday's study session, glancing up as he finally returns with a coffee in his hand. "More awake?"

"Yeah, sorry about that." He rubs at the back of his neck, his bicep bunching as he stretches his arm up. Not that I'm looking. It was hard enough not staring at him shirtless in the gym last week.

He places a white paper bag on the table as he sits back down, pulling out a blueberry muffin and a plastic knife. He cuts it in two and slides half over to me. "I only wanted a taste," he explains.

Fine with me. I love these things.

I take a bite and ask him what he wants to go over specifically for the test tomorrow, but he shrugs, asking me to read my notes to him aloud.

Okay, whatever.

He asks a few clarifying questions over the next twenty or so minutes, but otherwise stays quiet, listening to me.

By the time he's finished with his drink, he's more awake, and asks me to pause so he can throw away his cup. On his way back to the table, a guy stops him, and I'm only half paying attention until I hear them mention calculus.

I tune my ears in, listening as the stranger thanks Ethan for all the help he gave him last semester. The guy actually says he wouldn't have passed the class without him. Say what now? Was Amber right when mentioning it was Calculus he and Christian took together?

Ethan's gaze shifts to meet mine briefly, a guilty expression crossing his face before he excuses himself and returns to the table.

"What was that about?" I ask, pretending not to have overheard them.

"Nothing."

Yeah, right. "Do you know him?"

"We were in the same class last semester."

I shut my textbook, folding my hands atop it. "Which class?"

He strokes his beard. "Why the twenty questions?"

Ugh. He's acting like me now. "Have you taken Calculus?" I ask outright.

"Yeah," he answers warily after a moment.

"I did, too. Who'd you have?"

"Walker."

That's the guy that fails half his students every year. I'd purposely avoided his class and took it with another professor, and even then I got a C plus. It's the only C on my transcript.

"So do you have to retake it?"

"No."

"You passed?"

"Mm-hmm."

Seriously? How? "What grade did you get?"

His gaze searches mine, lips twisting. "You really want to know?"

"Stop being cryptic."

He smiles, the first one I've seen from him today, the familiarity of it easing me. He kind of freaked me out earlier being so solemn.

"I got an A minus."

I blink, waiting for him to say *gotcha* or tell me he's joking, but he doesn't. "Why the hell am I tutoring you in Psych if you're getting A's in Calculus?"

He holds his hands out in front of him. "You're the one who offered it off the bat, not me."

I open my mouth to argue, then shut it just as quickly. He's right. I never asked him if he needed help, only assumed. "What's your GPA?"

"Three-point-nine."

What the fuck? That's higher than mine. "But you're a boxer."

A shadow of annoyance crosses his face. "So? That means I can't be smart?"

"No," I burst out, unable to help myself. "You're not allowed to be gorgeous and athletic and charming *and* smart."

62

There's silence, my mouth gaping open as I realize what I said, his eyes wide as the two of us stare at each other.

What is wrong with me? Why would I say that? Why was I even thinking it? I don't think that way about him.

Yes, I found his picture at the lab the other day handsome. But that was more of an observation. The word gorgeous has a different implication. As if I'm… interested.

That's ridiculous. I'm not interested in anyone.

The tell-tale sign of his lips curving at the corners has me jumping out of my chair, grabbing my things to stuff in my backpack. I point a finger at him menacingly. "Don't say anything. It was an objective observation." He opens his mouth and I cut him off. "Not a word."

He mimes zipping his lips and reaches out to circle his fingers around my wrist, tugging me back in my seat. "You don't have to pack your things. We can still study together."

I slump in my chair, resting my forehead in my hands, elbows braced on the table. "Were you laughing at me the whole time?"

"Not the whole time."

I make a motion to stand and he laughs, tugging me back down again. "To be fair, your dad told you the first time we met I wasn't like most of the other guys there."

"I thought he was just being nice. You're paying him to help you beat up people."

He chuckles. "I love boxing, but it's not my whole world. Yeah, I'd like to compete, but it's not sustainable for a long-term future."

"So what's your major?"

"Civil engineering."

I hide my face in my hands again. He has a nearly perfect GPA in his junior year with that major? I'm a fucking idiot.

"You don't even take notes," I mumble.

"I'm a good auditory learner. I hear something and it just kind of... sticks."

Of course it does. Meanwhile, I have to study my notes ten times to remember it well enough for a test.

I mentally review our past interactions, the assumptions I made, the incredible patience he must have shown. "God, I've been such a bitch to you."

"No, you're just... prickly."

My lower lip quivers for a moment before I firm it. Prickly. That's a good word for me.

Why is he helping me? This was supposed to be an equal exchange. He helped me out of a jam and I help him in class. But it's unbalanced now. "If you don't need me to tutor you, what can I do? This needs to be equal."

"Lexie, you don't have to do anything extra. Let's just continue the study."

"No, you were the one who helped me out to begin with. I need to make it up to you. I didn't even pay you my share of the pizza from the other night."

"Don't worry about it."

I shake my head, knowing I'm being stubborn, but that's who I am. Prickly and stubborn. "I don't want to owe you."

He rests his elbows on the table, blowing out a long breath. "We're partners in this, right? That means we do things for each other. Sometimes I pick up the slack, sometimes you do. And we do it because we want to, not because we're obligated."

The question burns on my tongue, but I'm afraid to ask it. *Why would you want to help me?*

Guys don't do things out of the goodness of their hearts. Even if they are gorgeous and athletic and charming and smart.

Especially then.

But Ethan... He doesn't seem to follow the normal rules, does he?

"So can we be partners?" he asks softly. "Without worrying about keeping score?"

I waver. This isn't the dynamic I'm used to.

"Your Snookums wants to finish the study with his Pookie Bear."

A huff of laughter escapes me. "We're not actually calling each other that."

"Speak for yourself."

I give him a shaky smile, something about this moment feeling defining as I nod. Like we're actually a team rather than acting out of necessity.

His earlier bad mood appears forgotten as he smiles back, the two of us silently agreeing to continue studying, not acknowledging aloud how this changes things.

Because there's no doubt... things are different now.

———————

"Lexie," Travis calls out as I open the front door to our apartment. "What was the name of that guy on our school bus? The one I had a crush on."

Wow. What a way to be greeted. "Um..." I rack my brain, trying to remember. "Adam."

"Oh my God, yes. It was on the tip of my tongue. I kept thinking Allen for some reason."

"Must not have been a big crush," Isaac says from his spot on the couch.

"I could only see the back of his head on the bus. Look him up. Adam Eldridge."

I set my stuff down on the kitchen counter, peeking over at Travis and his boyfriend huddled in front of a laptop in the living room. "What are you doing?"

"Looking up our old crushes from high school," Isaac says. "I want to see who Travis was into."

Okay, that's weird. I wouldn't want to know anything about who my significant other formerly liked. If Ethan told me...

Whoa. Where'd that thought come from? I don't care who Ethan liked. Or likes currently.

I mean, I'm assuming he's not into anyone right now since he's pretending to date me. That'd be awkward, otherwise. But I did practically strong-arm him into this. Am I putting his love life on hold? Should I ask him later?

What kind of girl would he be into? Probably someone outgoing and beautiful and kind. Someone he can laugh with. Someone who has their life together. Who isn't struggling to make ends meet. Who isn't prickly and stubborn.

I blink away the sudden moisture in my eyes, turning toward the fridge so the guys can't see me. What the hell is wrong with me?

"Lexie," Isaac says. "When are you coming into the salon again? I need to touch up your roots soon."

I stroke a hand over my hair, studying the tips of my auburn locks. It's still a little weird to see it this way after being a brunette for so long. "I don't have the money," I reply honestly, pivoting around to face him.

He gets off the couch and comes over to join me in the kitchen, reaching out to fan my hair forward over my shoulders. "You think I'd beg you to let me dye your hair and then make you pay for the upkeep? Besides, I'm still learning. You'd be doing me a favor."

That first time in the chair had taken over five hours, but he needs the practice for his cosmetology program. I wanted him to like me, so I agreed, especially after Travis refused to let him bleach his hair.

If Isaac is happy with me, then Travis is, too. I need all the brownie points I can get to help me stay here.

"Just let me know when. My schedule is pretty open." On account of the no shifts at work. I'd even called up my old bar asking if I could come back, but apparently, they hadn't taken too kindly to me quitting in the first place.

"Who was your crush in high school?" Isaac asks me. "Please tell me someone better than this Adam guy. Your school had to have some hotties."

I exchange glances with Travis, my stomach bottoming out.

"Lexie never bothered herself with immature high school guys," Travis tells him casually. "She was too busy working or studying."

"Like you should have been doing," I remind him. I walk out of the kitchen, mouthing *thanks* as I pass him.

"Well, you have time now," Isaac says to me. "Who was that guy I saw you on campus with last week? He was cute."

"What?" Travis and I say in unison.

Travis stares at me, confused. He knows I don't willingly talk to guys, much less hang out with them. Not after what happened with Cody.

"You didn't tell me you're seeing anyone," he says, a hint of hurt in his tone.

"I'm not," I insist.

"Tall, muscular, dark hair and beard," Isaac elaborates. "He was carrying your bag and you got in an SUV with him. I saw you when I was picking up Travis from class..." His head turns between me and Travis. "Sorry if that was supposed to be a secret."

Travis's brows pop up further, just as mine relax. "Oh, that's Ethan. He's..." What is he exactly? How do I explain this? "He's, um, my fake boyfriend for this psychology study."

Both Travis and Isaac blink at me, dumbfounded. Yeah, it's admittedly pretty out of character for me.

"Your what now?"

I relay what happened last week, Travis's expression growing only more confused.

"Wait, so if you're only pretending for this thing at the Psych lab, why were you getting in his car?"

I scratch at the back of my knee, suddenly itchy. "We were invited to this study group. I couldn't say no."

He huffs out a disbelieving laugh. "You voluntarily hung out with people?"

I cross my arms over my chest. "I'm not that bad."

"Um, yes you are." He laughs again, but something about his statement strikes a nerve.

After hanging out with Ethan all those days last week, spending the weekend by myself had felt... lonelier than usual. I'd expected to see him at Marty's when I'd gone to work on the books Saturday morning, but he wasn't there.

"What's this Ethan guy's last name?" Isaac asks, returning to his laptop. "I only saw him from far away."

"Hudson."

Travis turns to me, lowering his voice. "I'm surprised you're doing this. Are you all right?"

I squint my eyes dramatically at him. "Are you questioning my mental state?"

His mouth quirks on one side. "I mean when you're with him. Are you... safe?"

"Yes." The answer comes with no hesitation. Somehow, despite meeting him only a week ago, I already know that.

His brows lift in surprise at the immediacy of my reply. Or maybe the content. I'll be the first to admit that trust doesn't come easy to me. It's even hard to let my guard down completely around Isaac, and he and Travis have been dating for five months.

"Oh my God, is this him?"

I glance toward Isaac, who has Ethan's Facebook profile pulled up on the screen. "Yeah."

"Damn, girl. That's your fake boyfriend? You need to hurry up and make him your real one."

Travis moves in closer to look, turning sharply back toward me. "Lexie, he's a fox."

Oh, no. That's Travis's top honor of hotness.

"He's okay looking, I guess."

Isaac turns to me, his expression clearly conveying his disgust with me. "You need your eyes checked? Look at these." He scrolls through Ethan's pictures, stopping on one of him shirtless at the gym, his arm slung over the shoulders of another guy I've seen there before. "Hello, how are you not jumping all over that?"

I can't tear my gaze away from the screen, studying his broad shoulders. His heavy pecs. His ridged abdomen. He even has a dark trail of hair along his abs leading directly…

I turn, breaking contact. I already saw it in person. It's not like the sight is new.

*And you were scared to look at it then too.*

Shut up.

"Looks aren't everything," I comment. "And he wouldn't want you ogling him, anyway." Actually, knowing him, he'd probably love it.

"Is he a douche?" Isaac asks, still clicking through his pictures.

"No, he's nice." The way he'd bought me that ice cream as an apology. How he'd stood up for me with Savannah. Insisting I don't owe him anything when we both know I do.

Out of the corner of my eye, I catch Travis staring at me, but I don't meet his eye.

I return to the kitchen, throwing a Hot Pocket in the microwave. "I have to get to work soon."

"We made spaghetti earlier if you want any leftovers," Travis says.

"I'm fine." I'm not a moocher.

"I'm beginning to think you don't like my cooking."

I stare at my sad meal rotating in the microwave. "Travis, I'm fine."

"Well, have some when you get home from work."

69

I nod, listening to them continue to look up boys they liked in high school, giggling over each other's crushes. What would it be like to be so comfortable with someone you could do that?

And why do I care? It's not like that's in the cards for me.

There's no use dreaming about what you can't have.

# CHAPTER SEVEN

## ETHAN

LEXIE'S HAIR shines in the sun, a halo of dark fire around her head as she sits on a bench outside the Psych building, waiting for me. We decided before meeting here last week that we should always walk into the lab together, like a normal couple would.

"Hey, how'd you do on the test yesterday?"

She squints, holding a hand up to shield her eyes against the sun as she looks up at me. "Good. You probably got an A, Mister Three-point-nine."

I give her a broad smile, glad she can joke about it now. And her blurted admission of what she thinks of me? Perfection.

I know better than to bring it up, though.

"Don't be a hater."

She rolls her eyes, standing and handing me her backpack. "You'll carry this for me, right, Snookums?"

Wow, someone's in a good mood. "Of course, Pookie Bear."

We walk up the stairs to the fourth floor where the Psychobiology lab is, Dr. Clark greeting us warmly. "We're splitting up the group today," she tells us. "You two will be with Justin down the hall using the fMRI machine."

Great. He'll probably ask me if I went to the doctor. I did… but it wasn't the news I was hoping for.

"They must be doing those brain scans today," Lexie whispers as we follow our professor to a room with a computer and multiple monitors. Against one wall is a long glass window showing another room with a huge piece of equipment in the center. It's kind of intimidating looking.

"Hope you're not claustrophobic," I whisper back.

"No, I'm fine."

"Hey, guys," Justin says, his back to us as he does something hunched over a tray table in the corner of the room. "Just give me a sec to finish up here."

Dr. Clark leaves us and I look through the window, studying the machine, asking if I can go in the room to examine it.

"Yeah, but no touching."

I open the door and wander over to it, leaning over and sticking my head in the hole.

Lexie follows me, elbowing me in the side. "Don't do that. It could be on."

"It's fine." I turn to face her, finding her right there, our faces only a few inches apart.

She blinks, lips parting, and my gaze zeroes in on her mouth instinctively.

Her tongue darts out to wet her bottom lip, the action surprising me. Did she do that on purpose? There's no way, right?

"All right, which one of you wants to go first?" Justin calls from the other room.

She steps back, whatever connection between us lost. Was it only on my part?

"I will," she says, turning back. "What do I need to do?"

I follow her, lingering in the doorway by her side.

"First, remove anything metal. Jewelry, coins, keys, and anything with magnetic strips like credit cards."

"I'm clear."

"Great." He motions to the table beside him, medical equipment laid neatly in a row on top. Behind it is an IV stand. "I'll need to set up this IV line."

She blinks, her face leaching of color. "What?"

"It's a contrast medium. It helps us see more detail in the image."

If I wasn't paying such close attention, I'd miss the way she compulsively swallows, the tremble in her lower lip, how her gaze darts around the room.

"You never said anything about needles."

"It's standard procedure for an fMRI. We'll remove the IV when we're finished. Should be about thirty minutes total."

The man's clearly not picking up on her apparent anxiety. Some researcher he is.

"You have a needle phobia?" I whisper to her as Justin turns his back to grab a syringe. I admit, I'm not crazy about needles either, but after this past weekend getting poked and jabbed at the clinic for a million tests, they've become sort of routine.

"No," she claims, clearly lying.

"You sure?"

She glances at me, panic in her eyes for a moment before she blinks and it disappears. "Maybe a… strong dislike."

"You want me to go first?"

I expect her to scoff, full of bravado, but she actually takes me up on my offer, nodding. Her gaze is back on the syringe, brows pinched together.

I move in front of her, blocking her view. "Are you okay to go through with this?" I murmur. "We can say you're sick or something." It's not a lie. Something's obviously going on with her.

"I'll be fine." She wipes clear any kind of emotion she was just feeling. "Totally good by the time you're done."

My hands itch to reach out and comfort her.

But that's not the sort of relationship we have.

"I'll actually go first," I announce.

"All right."

He motions me over to him and questions me a bit more about things that could interfere with the machine, then sets up the IV, Lexie's back to us as he does it. "The procedure itself will be painless, but you'll need to stay still. You'll hear some loud thumping sounds when you're inside, but that's normal."

He goes over a few more things about what I should expect and leads me in the room where I lay on the fMRI table, my head wedged between two cushions.

"This will help with the noise," he says, handing me a set of earplugs.

I stuff them in, trying to get comfortable, but it's impossible.

"We'll get started now," Justin says over a loudspeaker, the sound muffled. "Remember to keep still."

The table slides forward, the machine making a knocking noise as it revs up. After a while, a screen flickers to life, images appearing one after the other. These are different than the ones from the eye tests last week, except for one.

Lexie's picture.

My gaze traces her features, lingering on the creamy, ivory skin, those full lips curved in a half smile, her hazel eyes that seem more brown than green in this photo.

What's activating in my brain right now? The right regions?

I don't love her, but I can't deny I'm interested. There's definitely attraction. Lust too, if I'm being honest. And she's intriguing for sure with her strange dichotomy of confidence and reluctant vulnerability. When she lets her guard down enough, she's witty and clever. Amusing her is an ongoing mission I'm determined to win.

You have to earn the right to be close to her, and it's a challenge I'm so far enjoying.

Whatever is showing up on their monitors must be okay, though, because the test continues without interruption, my eyes heavy by the end after laying down so long.

Justin returns to the room and unhooks my IV, pressing a bandage to the area, and I follow him back into the first area.

"How'd I do?" I ask, curious as to what showed up.

"Fine," he replies, leaving it at that. Maybe he can't discuss the results with me. "You're up, Lexie."

She nods, eyes wide again as he heads to the table and grabs the second syringe.

He goes through the same spiel he did with me about removing anything metal or magnetic, and as he approaches her to inject the contrast medium, she steps back, her earlier promise to be fine by the time I'm done forgotten.

He pauses. "You okay?"

She swallows, staring at his hand. "I have a bit of a thing about needles."

"Sorry, it's standard procedure for the study. Everyone has to get it for the results to be uniform."

She trembles as he approaches again, and I hold a hand up to stop him. "Give us a sec, okay?"

He glances at the clock on the wall. "Okay, but we have to keep on schedule. We only have the machine booked for the next half hour before another researcher needs it."

I pull her over to the corner, sitting her in the chair there, and kneel next to her, wrapping a hand around the back of her neck. She's so worked up, she actually lets me do it without resistance, the muscles there rock hard.

"You've got to relax," I whisper, massaging her neck.

She releases a breath, swaying forward as the tension releases. "I'm sorry. I thought I'd be okay by now."

"You will be okay. I won't let anything bad happen to you." I reach out and take her hand, surprised when she grips it like a lifeline. "Just squeeze my hand while he's doing it."

She nods and I signal to Justin to come over and do it.

Her grip tightens painfully as he takes her arm and swabs her inner elbow with an alcohol wipe.

"Hey, not so tight," I joke. "I need my hands."

She gives me a shaky smile. "You're a boxer. You can't take a little pain?"

"You can do whatever you want to me."

The words slip out, a definite sexual undertone to them, and her gaze sharpens, some of the worry leaving her face.

Justin uses the opportunity to stick her then, and I move my hand on her neck so she can't turn her head to view her arm. "Look at me. Don't worry about that."

She somehow clenches my fingers harder, enough that I'm worried it might bruise, but that's okay. Whatever she needs to get through this.

"It's cold," she murmurs. "In my veins."

"Some people report a flushing sensation," Justin says. "It'll pass soon."

He finishes up and attaches the IV line, but I keep her attention on me, still rubbing the back of her neck, enjoying the rare chance to touch her freely. Her skin is warm and soft, muscles gradually loosening as the worst of it is over, but I don't let go just yet.

She holds eye contact with me, her normal barriers gone, and as Justin moves to the other side of the room, waking up the computer, she whispers, "You keep seeing me at my worst."

Her hand is still gripping mine, not quite as tight now, and I run my thumb over her knuckles, soothing her. "Nothing's scared me off so far."

"Let's get you in the other room," Justin says.

She nods, making the mistake of looking down at her arm, and freezes.

I tip her chin back up. "Don't look at it. Think about something else."

She squeezes her eyes shut for a moment, then stands, letting go of my hand as she follows Justin and situates herself on the fMRI table.

I watch through the window, holding my breath as he returns and starts up the machine, her head disappearing from view as the procedure begins.

I take a seat in the chair Lexie just vacated, watching the monitors for a few minutes, but I have no idea what it means. My leg jiggles and I have to force myself to stop, laying a hand on it.

"I've always wanted to read her mind," I joke aloud. "Now I can."

He looks over his shoulder, glancing at me, but doesn't respond. Guess it wasn't funny.

I stand, crossing my arms, and get closer to the biggest screen, studying it. "Looks like a walnut."

"Brains look like that," he confirms.

After another minute, he frowns and pushes the intercom button. "I need you to stay still, Lexie."

I stare through the window but can't see anything wrong. "What's going on?"

"She's shaking or something," he mutters. "Look at this. Her amygdala's lighting up when it shouldn't."

I'm guessing that's bad from the way he says it.

"Can you shut off the machine for a second? I'll go in there and talk to her."

He wavers. "That's not part of the procedure. No one else has contact with their partners while they're in there."

"And no one else was probably as freaked out as her. This will even the playing field."

He looks at the clock again on the wall. "I can give you a couple of minutes. Any longer and we'll have to scrap it and move on."

77

Does that mean they'd kick us out of the study if she's unable to complete this? She'll be crushed.

I join her in the room, crouching next to her on the side opposite of her IV. She's still half inside the machine, head immobile so she can't see me. "Lexie."

She reaches up and takes out one of her earplugs. "What is it?"

"You're moving too much," I whisper, not sure if there are microphones in here. "They can't get a clear image. And some part of your brain is lighting up that shouldn't."

Her fist clenches reflexively at her side and she lets out a sound of frustration. "I can feel it. The… the needle. I know it's there."

"Think about something else. Something you love." I slide my hand over hers, a featherlight touch, up over her wrist, her inner forearm, trying to relax her. "Concentrate on it."

Her body visibly relaxes as she takes a deep breath and releases it. I continue to stroke her arm, tracing the veins on her wrist, pleased when goosebumps race across her skin in response.

"Is that okay?"

"Yes," she whispers after a moment.

"You thinking of something you love?"

She doesn't respond right away.

"Lexie?"

"I don't know what to think of," she admits. "There's nothing I… love."

My eyes squeeze shut, my movements on her arm slowing. "Of course there is." Everyone loves something. "What about your mint chocolate chip ice cream?"

She releases a breath that almost sounds like a laugh. "You want me to think of ice cream when I see your face?"

"Yeah. Make it a positive association."

"Okay," she whispers.

I nod, satisfied now that she seems more relaxed. "I have to go. Keep thinking of ice cream."

"Ethan?"

"Yeah?"

Her hand finds mine, squeezing softly. "Thank you."

I impulsively press a kiss to the back of her hand. "Any time."

I leave before she can tell me I crossed the line, avoiding Justin's eye as I shut the door behind me. I hope he didn't hear any of that.

He starts up the machine again and I silently watch the screen, wishing I could interpret it.

After a few minutes, I ask, "Is she doing better?"

"Not as great as I'd like, but better. Whatever you said must have helped some."

So maybe he didn't hear.

"What are you guys looking for?"

He points to an area of her brain on the screen. "The ventral tegmental area is one we want to see light up. Same with the hippocampus, hypothalamus, and a few other places. Those are all associated with emotion regulation and reward processing."

"What does the area you said earlier do? The one that was lighting up." The amygdala, I think he called it.

"It activates when someone's afraid. We usually see a decreased amount of activity there when looking at a partner's picture."

Right. Not in Lexie's case, though.

"Did you, uh, go to the doctor?" he asks cautiously, keeping his attention on the screen.

"Yeah." I reach a hand up to stroke my beard, scrubbing the wiry hair. "You were right."

"Aw, man. I'm sorry."

"No, it's fine. I mean, not *fine*, but I needed to know." It's a wonder I could focus on something besides diabetes for the last hour. It's all I've been able to think about otherwise.

They'd done a blood sugar test on Friday which indicated I have it, then a different fasting blood sugar test first thing Monday morning which gave the same results. The past two days have been filled with appointments with an endocrinologist and nurses throwing information at me, learning how to use a glucose meter and insulin syringe, worrying whether my sugar levels are too high or too low.

But even with all that, I'm still glad I know now. It's hard to imagine what might have happened if I didn't.

"Thank you for reaching out," I add. "It could have, I don't know, saved my life."

"Yeah, of course."

I clear my throat, not wanting to dwell on that too much. "Could you not mention anything to Lexie? I haven't told her yet." Haven't told anyone. How do I even broach the topic? "I'm still wrapping my head around it all."

"You got it," he says. "Researcher-patient confidentiality."

"Thanks."

I return to the chair in the corner, waiting until Lexie's finished and Justin brings her back, noting how pale her face is again.

Damn. I should have gone in there to help when he took out her IV.

I stand and sling an arm over her shoulders, hating the way she hunches in on herself.

"You okay?"

"I'm fine," she murmurs. "Just want this day to be over already."

"We have anything left to do?" I ask Justin.

"No. You're both free to go. Drink plenty of liquids to flush out that dye."

Yeah, drinking a lot of water hasn't been a problem lately.

"Come on." I lead her out of the room and down the hall, passing by the main lab.

I pause in the doorway, catching Dr. Clark's eye. "We'll see you next week?"

She holds up a hand in a wave. "Yeah, thanks guys. I'm excited to see how your brains look."

Don't hold your breath.

We continue on, Lexie speeding up so my arm drops from her shoulders.

"You have somewhere to be?"

She glances over her shoulder, a flash of guilt crossing her face. "Yeah. I have to run."

So that's how she's going to play it? I thought I'd at least get a little explanation of what happened in there.

I nod, slowing my gait so she can make a quicker escape.

At the stairwell exit, she pauses, turning back toward me briefly. "I'll be at Marty's tonight working on the books. In case, you know, you're there too or something."

Does she want me to be there? "Okay."

"Okay," she repeats, disappearing through the door.

Maybe she'll be ready to talk later. Maybe she'll answer some questions.

I chuckle aloud. And maybe I'm deluding myself.

# CHAPTER EIGHT

## LEXIE

STUPID FREAKING NEEDLES.

Why didn't they put that on any of the forms we filled out initially? Was it there and I glossed over it? Did they purposely withhold the information so it would be a surprise?

Or am I the only person it's a big deal to?

*Mom laying on the couch, arm outstretched on the coffee table, a syringe dangling from her blue fingertips.*

I squeeze my eyes shut, pausing on the stairs as I grip the railing. Not here. It was bad enough reliving that stuff in the lab.

I push the memory away, continuing down, shoving open the bottom door with more force than necessary as I exit.

While I'd normally head over to the computer lab to get some work done, I'm not up to it today. I drive home and review my notes from class earlier, eyeing the doorstop of a book I still need to finish for Russian Lit, but I can't focus enough to fully comprehend it right now.

*Rushing over and placing trembling fingers on her neck, unable to find a pulse, lips blue too. Her skin pale, a fresh puncture wound next to the scabbing along her inner elbow.*

I slam my notebook closed, standing and pacing my room, past the mattress on the floor, the desk and chair that Travis's last roommate left behind, to the window with a sheet tacked up over it, and spin around, repeating the path until the image leaves my mind.

It's in the past. It can't happen again.

I grab my bag and head out of the apartment, thankful Travis isn't home yet from class. He would know something was wrong.

The same as Ethan did.

No, I'm not thinking about him either. Even though I stupidly told him where I'd be tonight, like it was an invitation. Even though I owe him an explanation for earlier. And an apology. And gratitude.

Ugh.

Could I have done anything more embarrassing in front of him? Maybe only if my lunch had come up the way it had threatened to.

And yet, he had still stuck by me, willingly helping, despite not asking him to. Was it just for show because of Justin? It was definitely the kind of stuff a boyfriend would do. Especially when he had pressed that lingering kiss to the back of my hand.

Wait, didn't I just tell myself I'm not thinking about him?

I make my way to Marty's Boxing Gym earlier than I intended to go, but Marty only said to be here tonight, not a specific time. I ignore the male interest that greets me as I walk in, not making eye contact with anyone. You'd think they've never seen a girl before.

Even so, I can't help taking a second look every time I pass a tall guy with dark hair, searching for a matching beard and mischievous green eyes.

But no such luck. He must not have cared about seeing me tonight. And why would he after I practically ran from him in the Psych building?

I just couldn't handle much more then. I'd been too exposed. Too weak. Too raw.

All right, for the last time, stop thinking about him.

I knock twice on Marty's glass door, waiting till he raises his gray head and signals for me to enter.

"You finished with that ledger yet?" He's not one for preamble, is he?

"Almost." It was a lot of grunt work, but breaking it up over a few nights this past week made it more manageable. "Once I record everything, I'll start reconciling and see where we stand."

"You doubt my bookkeeping skills?" His tone is gruff, but I'm used to that.

"I'm just doing my due diligence."

"Good. We need more people like that around here."

"Um, thanks." I'm not sure it was even a compliment.

"You need this?" He points to the computer on his desk.

I nod. It'd be a lot easier if I had a laptop, but my last one finally crapped out on me a few months ago and I haven't had the money to replace it. For now, I'm making do with the computer lab on campus.

"Sounds like a good excuse for me to get on home, then." He stands, smoothing down the front of his wrinkled white dress shirt over his flat stomach. For an old guy, he's still in great shape.

"I wasn't trying to kick you out."

"I was looking for an excuse to leave. The gym doesn't need me as much anymore. It runs all right on its own for the most part." He doesn't appear particularly saddened by that statement. "Steve's closing tonight, so the place is in good hands."

He rounds the desk, hightailing it out of here. Was he just waiting for me to show up so he could leave?

I shake my head and settle in at his desk, pulling out the ledger and getting to work.

The next time I look up, my neck has a crick in it. How long have I been at it?

I focus on the lower corner of the screen. Two hours? Wow. Well, at least the tedious part is done after transcribing everything.

I stand, stretching until something pops in my back, and glance out the office window onto the main floor. There are fewer guys out there now, most hanging out around the rings on the other side of the room. There's a huge guy with shaggy blond hair in the closest ring duking it out with another equally big guy, three men on the sidelines watching them.

In the farthest ring is one of the gym's trainers, working with a dark-haired man whose back is to me. Could it be…

No, it's probably not. A ridiculous number of guys here have dark hair.

I sit down, staring at the computer, but my concentration is broken. My gaze cuts to the window, hoping I can see the man's face, but no such luck.

Okay, would it be such a big deal if I went over to the ring and double checked? Then at least I would know for sure and wouldn't spend all my time in here wondering.

I meander out there, pulling my sweater tighter around me, and take a wide berth to avoid the first ring, the guys on the sidelines calling out increasingly filthy suggestions about what the two men in the ring should do to each other. Why are boys so weird?

As I near the farthest ring, the boxer in there turns, showing me his profile, and my stomach sinks in response. It's not Ethan.

"You finally taking a break?"

I jump, thankfully keeping the scream contained in my throat, and whirl around, finding my fake boyfriend there. "Why are you trying to scare me?"

He holds his hands up. "I asked you a question. It's not like I came up and goosed you."

I hold a hand to my chest, willing my heart to slow down. "Where were you? I didn't see you out here."

His mouth crooks up on one side. "You were looking for me?"

Damn. He got me.

I roll my eyes. "I was just curious is all."

He nods, but doesn't take it further, letting me keep my dignity. He points to the punching bags about twenty feet away. "Practicing. Steve's with Johnson tonight."

"You normally train with him?"

"My first choice is your dad. His style meshes with mine the most. But Steve's my second choice." He holds a hand up to the side of his mouth. "But don't tell him that," he stage whispers, "He thinks he's number one."

Does he ever stop with the antics? Even if, I have to admit, they're occasionally amusing? "So you don't have anyone to punch tonight?"

He strokes his beard thoughtfully. "Well, I could practice blocking."

"With who?"

"You."

I can't help but laugh. "Yeah, right."

He grins, those incredibly straight white teeth on display. His orthodontist must have charged a pretty penny. "Come on. I thought you would jump at the chance to hit at me. Get some of that aggression out."

I shake my head at him. "I don't box."

"Lawrence didn't teach you anything?"

"I didn't say that."

"See? I knew it." He holds up his fists in a blocking position. "Show me what you've got. If anyone has a wicked right hook, it's you."

I twist my lips. I guess I should do something he wants after earlier today. I owe him. "Okay, but I'm putting on gloves. I'm not accidentally breaking my hand when I hit your thick skull."

He pumps his fists up. "Yes."

God, he's so ridiculous.

We head over to the rack along the east wall with all the gloves and I search through for the smallest looking ones.

"You wrapping?" He holds up a roll of hand wrap.

I don't need it since I'm not seriously hitting him, but I still find myself nodding for some reason, avoiding his eye.

"Should I wrap it?" he asks when I make no move to take it from him.

I nod again, though I'm perfectly capable of doing it myself. I learned how years before he even picked up a glove.

He unrolls it, taking my hand as he loops it over my thumb and back the opposite way around my wrist, his touch as steady and sure as it was earlier today in the lab. Fingertips work-roughened where they hold my hand still, warm against the cool of my skin. Gaze focused completely on his task, the playful air usually about him gone for the moment.

I hold my breath, barely inhaling as he leans in closer to check his work, unable to help taking note of the way the hairs at the nape of his neck curl slightly with sweat.

He continues wrapping my hand, something hypnotic about it, just like the way he'd soothed me in the lab today, tracing those fingertips featherlight over my skin, stirring something within me...

I couldn't process it at the time with everything else going on, but now that I've had a chance to calm down, I realize maybe it wasn't only the situation earlier making me feel like he had some kind of weird pull over my body. Maybe it wasn't just the adrenaline making me feel something that wasn't really there.

Because I feel it again now.

# CHAPTER NINE

## LEXIE

THERE'S a strange lightness in my stomach, the warmth of his touch permeating me, filling me with something I don't quite understand. No one in memory has ever touched me like this. With purpose. With care. With concern.

We held hands multiple times last week, even walking into the lab today, but it didn't feel like that then. Like something… more.

Wow, maybe that needle addled my brain more than I thought.

I jerk my hand back, his head lifting in surprise. "I can finish it myself," I mumble, making quick work of the wrap on both hands.

He watches me, brows lifting. "I can't even do it that fast."

"It won't hold for a whole fight, but we're not doing that." I slip on the gloves, eyeing him. "You're only defending, right? Not hitting back?"

He frowns. "I'd never hit you."

I release a sigh. Too much honor will get you killed in the ring. You have to play a little dirty sometimes.

I come at him, and he barely blocks me from hitting his face in time. "What the fuck, Lexie?"

"Lesson one. You need to be ready for anything, at any time, from anyone."

He steps back, bringing his hands in front of him in a defensive position. "Is that your life motto or something?"

I shrug. It kind of is.

Not that I was prepared today.

"You blocked well. But you could still work on your reaction time." I circle him, glad that the only guys left here aren't paying attention to us. "Do you get hit in the ring normally?"

He grins. "You'd like that, wouldn't you?"

"I said no such thing," I tell him primly. "Your hand should be closer to your chin."

He moves it, and parries as I come in again, slapping my hand out of the way.

"Have you ever competed?" he asks, eyeing me speculatively. "Your form is surprisingly good."

"Just because I don't like boxing doesn't mean I can't do it." I take a jab at him, and he ducks neatly out of the way.

"I find it odd that you're good at something you claim to hate."

"I didn't always hate it," I murmur, studying him for weak spots. His stance is pretty spot on, though.

"What changed?"

I roll my neck, loosening the muscles. God, it'd felt nice when he massaged the area in the lab. "Nothing did, really. I thought I could change things, but I couldn't."

"Change what?"

I go for an uppercut, but he slips away, light on his feet.

"What did you want to change, Lexie?"

"Why do you care?"

I press my lips together tightly, wishing I hadn't said that. I don't want to hear him say he doesn't.

"Because I want to know you. We're partners."

It's the same as he said at the library the other day. And I still owe him for earlier…

"I thought—" I clear my throat, getting rid of the crackle in my voice. "I thought if I could get great at boxing, Dad would take me with him. To live. I would practice with him whenever he came to visit. But he laughed when I suggested it."

He lowers his hands, but I don't bum rush him like I should. "How old were you?"

"I don't know. Ten? Eleven? He probably doesn't even remember it now."

"And you did that because you didn't want to stay with your mom?"

Did I tell him that before? Or is he guessing? "Yeah."

He steps closer, something about the action setting me on edge after all his questions. "Why did you freak out so bad about the needle earlier?"

My heart pounds, face growing hot, and I look down at my gloves, still at the ready. If anyone else asked that, I'd ignore them, but Ethan deserves some kind of response.

"I've had… not good experiences with them. I don't want to talk about it."

"That's not really an answer."

I stare at him. "I know." But how the hell am I supposed to tell him what I watched my mom go through? Her lifelong struggle with addiction. Finally getting clean for a few months and then coming home to find her shooting up again. And especially how I last found her.

No. That'll invite too many questions. Bring up too many painful memories. It's better to keep it buried in the past.

"How am I supposed to help you if you don't tell me what's going on?"

"I never asked for help."

91

We stare at each other, the group of guys at the big ring earlier loud in the echoing space as they finish up.

"Come on," Ethan says. "You need the heavy bag."

"What?" That's not what I expected him to say.

"Punch it out." He leads me to the oversized punching bags suspended from the ceiling beams. "If you can't talk about it, you still need to get it out."

I roll my eyes behind his back. "That doesn't actually work."

"Humor me, then. What could it hurt?"

My hands for one. My knuckles aren't used to hitting anymore.

I sigh as he positions me in front of one, and I give the bag a half-hearted hit.

He crosses his arms. "You swung at me way harder than that."

"Fine."

I ready myself, shaking out my arms and bouncing on the balls of my feet, limbering up. The ritual of a decade ago comes back easier than I thought it would as I start out slowly, my muscles warming, and jab at the bag, the contact better than I expected.

"Did you quit boxing when your dad said you couldn't come with him?" Ethan asks after a minute.

"Yeah."

"Out of spite?"

"More like I was angry and didn't want to be reminded."

I punch the bag harder, that crestfallen sensation from ages ago returning, burning in my chest. Dad hadn't even seemed to notice how important the idea had been to me, oblivious as usual.

And then he'd left again, like he always did, leaving me with her. She'd fake acting like a good mom whenever he came to visit, hoping he'd stick around this time, want to be a family again, but he'd given up on her long ago.

I guess I was lucky he came back around occasionally for me.

My glove connects with the bag with force, more memories returning. Mom screaming at me it was my fault Dad had left, making me swear never to tell him she was using, leaving me by myself when she went on binges with her friends.

Sitting at home praying she'd come back, terrified this would be the time something would happen, living in a constant state of fear and anxiety…

"Lexie."

I turn to Ethan, surprised at the volume of his voice, and blink, finding moisture on my lashes. Oh my God, am I… crying?

I back up, bumping into another punching bag, his hands coming out to steady me.

"Hey, hey." His hands slide from my shoulders to my back, bringing me into his chest, the scent of clean sweat mixed with whatever cologne he uses overtaking me. "Everything's good. I didn't mean to make you—" He cuts himself off before he can finish that statement. "I just wanted to know more about you. You don't give me anything."

One of his hands idly rubs my back, the action probably commonplace for most others, but for me has my body in sensory overload. I melt against him, weak again in the face of his touch, allowing myself to press my cheek to his hard chest.

"I'm sorry I fell apart in the lab today," I whisper. "That wasn't fair to you."

"You can't help how you react to things."

"I don't know if I would have gotten through it without you," I admit, the light scratches he makes along my back opening up some kind of reserve within me.

"You would have. You're strong."

I squeeze my eyes shut. He's kidding, right? I run from my problems all the time. Like I did earlier with him, actually. "Well, thank you, anyway. I might have blown it all otherwise."

"It was no problem. Seriously." His hand moves up my back, trailing over my neck, to my chin, tipping it up so I meet his gaze. "And you don't owe me anything for it."

Damn. How'd he know that's where my mind had gone?

I step away, realizing how close our faces are, and undo the velcro fasteners of my gloves. "I'm all done boxing for the night."

He's quiet for a moment. "Yeah, me too."

He grabs his gym bag and follows me to Marty's office, where I close out of the accounting software up on the screen and shoulder my backpack. On the way out, he waves to Steve, still working with that guy in the ring, and we walk up the basement level steps to the street, his SUV parked next to my rust bucket.

I open my door, the hinges screeching as they always do. Crap. I meant to do something about that.

"Wait a second," he says, opening his passenger door to search for something inside. He turns back around after a minute holding a can in his hand, triumph on his face. "Look what I've got."

I take a closer peek, the words *white lithium grease* in bold letters on the front. That means next to nothing to me, though. "I have no idea."

"Watch and be amazed," he tells me, opening my driver's side door wider to spray the contents of the can on the hinges. He opens and closes it a few times, working the grease in, and somehow, magically, it stops squeaking.

"Holy crap."

"I know, right?" He walks around to the other side of the car and does the same on the passenger door, then both backseat doors. "I noticed the sound when I dropped you at your car last week."

"You had that stuff at home?"

He flips the can in mid-air, pretending to blow it off like it's a smoking gun. "Got it at work."

"Where do you work?" How have I not asked him that already?

"Bill's Hardware."

"Oh, that's, what? Five minutes from here? Down that way, right?" I point in a southward direction. "With the red sign."

"Yep." He tosses the can back in his passenger seat, the action serving as a natural end to our conversation.

But for some reason, I find myself not wanting to leave just yet. Travis texted earlier that he's spending the night at Isaac's, so it'll be me alone at home tonight.

"Do you, um, like working there?"

He squints at me. "Are you making small talk? The Lexie I know wouldn't do that."

I bite my lip, not keeping my grin very well contained, and push his shoulder. "Shut up."

Delight flares in his gaze. "If an alien's taken over your brain, blink twice. Three times if you're possessed by something else."

"I can have conversations," I insist. "I just don't make small talk with people I don't know." One of my shoulders lifts in a shrug. "But I know you now."

He nods, grinning back at me. "To answer your question, yes, I like working there. My brother is the assistant manager, so I can get away with pretty much anything."

"And which brother is this? Wait, don't tell me." I mentally go through the family information of his I memorized on the off chance it comes up in the lab. "I'm going with Scott, since he's the oldest."

He points at me, brows narrowing slightly. "Yes. You remembered my brother's name?"

"Yeah. I told you, I don't want to be tripped up if they ask us something during the study."

"They haven't asked us anything personal other than, what? How we met?"

"Yeah, it's annoying. All that time spent studying your answers for nothing."

He holds a hand to his chest, acting affronted, even as he smiles. "Learning about me meant nothing to you?"

My lips twist. "You know what I mean."

He nods, sticking his hands in the pockets of his gym shorts. "What are you up to for the rest of the night?"

I sigh, raking a hand through my hair. "Finishing up *War and Peace* before class tomorrow." Something occurs to me then. "Hey, you read it, didn't you? Not just watched the movie?"

A smirk crosses his face. "Guilty."

"Well, if I fall asleep tonight reading it, I'll ask you tomorrow in class how it ends."

He nods. "It's a deal. Good luck with it."

There's an awkward pause as the conversation dies out. Two other people might hug goodbye at this point, but that's not who we are. It was already bad enough he had to comfort me not once, but twice today.

"Goodnight, Ethan."

"Night."

I get in my car, the engine taking a couple tries to catch, and reverse out of the space, Ethan watching me all the while. He raises his hand in farewell as I speed away, and I cautiously lift mine in return.

Does he wave goodbye to everyone or something?

Flicking on the lights as I walk into my empty apartment ten minutes later, I set my stuff down on the couch, retrieving the novel I need to finish out of my bag. I settle into the cushions, pulling Travis's plush throw blanket he keeps across the back of the couch over my legs, and prop a pillow under my head.

There. All set to knock this book out.

Except, despite wanting to find out what happens to Pierre and Natasha, my mind can't focus. It keeps going back to... Ethan.

Him lightly stroking my arm in the lab, massaging my neck. Then wrapping my hand and rubbing my back in the gym. Has anyone else been so tactile with me? And, to be fair, have I let them?

So why am I letting him?

I shake my head at my inane train of thought. Because he's my fake boyfriend, that's why.

*You two didn't have any reason to do that at the gym.*

We just need to be… comfortable with one another. It's part of the act. The more at ease we are with each other, the more natural we'll seem as a couple in the lab.

And besides, with any other girl, the things Ethan was doing would be barely anything. Just another day.

But to me…

I pick up my book, forcing the words in my line of sight, putting anything from earlier today aside. It didn't mean anything special.

Even if I thought for a moment it might have.

# CHAPTER TEN

## ETHAN

ALL RIGHT. New test strip? Check. Fresh lancet? Check.

Oh, shit. I nearly drop the glucose meter on the floor of the bathroom stall, catching it before it hits. I should have gone back to my car to do this, even if it is out of the way. A public school bathroom is probably the least sanitary place I could have done this.

Okay, I need to hurry up. If I have to be at class at two, then I should start lunch by one-thirty, and I have to take the insulin a half hour before I eat. It's already five after one now...

I prick the side of my finger, squeezing the blood that forms onto the edge of the strip. The monitor counts down, and that number means... Crap. I forgot.

I check the instructions the doctor sent and unzip the kit I bought that holds all my supplies, tucking the meter back in and pulling out a syringe and bottle of insulin. I measure the correct dosage and pull up the bottom of my shirt, finding a place on my stomach I haven't injected into.

Next month, I'm springing for the pre-filled pens, even if they are more expensive. This process is already getting old.

The main bathroom door swings open, and I freeze before remembering they can't see me in the stall. Not that I'm doing anything wrong, but it still feels that way. Like it's something secret. Shameful.

No, I shouldn't think like that. Everyone at the clinic said it wasn't my fault, that there was nothing I could have done to prevent this.

But that doesn't change that I have to live with this forever now.

I put everything away and unlock the stall door, heading over to the student center where the cafeteria is. Looking over the options, I hesitate, wanting to go for my normal burger and fries, but I guess I shouldn't eat like that anymore. I should probably get something like a… salad.

Gross.

I compromise by getting a grilled chicken sandwich and baked potato, wolfing it down before making the trek to Psych. That's healthy, right?

About fifty feet from the lecture hall entrance, I spot Lexie, ignoring everyone around her as usual as she strides along the path.

"Pookie Bear!" I call out, waiting for her to turn around. Things got so serious between us yesterday, she needs some levity.

She slows, a frown on her face as she glances over one shoulder, shaking her head.

"When will you let that go?" she asks as I catch up to her. "I never agreed to that."

"You agreed the moment you called me Snookums."

She rolls her eyes, shifting her backpack to her front and unzipping it. "I almost regret getting you this now." She pulls out a bag of Skittles, handing it to me carefully.

I glance back and forth between her and the candy, taken aback. "What's this for?"

She doesn't look at me, adjusting her bag the right way again. "You said you liked it. I mean, you must if you named your dog that."

"You went and got this for me?"

She shrugs. "Yeah…"

I grab the handle to the lecture hall door and open it for her, waiting till we're inside to drop an arm over her shoulder. "My Pookie Bear loves me," I whisper in her ear as we walk up the steps to our normal row.

She tries, but she can't hide the amused quirk of her lips. "Get over yourself."

This is a good sign. She did something special for me. Yeah, I probably shouldn't be eating these now, but she didn't know that. If I just have a few, it shouldn't raise my blood sugar too much.

When we're in our seats, I rip open the package, pouring out a few Skittles in my palm. "What flavor do you want?"

"Anything but green," she says, choosing an orange one and popping it in her mouth.

I take a red one, savoring the sweetness. "No lie, green's my least favorite, too. It's like we're a match made in candy heaven."

She smirks, taking another piece from my outstretched hand. "Wouldn't it be a better match if you loved all the ones I hated? That way nothing would go to waste."

"We already have enough yin and yang going on. Let us have one thing we agree on."

Her gaze flicks up, her playfulness dimming as she straightens in her seat. "Incoming."

I look over my shoulder, finding Christian and Amber walking down the row, Amber giving us a little wave.

"How did you all do on the test?" she asks as she sits down. "Dr. Clark posted the scores this morning. Christian and I both got A's."

I glance back at Lexie, raising my brows.

"I got an A," Lexie says.

"Me too," I add. I lean to the side, whispering in Lexie's ear, "You should tell her how much you liked the study group."

"Why would I do that?" she murmurs back. "I hated it."

"To be nice. We should be friendly since we're in the Psych study together."

She lets out an aggrieved sigh, but leans forward to talk across me, angling her body toward Amber. "The study group last week really helped. We should, um, do it again sometime."

Amber's eyes light up with excitement. "We should. Maybe next Thursday after class? We have another test the following Tuesday."

"Sounds like a plan." I grab Lexie's hand, intertwining our fingers. She can't be mad about going this time if she's the one who suggested it. "How was the fMRI for you guys yesterday?"

Christian frowns. "We did the kissing test."

Lexie's fingers clench against mine. "The what?" she asks, her voice sharper than normal.

Dr. Clark taps her microphone from the front of the room, everyone quieting. "All right guys," she says. "We've got a lot to cover today about research design and methods."

Lexie lets go of my hand to retrieve her plethora of items from her backpack, and opens her notebook to a fresh page, scribbling something down before turning it to me.

*What did he mean by kissing?*

I glance at her, shrugging my shoulders. I'm just as clueless as her.

She writes something else.

*Well, ask him.*

I take the pen from her, writing down my own message.

*I will after class. I'm trying to listen to Dr. Clark and you're being a bad influence.*

Her lips thin as she tilts the notebook back toward her and plucks the pen out of my hand.

Seriously, what did Christian mean by that? Are they going to study the way we kiss or something? I'm definitely not opposed to the idea, but Lexie's another story. Will she go for it?

We're already a third of the way through the study. She survived a near panic attack yesterday. She won't bow out now over a little kiss, will she?

Her leg jiggles up and down next to me, obvious tension in her. I casually drop my arm over the back of her seat, leaning in to whisper, "Relax. We'll figure it out."

She nods, her leg ceasing its frantic motion.

At the end of class, I catch Christian's attention before he leaves. "Hey man, what'd you mean by the kissing test earlier?"

He shrugs, scratching at his jaw. "It was pretty easy. They took cheek swabs before and after we kissed."

"It was weird kissing with Dr. Clark right there, though," Amber adds. "So be prepared for that when it's your turn."

When will it be our turn? Next week? Later than that?

"Thanks, guys. See you on Tuesday."

I stand, grabbing Lexie's hand as we exit, keeping hold of it even when we're out of the building, and steer her to a nearby bench, sitting us down. "So…"

"Yeah," she says, letting go of me to stuff her hands in the front pocket of her hoodie.

"So we'll have to kiss. Not a big deal."

She looks over at me but stays silent.

"It's only a big deal if we make it one." As much as I enjoy teasing her, I know her boundaries, and this seems to be a major one.

"Right," she mutters.

I let out a long breath. "Is this a dealbreaker for you? Are we out of the study?" Though the money wasn't a huge incentive for me at the start, I could actually use it now that I have all these diabetic supplies to buy.

She pulls her hands out of her pocket, only to cross her arms over her chest. "No."

Wow, such eloquence. "Is the thought of kissing me that repulsive?"

Her stone-faced expression softens some. "It doesn't have anything to do with you."

"It kind of does." I can't help my peevish tone, despite not wanting to piss her off.

"I'm sorry," she whispers. "You're right. It won't mean anything."

Even though I wanted her to say that, it still stings. I need to remember she doesn't feel the same way about me.

"Okay."

"Okay."

We sit in silence for a few moments before I blurt out, "Are you worried about it looking real in front of Dr. Clark and Justin? Because we could practice if you want."

She finally cracks a smile. "You're ridiculous."

Is the idea so crazy, though? "Will we be okay to wing it? Especially if they're watching closely?"

She shifts on the bench, facing more toward me. "I'm sure it'll be fine."

"Miss Overprepared doesn't want to prepare?"

I don't know why I'm pushing the idea so hard, but some part of me doesn't like that she's so resistant to kissing me. If she gave me a reason, that'd be one thing, but she hasn't.

"This is different. This is… intimate."

I swallow, the word on her lips making my belly curl. "It doesn't have to be," I tell her, despite my body's reaction.

"Ethan…" She picks at her thumbnail, talking to it rather than me. "We've become… friends. And friends don't kiss each other."

Well, at least she acknowledges there's some kind of connection between us. "They do when there's a thousand each on the line," I remind her. "Isn't that why you're doing this?"

"Yes. I didn't say I wouldn't do it. Just that it'll be weird."

Please don't let her tell me I'm like a brother to her. I've never had any kind of brotherly feelings toward her.

"Why will it be weird?" I force myself to ask.

I brace myself for her to tell me she's not attracted to me, that I have garlic breath, that I'm so far in the friend-zone, there's no chance of escaping.

"I don't know. It just will." She stands, shifting her weight from one foot to the next. "I have to get to Russian Lit. Can we talk about this later?"

That means we'll never talk about it. Out of sight, out of mind.

"Sure." The words are barely out of my mouth before she's gone, racing past people toward the Humanities buildings.

I blow out a breath, stretching out my legs, and pull my phone out of my pocket, checking the time.

Crap. A text from Mom.

**Mom**: *Can you come to dinner tonight? I want to talk to you about something.*

That's weird. She's never vague like that. Raising five boys, you have to be direct.

**Me**: *What time?*

**Mom**: *Six.*

I've got a little over two hours then.

**Me**: *Is it serious?*

She can't leave me in suspense like this.

**Mom**: *I'd rather talk about it in person.*

Okay...

Guess I'm going home for dinner.

# CHAPTER ELEVEN

## ETHAN

I PULL up to Mom and Dad's house, parking on the street since the driveway is full. I expected Jacob to be here because he's still living at home, but Scott's truck is here too.

An older model Mustang pulls up behind me, and I hold back a groan as my younger brother, Jordan, swaggers out, thinking he's hot shit after buying his car last month.

"Still in that mom-mobile?" he asks, grinning from ear to ear.

I glance at my SUV. "It's a RAV4. Not a minivan."

He shrugs. "I'm just fucking with you."

Yeah, hilarious. I'm not this annoying to Lexie, am I?

"Mom didn't say you'd be here," I comment, walking up the driveway.

"What? You wouldn't have come if you knew?"

I reach for him, putting him in a headlock, and noogie the top of his head. "Obviously, dipshit."

He wriggles out of my hold, straightening his hair. "You said you'd have lunch with me at school this week. You haven't even texted."

"I've been busy." I try the front door handle, finding it open, and let myself in. Damn, it smells good in here. "And I said I *might* eat with you. I can't be seen too much with a freshman." Jordan's best handled in small doses. Our relationship improved tenfold when I moved out two years ago.

I clap Jacob on the back as I pass him in the hallway leading to the kitchen, and find Mom bustling about, directing Scott on what should go in the salad.

I walk up to her, giving her a brief hug. "What did you want to talk about?"

Her gaze flicks to Jordan, who walked in behind me. "Let's do it later."

"Ooh, so secretive."

"Mind yourself," she warns, using her mom tone. "And grab a stack of plates and set the table."

I open the cabinets, pulling out the set of Corelle she's had since before I was born. "Is Brian coming?"

"No. He said he couldn't make it. Your father's working late too."

Okay, so that means there's five of us tonight.

I put out the plates on the table in the eat-in kitchen, grabbing silverware next, and top it off with napkins. Mom will nag if there are no napkins.

She slips on two oven mitts and opens the oven, pulling out a bubbling pan of lasagna, a gooey layer of melted cheese over the top. So that's what smelled so good.

Oh, shit. That's probably on the *eat in moderation* list the doctor gave me, along with those Skittles from earlier. Rather than outright banning me from certain foods, they said I should only have a small portion and pair it with something that will keep my blood sugar levels from spiking too high. And looking around the kitchen, it looks like my best bet for that is... salad.

Seriously, who likes eating rabbit food?

"Dinner," Mom calls out, her one and only prompt to get to the table. She gave up years ago trying to track us all down to eat together at the same time.

I settle in my usual spot by the bay window that overlooks the street, watching Mom as she carefully places the lasagna on a trivet, the large bowl of tossed salad next to it.

She serves herself the first piece, a longstanding rule to make sure she got enough food before the rest of us devoured it. After that, we go in ascending age order, Jacob going next since he's the youngest, if only by ten minutes. It wouldn't matter if we went descending, though. I'd still be stuck in the middle.

When it's my turn, I attempt to calculate what a *moderate* portion is, erring on the side of caution. It looks awfully sad on the plate.

"There's plenty more, Ethan," Mom says, using tongs to scoop salad on her plate. "Scott can't eat all that."

"No, it's fine. I'm going to have some salad with it."

She drops the tongs, a loud clatter echoing in the now silent room as everyone stares at me.

"You're what?" Jordan asks, theatrically sticking a finger in his ear as if he's cleaning it to hear better.

"I'm having salad," I mutter.

"But it has lettuce in it," Jacob says.

"And vegetables," Scott adds.

Yeah, don't remind me.

Mom stands, rushing around the table to cradle my head. "Is it happening? Is my baby finally becoming an adult?"

Everyone snickers, and even I have to smile. "I'm not allowed to eat salad?"

"No," they all say in unison.

Sure, it's out of character, but not totally unreasonable. "I'm... training," I tell them, making up something on the spot. "For an upcoming match. I have to clean up my diet to make weight." Yeah, that makes sense. And is something I probably should be doing anyway.

Mom drops her hold on my head, pursing her lips. "I should have known it had to do with boxing."

She's made her disapproval of the sport clear since I started last year, citing statistics on injuries and concussion rates to me, but it's not like she has a say in what I do.

"When's your match?" Scott asks, finally serving himself a massive slice of lasagna. Lucky. "I'll bet on you."

"Don't waste your money," Jordan says. "There's no way he's good enough to beat anyone."

I ignore his obvious attempt at riling me up.

"I don't know," I tell Scott. "Nothing definitive has been set up yet. And it's an amateur bout. No betting."

"You've been training for a while. When are you going to get in the ring for real?"

"It'll happen. Don't worry."

I take a huge bite of lasagna so they don't ask me any more questions, immediately regretting my decision as it burns the roof of my mouth.

I keep to myself as the dinner continues, letting the usual chatter wash over me. The only person quieter than me is Jacob, who decided from an early age he had no interest in competing with the rest of us trying to get a word in. Despite being twins, he and Jordan couldn't be more different.

The twins take care of cleanup after dinner, and Mom drags me upstairs into the home office she and Dad converted from Scott's old bedroom years ago.

"Is this where we're having our secret meeting?" I ask her, still clueless as to why she wants to talk.

"Yes." She opens her laptop, navigating to some site I don't recognize. "I didn't want to bring it up in front of your brothers, but I suddenly have multiple insurance claims for you this week. Two visits to the endocrinologist? What's that about?"

What is she doing? Trolling her health insurance account? Don't claims normally take a long time to be processed?

"Is this related to boxing, too?" she asks when I'm silent. "Did you hurt yourself?"

"No, Mom." I sigh, scrubbing a hand down my beard. "Everything's fine. Don't worry."

For some reason, I don't want to tell anyone just yet. It's… private.

Her brows narrow. "Everything's fine? You haven't been to a doctor since high school when I would drag you for your annual physical. I don't buy that you all of a sudden need to see a specialist if something isn't wrong."

"I don't want to talk about it." Great. Now I sound like Lexie. She must be rubbing off on me.

Her lips pinch together. "Fine."

That obviously means she's not fine, but I take the reprieve anyway. I know this isn't the last I'll hear about it from her, but I'm not ready to share. I can only imagine what everyone will say, the questions they'll ask. I'll be the Hudson boy with diabetes.

Not the smart one. Not the class clown. Not the boxer.

The one with an incurable disease.

"I'm not trying to be difficult," I promise her. "I'll let you know when I'm ready."

She reaches out, squeezing my arm. "You really are an adult, aren't you?" she murmurs. "All of you used to need me so much, and now you're grown and off living your own life. Just try to keep me in the loop, okay?"

"Mom…" I pull her into a bear hug. "I still need you." But not about this. Not yet. "I'm here eating the insanely delicious food you made, aren't I?"

"I haven't even heard from you since the semester started." She extracts herself from my hold, smiling warmly at me. "But that's fine. That means I did a good job raising you if you don't need me as much."

I squint at her. "Are you trying to get me emotional? Because it won't work."

She laughs, wiping briefly at her left eye. "No, but I might."

"I'll call more often. Promise. Things have just been busy." School. Boxing. Work. Now this thing with Lexie. Not that it's too much to handle, but I'll admit Lexie's occupied most of my mental real estate lately.

And now that we might have to kiss next week? I can't say I've ever been looking forward to something as simple as that.

I head back downstairs, catching up with Jacob on the programming boot camp course he's taking online, then shoot the shit for a bit with Scott about some things at work. Jordan hangs around us like a pesky fly, but soon gets bored when he realizes there's nothing he can contribute to the conversation.

I leave at nine, finding Tyler and his girlfriend, Mia, watching some horror flick on the couch in the living room when I return home. She's curled tightly against his side, her palm over her eyes, peeking through.

I shut the front door, creeping as quietly as I can toward them. Mia glances back, spotting me, and I hold a finger to my lips in a shushing signal.

Upon reaching Tyler, I brush my fingers lightly against the side of his neck, savoring the choked cry he makes as he whips around.

"What the hell, man?" His nostrils flare in annoyance, and beside him, his girlfriend dissolves in a fit of giggles.

"C'mon. It was too good of an opportunity to pass up."

"Do you know how disturbing this is?" He points to the TV dramatically. "You almost made me shit my pants."

I flop down on the loveseat, not paying attention to the possessed doll on the screen. "Now that I'd pay to see."

He rolls his eyes. "You would."

Mia finally contains her laughter and gestures toward the coffee table. "I made some brownies if you want some."

"You're going to reward him after what he did to me?" Tyler asks her. He puts his arm around her, pulling her into his side, and kisses her temple. "You're too softhearted," he murmurs affectionately.

And that's my cue to leave.

Seeing Tyler happy for a change was heartwarming at first, especially since I like to think I had a little something to do with the two of them getting back together, but I never would have taken him for a PDA kind of guy. Thank God we don't share a bedroom wall, at least. I've already heard my fair share of them at night.

I stare at the brownies longingly as I get up, knowing I shouldn't press my luck. I already have to inject my long-acting insulin before bed to stabilize me throughout the night. I don't need to add a second fast-acting insulin to the mix too. You can never have just one of Mia's desserts.

Returning to my room, I sink onto the bed, thinking about what next week holds. Shifts at work the next three nights, a test in Geotechnical Engineering on Monday, a scheduled training session with Steve at the gym on Tuesday, and on Wednesday...

Kissing Lexie?

# CHAPTER TWELVE

## LEXIE

"SO WHEN WE use variable costing, all manufacturing overhead costs are charged to expense in the period that a product is produced." Dr. Perkins writes out what she's saying on the whiteboard at the front of the classroom. "This is in direct contrast to…" She glances over her shoulder, expectantly awaiting an answer.

I glance around, but no one appears keen on answering her. It's absorption costing.

"Absorption costing," she says, disappointment in her tone.

Damn. I should have answered her.

I angle my gaze down, focusing on my notebook and writing down what she says. When she goes off on a tangent about product cost versus period cost, my mind drifts, returning to the one thing I haven't been able to get out of my head since last week—kissing Ethan.

I'm actually surprised he didn't bring it up in class yesterday. Then again, I'd hightailed it out of there as soon as Dr. Clark had dismissed us, claiming I needed to be at Russian Lit early to review for a quiz.

I mean, it wasn't a complete lie. I needed to look over the new book we're on, *Eugene Onegin*, but only so I wasn't a deer in headlights if Dr. Kroft called on me. He doesn't seem to understand that not everyone gets these books as well as him.

Okay, I need to focus. Dr. Perkins is talking about... Oh, it's still product cost. The material in this class isn't the most exciting, but neither is accounting in general. If I can get a job in the field, though, it'll make for a nice, comfortable life. A stable career. No moving from place to place. No more worries about if I'll have enough for rent. I can buy a house of my own, in a nice neighborhood with no junkies on the corner. With a backyard instead of a filthy, piss-stained alley. Where cops patrol to keep people safe rather than looking for someone to bust.

I shake off my train of thought. I won't be able to buy any house if I don't pass this class. I should concentrate.

Even though I know what's coming up in just an hour and a half.

*Kissing Ethan.*

No, I can't be sure about that.

*But Christian and Amber say they did it.*

Maybe they assign the tests randomly.

*Or more likely they rotate them because everyone can't do the same tests on the same days.*

Okay, what would be the worst that could happen? We give each other a quick peck on the lips and call it a day. Like Ethan said, not a big deal.

*But what if it gets around campus that I'll kiss anyone? Guys will line up at my door, expecting...*

No, this isn't high school. That's not happening again. I'm older. Wiser. Stronger. Not the naive fourteen-year-old who thinks the popular jock is paying attention to her because he actually likes her.

I press a hand to my chest, willing my heart to slow down. This is college. No one cares about that kind of stuff anymore. Hell, with as many people that go to this school, most probably don't even know who I am.

And that's the way I want it to stay.

I tune back in to Dr. Perkins, diligently taking notes, and push all thoughts of Ethan away for the rest of the class, heading over to the Psych building for the study before three.

This time, he's waiting on the bench outside, watching me as I approach. His normal grin lurking about his lips is absent, and all I can think of is our conversation last week. The one where he outright asked why the thought of kissing him was so terrible.

I don't blame him for the question. Just based on his looks, he probably gets plenty of notice from girls. Savannah hit on him five seconds after meeting him. And he's not only the jock I initially assumed he was. He's smart. Funny. Pays attention to what I say. I practically shouted his good qualities at him that day in the library.

I nearly stumble over nothing as I realize the direction my thoughts are going. What am I thinking? He also lacks boundaries. Doesn't take things seriously. Too cocky for his own good.

And besides all that, I'm just plain not interested.

Even if my heart speeds up as I approach him.

That's only because I'm nervous, though. Who knows what they'll make us do today up on the fourth floor?

He's deceptively casual as I stop in front of him, his arms spread wide over the back of the bench, one leg crossed over the opposite knee.

"Are you ready?" I ask when he makes no movement to get up.

His head tilts as he studies me. "Are you?"

What's he up to? Is he trying to pull some kind of reverse psychology trick on me?

I grip my backpack straps, meeting his gaze. "Yeah."

He finally stands, not stepping to the side like he should, but directly in front of me. There's not much space between us and I have to resist the urge to step back, especially when he moves even closer, forcing me to tilt my head up.

"What are you doing?" I ask, confused.

His lips twist, but not in an amused way like they have in the past. "Lexie, you look like you're about to run scared. We're supposed to be a couple in love."

"I know," I mumble, my chest tightening for some reason in response to his assessment of me. "We are in love. Upstairs."

"If they're watching us closely today, you can't look like that. Can't shy away from me. Can't flinch."

"I know," I repeat. No, I don't have the best track record in the lab of pretending everything is okay, but I can manage this.

"So show me you won't."

What? How am I supposed to prove it to him? "I'm next to you, aren't I?"

"And if I do this?" He brings a hand up, wrapping it around the back of my neck.

I flinch, just like he said I would, and he drops his hand.

"We're not in the lab," I argue, the ache in my chest intensifying. "It doesn't count."

The look he gives me shows what he thinks of that.

"I'm ready now," I tell him. "Do it again."

He stares at me, unmoving.

"What are you waiting for?"

"You're tense. I can actually see how tense you are."

I consciously relax my shoulders, but they bunch right back up. Damn it.

His expression softens. "If I can't even touch you," he says gently, "how am I supposed to kiss you in the lab?"

Ugh. Why does he have to be so logical? What happened to goofy, go with the flow Ethan? He would have been okay winging this.

"You let me touch you last week," he whispers, the softness of his tone implying an intimacy I don't want to be reminded of.

"That was different." I was freaked out. Could barely process anything.

He lets out a sigh. "I was afraid it might be like this. Maybe we should drop out of the study if you're that uncomfortable."

"No." I need the money. "We can do it. *I* can do it."

"There's no shame—"

I reach up on my tiptoes, squeezing my eyes shut as I crush my lips to his. See, I can do this. It's not like kissing Cody. Ethan won't do anything to me.

Even so, I'm still trembling as I break away, my stomach doing cartwheels. Opening my eyes, I expect to find him grinning at me, impressed, but his face remains impassive.

"Mashing your mouth against mine for five seconds isn't a kiss," he says. "There's no way they'll believe that."

My shoulders drop, defeated. He's stupidly right. "What did you have in mind, then?" Seriously, what else am I supposed to do?

"You have to relax. Trust me. And follow my lead."

I nod, figuring I have nothing left to lose at this point. We're due upstairs any minute.

His hand returns to the nape of my neck, gently massaging until the tension melts away, the same as he did last week. Did he take a class to learn how to do that or something?

He leans down, stopping before he reaches me, our breaths mingling. His is fresh and minty. Mine probably smells like the pb&j I scarfed down earlier after class.

"Trust me," he whispers, tilting my face up, his lips featherlight as they make contact with mine.

Whoa. That's new. And not... unpleasant.

My eyes drift shut, body still as his mouth moves over mine, silently coaxing. Patiently encouraging. Wordlessly persuading. But for what, I'm not sure.

His slight hold on me never tightens, allowing me to slip away anytime I want. I'm in control, no expectations to reciprocate.

Cody's kisses weren't like this. I didn't know it could be this way. A gentle exploration. A soft meeting of two mouths. No domination. No conquering.

I find myself reacting, returning his kiss, the barely-there noise he makes in response making my belly dip low.

I step back, surprised at my body's betrayal. This isn't something to enjoy. It's supposed to be something to get through, to endure.

His gaze searches mine, but I have no idea what he sees, other than confusion.

What kind of kiss was that?

"You ready now?"

I nod, not sure what to say, and follow him in, still caught up in a moment that wasn't even anything.

He waves to Christian and Amber as we reach the lab, but there's no time to speak to them as Justin informs them they'll be joining him for an fMRI test and leads them out of the room.

That must mean Ethan and I are kissing today.

My stomach does a strange flip-flopping motion, not sure if it wants to sink or float. My mind tells it to sink. This is terrible. I don't want to kiss Ethan again.

But my body... Well, it apparently didn't get that memo.

Maybe outside was a fluke. Maybe it won't be like that a second time. His lips soft but firm. Testing yet controlled. Warm and delicious and...

All right, no more thinking about it. I'm blowing what happened completely out of proportion.

Dr. Clark greets us and explains how she'll be taking swabs of the insides of our cheeks, testing our saliva at different points to measure our levels of oxytocin.

Isn't that a drug? No, wait. That's OxyContin. Yeah, there'd been some of that around the house over the years, too.

"What's oxytocin?" Ethan asks, never shy about asking questions.

"It's a hormone generally associated with, well, love. Relationships, sexual activity, trust. It's all tied together. We're looking to see if your levels change based on various interactions with your partner." She leads us over to a tray of long Q-Tips. "Now, if you don't mind, I'll go ahead and take the first sample to establish a baseline."

She swabs our mouths and sticks the Q-tips in clear-capped cylinders, labeling the sides with a Sharpie.

"If you could take a seat over here," she continues, motioning to two chairs, "we'll move on."

We sit down, angling our chairs toward each other when she indicates for us to do so.

"Now, you'll stare into each other's eyes for the next two minutes."

Excuse me?

"No talking. No looking away. Once you're ready, I'll set the timer."

Ethan's brows raise as he looks at me, as if to ask *you ready?*

I nod, preparing myself. I mean, how hard can it be to look at him?

There's the quiet beep of the timer starting, and we're off, the first twenty seconds or so okay given that all I can think of is how weird this is.

But after that, I start to really focus on him. Superficial things like how green his eyes are, how the shape of his brows complement his face. And when my gaze strays south toward his lips, I snap it back up, reminding myself to keep eye contact. There's no need to concentrate on his mouth. The slight pressure he kissed me with, enough to have an effect without becoming overwhelming. The gentle bristle of his beard as it had brushed my face. That low sound he'd made as I kissed him back.

The next time we kiss, will he make that sound again?

Will I make one?

I swallow heavily, shifting in my seat, unable to get the image out of my mind now. Can he tell the direction of my thoughts? Is he thinking of that kiss too?

No, he'd seemed annoyed at me earlier, probably fed up with all the bullshit I've put him through so far. Asking him to be my pretend boyfriend and then not following through on simple things like touching and kissing. Things a normal girl would do. Things that shouldn't be a big deal to anyone else.

I thought I had put all those memories behind me. Cody kissing me that last time, his hand on my throat holding me in place, teeth knocking against mine as he'd struggled to keep me still.

No, no. I push the memory away. That's not happening again. Never happening again.

Ethan's brows knit, his hand coming out to reach for mine. Did he see something on my face? Did I reveal too much?

His hand drops as Dr. Clark immediately tells us not to touch, and I let out a shaky breath. There's no reason to be thinking about Cody right now. I'm supposed to be concentrating on Ethan. The guy who's nothing like I expected.

"Time's up," Dr. Clark says, swabbing first Ethan's inner cheek, then mine. Will they be able to tell we're not really in love? It's one thing to spin them a tale, but I can't change the chemicals in my body. My data alone will probably skew the study's results.

"You okay?" Ethan whispers as our professor turns to label the second set of samples.

I nod, putting on a smile for him. Not that I'm fooling anyone.

"Let's take a quick breather," Dr. Clark says, gathering the tubes. "I'll be back soon."

I stare at a spot about a foot in front of me, avoiding Ethan's eye as we're left alone, but that doesn't stop him from commenting, "Your face changed at the end there."

"Hmm," I reply, not answering him.

"What were you thinking about?"

See? Pushy. No boundaries. A reasonable person would leave well enough alone.

My first instinct is to tell him it's none of his business. But if I know him at all, that won't deter him.

"About the last time someone kissed me," I reply honestly.

"Someone like five minutes ago or someone before that?"

"Before you," I whisper.

"And based on your expression, it was... not good?"

"Not good," I confirm.

He scoots his chair closer, until his knees are touching mine. I look up into those familiar green eyes, the patience and understanding there nearly too much to handle. "Maybe we could replace that memory with a better one."

# CHAPTER THIRTEEN

## LEXIE

MY HEARTBEAT PICKS up as I process his words. "What?"

"When they ask us to kiss," he clarifies. "So now your last kiss will be a better one."

My mind goes back to how softly he had kissed me before. No, stop thinking of that. "It's not a real kiss," I remind him. Needing to remind myself, too.

"I know. I just thought..." He blows out a breath, resting his elbows on his knees, head hung low. "Never mind."

God, I'm such a bitch. He's trying to help, and I continue to piss all over him. "No, it's really... thoughtful of you." I slide my right hand up my left arm, squeezing my bicep. "You're actually a..." I swallow, the words stuck in my throat. "You're a considerate person."

His head tilts up, gaze meeting mine, something lurking behind his eyes I don't quite understand. "I'm not offering purely altruistically," he murmurs.

My heartbeat pounds louder, until it's all I can hear. What does he mean?

"You guys ready for the last part?" Dr. Clark asks, breezing into the room.

I straighten in my seat, like I was caught doing something wrong. I wasn't, though. Nothing even happened.

I think.

She sets down fresh supplies on the tray table on the desk. "One more swab and you'll be out of here. You have it easy today."

Easy? Is she kidding?

Then again, last week wasn't a walk in the park either.

"This one is measuring your oxytocin levels after you kiss. I'll turn my back and have you kiss for ten seconds. Don't use any tongue because we want to minimize the transfer of saliva."

Gross.

She turns her back to us. "Let me know when you're ready."

So she's not observing us? We could just tell her we did it and she would never know?

I look at Ethan, his gaze steady on me. Where previously I may have gone the route of tricking Dr. Clark into thinking we actually kissed, there's a part of me that wants to find out if that barely-there kiss outside the Psych building was a fluke. To make sure I'm not crazy. To put the memory out of my mind.

It won't be like that a second time, right?

He moves in close, tilting his head to whisper in my ear, "We don't have to do this if you don't want. We can quit while we're ahead."

"I'm not quitting," I find myself replying.

He leans back, satisfaction in his gaze. "That's my girl."

There's that low dip in my belly again. Even though I'm not his girl. I'm his co-conspirator. His partner in crime as we trick the researchers into thinking we're in love.

I'm hardly anything to him, I remind myself as his hand comes up to cup my cheek, fingertips warm.

And he's hardly anything to me, I tell myself as he announces we're ready.

I inhale shakily, no time to prepare as his lips are on mine again, just as soft as before, moving with purpose. I kiss him back, participating this time, my stomach somehow going lower until it's down to my toes, something fluttering like mad in there.

His hand moves from my cheek to the back of my head as he deepens the kiss, cradling me. There's tenderness in the action, a sensation of safety flooding through me, so different from the last guy who kissed me.

I welcome it instead of pushing him away, my hands finding his broad shoulders to balance as I lean into him. The scent of his cologne weaves itself around me, lulling me, putting me under his spell, wanting more. Wanting him.

Wanting him?

"You finished?" Dr. Clark asks.

I break away from him, shutting my eyes. I don't want him to see whatever might be visible in them.

"Yeah," he replies to Dr. Clark, his deep voice sending a shiver through me.

What's wrong with me? Why is he affecting me like this?

I turn from him, focusing on the long Q-Tip as she reaches out to swab me, standing and shouldering my backpack as soon as she's done.

"Are we free to go?" I ask when she's finished with Ethan.

"Yep. I'll see you in class tomorrow."

I wait for Ethan as he gathers his bag, the two of us silent as we exit and head down the hallway.

Is he feeling as awkward as I am after doing that? As confused?

When we reach the bottom of the stairs, he holds the door to the outside open for me, waiting until I'm through to say, "See? Not a big deal. You did great."

The lightness in my stomach grows heavy. Of course he's not confused or awkward. Of course it wasn't a big deal to him. He assured me beforehand it wouldn't be. He probably kisses girls all the time. Just another Wednesday to him.

I nod in response. I'm obviously not admitting it was absolutely a big deal for me.

"And maybe you have a better memory now?" he asks, brows raised in expectation.

What? Oh, yeah. Replacing the memory of my last kiss. "Yeah, thanks." Not that I'll ever forget what a nightmare Cody turned out to be, but one thing's for sure—I won't forget Ethan's kiss anytime soon.

"Will you be at Marty's doing your bookkeeping stuff tonight?"

"Yeah." Wednesday nights are turning out to be a good night to work on that there.

"I'll see you there, then."

He leans in close before I realize what he's doing and kisses my cheek, his beard tickling me.

He walks backwards away from me, grinning, before turning around and heading toward the other buildings on campus.

I touch my cheek once he's out of sight, walking in a daze to my car, pulling the visor down as I get in to study myself in the mirror. My fingertips brush my lips, but they don't appear any different. They only feel that way. Like the imprint of him is still there.

My phone chimes, startling me out of my reverie, and I snap up the visor, blocking my view of my mouth. There's nothing different about me. It's all in my head.

My messed-up head.

I pull out my phone, pressing the button on the side.

**Isaac**: *Are you free to touch up your roots today? I'm sick of practicing on these mannequins.*

Yes. The perfect distraction so I don't go back home and ruminate over the last twenty minutes.

**Me**: *Can I come to the salon now?*

**Isaac**: *Yes, come now! Save me from my boredom!*

I smile to myself. He's so dramatic.

**Me**: *Be there in ten.*

I reverse out of the parking space, turning up the radio loud to drown out any thoughts as I drive to Isaac's cosmetology school. Thirty minutes later, I'm in a barber's chair, a black cape wrapped around me, Isaac painting my scalp as he tells me about the ongoing saga of two of his classmates we overheard arguing earlier. I listen to him prattle on, not because I'm at all interested, but so my mind can't drift.

"So it turns out Liz had made out with Jeremy last year at a party, but never told Dave about it."

I stare in the mirror at what he's doing to my hair. Was the dye that red before? "And Jeremy was… his friend?" I might have tuned out at that part.

"No, they hate each other. Like mortal enemies."

Mortal enemies? That's a bit much. Then again, didn't I feel the same seeing Savannah the other week? At least I haven't seen her old ringleader, Ashley. That'd be even worse.

"So she cheated on Dave?" I ask.

"No, it happened before they got together."

"Then how can he be mad?"

"Lexie." He sighs. "The heart doesn't listen to logic."

I blink, unsure how to respond. I've never discussed anything personal with him. Travis always changes the topic whenever it gets to this point.

He sets his brush down. "All right, this is done for now. Just needs to process for a while."

"Okay." I'm not sure what that means, but whatever he says.

"I still wish you would have let me do rainbow hair," he complains, stripping off his gloves.

"Um, no." Not exactly a personality fit.

He takes a seat in the empty chair next to mine, spinning around. "So, what's going on with you? How's your boy toy?"

I sputter involuntarily. "My what?"

He grins at me, eyes crinkling at the corners. "Ethan. Don't think I forgot about our little convo last week."

"He's not my boy toy." Despite what we did earlier. That was for the study.

"I'd make him mine."

"Would you say that in front of Travis?"

His grin grows. "Hell yes. But he knows I'd share."

I bite my lip so I won't laugh.

You know, Isaac probably has a lot of dating experience. And he understands how guys think. Maybe he can give me some clarification on this new situation with Ethan.

"Back to the, uh, Liz and Dave thing, with the kissing." I stumble over my words, not sure what I really want to ask. "Have you ever, I don't know, kissed someone you're not into? Or like a friend?"

He twirls his chair again, shrugging. "Yeah, sure." Like it's just so normal.

"Did it change things?"

"No. I guess it could have, but I didn't let it. A couple years back, a friend and I got drunk at a party and made out. And it was a girl, if you can believe it." He chuckles to himself. "We laughed it off the next day. It was so stupid."

Getting drunk and doing something is different. You're not in full control of your body—which is exactly why I don't drink.

"But never any other time?"

"Oh, gosh. Well, there was this one other thing." He stops spinning his chair, facing me. "There was this guy. We were sort of in the same friend group, but more like a friend of a friend kind of thing. I couldn't stand him the first time I met him. So full of himself."

I nod, resisting the urge to scratch my itchy scalp. I'll stain my fingers red if I do.

"Anyway, we were at this mutual friend's party and we ended up kissing. Don't ask me how it happened. I couldn't tell you. And that time I wasn't even drinking, so I don't have an excuse."

"What happened after?" That's the part I need to figure out. How do I act around Ethan now that we've kissed?

He holds his hands open wide. "Nothing. We just never brought it up again. But it's not like we saw each other a whole lot to begin with."

I nod. Well, that's not exactly helpful.

He points a finger at me, jaw dropping. "You kissed your boy toy, didn't you?"

How'd he know that? "I..." Oh, there's no use lying. "It was part of the study today."

He scoots to the edge of his seat, eyes wide. "How was it?"

My hands knot together under my hairdresser's cape. "Weird? I don't know."

He grimaces. "He a bad kisser? A sloppy tongue will ruin things every time."

Sloppy tongue? Good Lord. "No, it wasn't that. The kiss was good. Better than I expected, actually." Way better. "I'm just not sure how I should act around him now. It's weird that we've done that."

"What'd he say after?"

"That it wasn't a big deal."

"Is that what you wanted?"

"Yes."

He studies me. "Are you sure?"

131

Of course I'm sure. "I'm glad he's not making it into a thing. Then I really wouldn't know what to do."

"Lexie, if you don't have feelings for him, then it shouldn't be weird to you either."

I blink at him. "I don't."

He shrugs, clearly not convinced. "If you say so."

"I don't," I insist. "He's ridiculous half the time, making jokes and trying to embarrass me. He pushes things too far." I struggle for something else to come up with. "He only listens during a lecture and somehow makes an A." Okay, that's not his fault. It's just annoying to me. "And he's too... perfect looking."

He bites his bottom lip, as if he's holding back a smile. "Okay, you realize none of that helps your case, right?"

I grip the edges of my seat, wishing I could leave, but there's still a bunch of dye in my hair. "How long till I'm done?"

He smiles, coming over to inspect my hair. "Touchy, touchy. Let's give it ten more minutes." He leans against the back of the chair, looking at me through the mirror's reflection. "How about I leave you alone with your thoughts? You think about all the ways you *don't* like your boy toy."

Ugh. How does Travis put up with him? I was just trying to get an idea of how to act around Ethan, not suggest I'm interested in him. I'm obviously not.

If Ethan wants to act like it wasn't a big deal, then I'll follow suit. There. Problem solved.

No thanks to Isaac.

# CHAPTER FOURTEEN

## ETHAN

I GLANCE behind me for about the hundredth time, but I still can't see Lexie from this angle. She's holed herself up in Marty's office for an hour already, barely looking at me as she entered the gym.

Not that I expected her to come over and kiss me hello, but something other than a brief glance my way would have been nice.

"That your girl?"

I glance over at Austin, his question punching me in the gut. I'd slipped up calling her that earlier, but she hadn't said anything about it. Probably because I'd kissed her right after. "No. A friend."

He shrugs, satisfied with my answer, and turns back toward the action, crossing his arms over his chest. Lawrence is almost finished with Johnson, then it's our turn.

"His elbows aren't low enough," he comments, just as Lawrence says the same thing in the ring. "He's getting tired."

"Sloppy," Lawrence shouts as he gets past Johnson's guard.

I'm silent, listening to Austin's quiet commentary, noticing everything Johnson's doing right and wrong as he mentions them. Would I have seen the same things on my own?

"You study a lot of other boxers?" I ask when they pause in the ring for a water break.

He shakes his shoulder-length blond hair behind him, pulling a hair tie out of his pocket to tie it back. "You have to find out your opponent's strengths and weaknesses. Then you can develop your strategy."

He sounds serious about it. If this is your livelihood, though, you have to be.

"And what would be your strategy against him?"

He scratches at his jaw, a calculating gleam in his eye. "Johnson's got a wicked right hook, but he tries to rely too much on knockouts. I'd stay away, tire him out while he throws punches. Then come at him when his stamina runs out."

Sounds like a solid plan. "Do you study everyone here?"

"Yeah. Especially those in my division."

"What's your weight class?"

"Light heavyweight. But I'm trying to get down to super middleweight."

Good thing I'm middleweight. I wouldn't want to face him in the ring based on what I've seen.

"You haven't competed yet, have you?" he asks, eyeing me.

"No. Still training."

"You interested?"

I shrug. "Sure. But I'm not looking to make a career out of it."

Where many of the guys here would dismiss me after a statement like that, he merely nods. Maybe he has other plans too. He doesn't look that much older than me. A couple years at most.

He jerks his head in the direction of a few guys skipping rope. "I'm going to warm up. Lawrence should be ready for us soon."

I should warm up too. But my head turns instead toward Marty's office, sidling further and further away from the ring until I can see through the window. She's concentrating on what looks like a spreadsheet on the computer screen, too focused to notice me staring at her.

My gaze traces the curve of her cheek I cupped earlier today, her skin delicately soft. God, how I'd wanted to brush my thumb over her lips, to have her part them in anticipation for my kiss. I'd felt how she kissed me back that second time, how she'd laid her hands on my shoulders, fingers gripping me.

That tug in my lower belly flares again, remembering how badly I'd ached to pull her onto my lap, to kiss the hell out of her, learn her taste, hear her moan for me. To get any kind of reaction at all. That's all I want from her. A reaction. To know this growing craving for her isn't one-sided.

Except, Lexie's made it one hundred percent clear she's not interested.

But that kiss…

*Was for the study. Not because she wanted to.*

Maybe I could change her mind, though.

*That's a dangerous road.*

True. Do I really want to head down that path?

I watch her, recalling the way she'd pressed her cheek against my chest last week in the gym, the rare smiles she's bestowed upon me, how she's let me in bit by bit over the past couple of weeks.

Yeah, I want to do this.

I want her.

"Ethan, are you ready?"

I whip around, Lawrence at the edge of the ring staring at me. Oh, shit. Does he know I was thinking about his daughter? Yeah, I joked to Tyler that he loves me, but I have no doubt he could beat me to a pulp if he wanted.

"Yeah." I jog over, twisting under the ropes to join him. I never did warm up.

"You been working on the stuff I told you to?" he asks. "Speed bag? Heavy bag? Jumps?"

I nod. "I can go longer on all of them."

"And you got your passbook, right?"

"Yeah, a few months ago." Just in case.

"Good." He claps me on the back, grinning. "I've got a fight lined up for you."

My stomach drops. "What?"

"A promoter I know is putting together an event. It's local, so it's the perfect time for you to start."

I loop my hands behind my neck, unable to lace them because they're already wrapped. "Yeah, great." This is what I wanted. To actually fight.

So why do I have a lead bowling ball in my stomach?

"When is it?"

"Two weeks."

That's it? "Who will I fight?"

"We won't know until the day of, but they'll do their best to match you to someone on the same level. It's amateur level only, no pros."

Okay, that's not so bad, I guess.

"If you can hold your own against this maniac," he says, gesturing to Austin, who's now entering the ring from the other side, "you'll do fine."

I nod, swallowing heavily as Austin removes his shirt. How does he seem so much bigger without it?

Normally, I'd take mine off too, but since I started injecting my daytime insulin shots in my stomach, I have some bruising I'd rather not explain to others. Then again, I could always just tell people I got punched.

"All right, Ethan. You're with me for the next two weeks until your fight. We don't want to overtrain in the week leading up to it, but I'll prepare you for everything you need to know."

It's good that I'm finally a priority for Lawrence, but the circumstances... Am I really ready for this?

"Let's work on offense tonight. Austin, you're defending."

An hour later, I'm sore as hell, my arms about to fall off, but I don't let on, determined not to give him a reason to doubt me. This is what I've been training for. Why I started going here with Tyler in the first place.

Lawrence checks his watch. "All right guys, I'm out of here. I'll see you Sunday, Ethan. Work on the stuff I told you to until then."

He exits the ring, walking over to Marty's office to poke his head in and speak to Lexie, but I'm too far away to hear what they're saying.

I turn around to find Austin wiping off his front with a towel. I look down at myself, my sweat-stained shirt cooling now, sticking to my torso. Great.

"Any pointers for me?" I ask. "I'm sure you were studying."

One corner of his mouth lifts in a grin. "You really want to know? A lot of guys don't do well with criticism."

"Hit me with it." I can take whatever he has to say.

He nods, slinging the towel over one shoulder. "You're too hesitant. You need to take more chances. Otherwise, you'll never make contact."

"Fair enough."

Maybe I should take more chances elsewhere, too.

Like with Lexie.

Or is slow and steady the way to go? She's so skittish. But nothing will ever happen if I don't try something.

Hmm. I need to think about this some more.

Austin continues on with a few other nitpicky things that Lawrence had previously mentioned too, and I make a mental note to work on those until they're second nature.

"Did you want to spar?" he asks when he's finished telling me his laundry list of improvements I could make. I asked for it, though.

"Uh…" I glance toward the office, Lawrence already gone from the doorway, but there's movement inside. Is Lexie packing up? "No, I have to get going."

"All right. Hit me up if you ever want to practice."

"Thanks, man."

I slip between the ropes and remove my gloves, unwinding the tape around my hands. The office door opens, Lexie's backpack on her back like she's about to leave, and I rush to finish, wanting to at least say goodbye to her.

I head in her direction, her steps slowing as she catches my eye.

"You all finished Miss Bookkeeper?"

She nods, covering her mouth with one hand as she yawns.

"Mind if I walk you out? I'm done, too."

She gives me a once-over, gaze lingering on my shirt. "You're not showering?"

Ouch. "Nah, I'm fine." I wouldn't get to walk her out if I did.

"I'm surprised you aren't trying to show off your abs to everyone again."

I grin at her. "You miss the show?"

I savor her eye roll, letting her lead the way out, and grab my gym bag before we make it to the door.

"I was thinking of going to the diner," I tell her as we walk up the steps back to street level. "Want to join? My treat." She's sure to say no if she has to pay. Is she still having money problems?

She hesitates, sticking her hands in her hoodie pockets, and I sweeten the deal by adding, "I'll even change my shirt."

Her lips quirk, but she says, "No. I have to get home."

Instead of letting her be, I ask, "Why?"

She shrugs, hunching her shoulders. "I'm tired."

"It's not because of earlier today? With the kissing?"

She's silent, coming to a halt in front of her car.

I'd already assured her it wasn't a big deal, hoping to put her at ease. In truth, that kiss had been all I could think of even as I'd said that to her.

"I know you said it would be... weird." I still hate that she used that word. "But I hope it wasn't that bad."

She leans against the hood of her car, her thigh next to a spot where the paint has peeled off. "It was fine."

Fine is one of those words that doesn't mean what it's supposed to, right? "Is this where a girl says things are fine, but they really aren't? And then you silently seethe about it and meanwhile, I'm a clueless idiot?"

A full smile graces her face then, an actual honest-to-God chuckle escaping her. My chest glows with pride in response.

"It really was fine. Better than I expected, actually."

And that doubles the warm feeling going on inside me. "We can kiss anytime you want." I tack on a grin so she doesn't take me seriously. Even though I'm completely serious. There's no way today could have been our only kiss.

She reaches out, lightly nudging my shoulder. "Don't push your luck."

Yeah, I think I might be doing more of that soon.

"I finally got a fight scheduled," I tell her. "Your dad set it up."

Her brows raise. "Congratulations. You ready?"

I rub the back of my neck, a shiver running over me. "As ready as I can be, I guess. I'm training with Lawrence again on Sunday. Did he, uh, say anything about me when he went in the office?"

She shakes her head, her hair swinging. Did she do something different with it? "He asked if I wanted to come over for dinner tomorrow night."

"Well, talk me up while you're there. I want him to keep training me."

"I told him I couldn't. We have that study group with Amber and Christian."

Now my brows raise. "You'll actually go again?" She said she hated it last time.

"Amber invited us. You made me be nice to her."

Yeah, I did, didn't I? "Well, we'll make sure we have enough chairs for everyone this time." Though I wouldn't mind a repeat of her on my lap.

"And if not," she says, sickly sweet, "I'm sure *Savannah* would be happy to sit on your lap." She makes a noise of disgust, and I don't blame her. The girl had been a total bitch to her.

"You know I'm not interested in her, right?"

She looks up at me, holding my gaze for a moment before looking away. "Lots of guys would be."

I shake my head. "The way she spoke to you… Putting down others for no reason isn't attractive to me."

"I put you down the first time I met you," she whispers. "I called you a meathead."

Yeah, but she said it about all the guys in the gym, not just me. "That was different. I took it as an affectionate term."

She smiles again, biting her lip. "And because you knew it wasn't true. I'm sorry I judged you wrong, by the way."

"Wow, an apology? Who are you?"

She playfully smacks my arm. Touching me is good, right? "I'm being serious here. You're not—" She takes a deep breath, looking back up at me. "You're not like I expected."

"Is that good? Or bad?"

"It's… good. Even though you drive me crazy half the time."

"That's what fake boyfriends do."

She rolls her eyes again, the relaxed vibe leaving her as someone approaches us from the basement level steps.

It's her dad.

His steps slow as he nears us, rubbing at his wet hair. He must have come from the showers. "What's going on?"

Lexie shrugs, sticking her hands back in her hoodie pocket. "We're just talking."

He glances between us, trying to figure out what our connection is. I don't blame him. Lexie's not the talkative type.

"Did Lexie mention we have a class together at school?" I ask him, attempting to put him at ease. "We realized it after that first day we met here."

He looks at her, brows pinched. "No, she didn't."

"I don't tell you everything, Dad."

I wonder if she's talked to him at all about those things from her childhood I suggested. Knowing her, probably not.

She moves away from her spot against the hood, pulling out her keys. "I'll see you in class tomorrow, Ethan. See you, Dad."

We both watch her as she gets in her car and speeds off, Lawrence looking at me after she leaves. "Are you guys..." He trails off, leaving the question open-ended.

"We're friends," I clarify. I don't think trying to explain our fake arrangement will go over too well.

He nods. "That's good. She could use some more friends. The only one I ever hear about is her roommate."

She has a roommate she's friendly with? This is the first I'm hearing about it. Then again, have I talked to her much about mine?

"How's she doing in school?"

He doesn't talk to her about that kind of stuff? "Good, as far as I know. We both got A's on our last Psych test."

He nods. "She was always smart. Way more than me or her mom."

Though I'm tempted to ask what the deal is with her mom, that should come from Lexie herself.

He fishes his keys out of his pocket, turning toward an older looking black car. "If you need help with her, let me know."

My brows narrow. "Help?"

"When she pushes you away. She does it with everyone."

He leaves me standing there, contemplating his words. While it's good to know it's not just me she does it with, it also pushes me even more to make it so she's *not* like that with me. I've already snuck my way in around a lot of her barriers.

So what will it take to get all the way in?

# CHAPTER FIFTEEN

## ETHAN

"SO WE'LL SEE you at six, okay?" Amber confirms. "It'll be at Heather's dorm this time. It's right next to Chapman Hall. Second floor."

"Got it," I tell her, my hand on Lexie's lower back as I steer her away toward the exit. Not that it needs to be there, but she hasn't removed it, at least. "See you in a couple hours."

"You have to get to Russian Lit?" I ask Lexie as we head down the lecture hall stairs.

"Yeah. And I fell asleep last night before I could finish the chapter I needed to."

"Here, I'll help." I hold open the door for her, walking with her toward the Humanities building. "All you need to know about Russian literature is that something depressing happens, they drink vodka, and a bunch of people die tragically. The end."

She groans. "That doesn't help."

"Okay, okay. What are you reading?"

"*Eugene Onegin*."

I mentally sift through the books I've read, bringing back the finer details of that one. "All right. Eugene. What a jerk, am I right?"

She sidesteps a guy standing in the middle of the path, returning to my side after. "Yeah. I guess."

"I mean, he rejects Tatyana, pretends to seduce Olga, then kills Vladimir—"

"He kills Vladimir?"

Shit. "You hadn't gotten to that part?"

"No, but it's fine. I need to know in case Dr. Kroft asks. How does he kill him?"

"Shoots him in a duel."

She scoffs. "God, why are men so stupid?"

I stroke my beard, pretending to mull over her question. "I'd take exception to that, but you're right. As a whole, we are impressively dumb."

Ah, and there's that laugh again.

"Okay, what else happens?"

I continue telling her what I can remember from the book, although it's been a few years since I read it.

"What class did you read this for?" she asks, making the final turn toward her lecture hall.

"It was just for fun. I went through this phase in high school where I only read classics. Well, listened to the audiobooks. I thought I was *so* much smarter than everyone else."

She gives me a deadpan look. "You read this for fun?"

"You took this class for fun, didn't you? You're an accounting major. There's no way your degree requires Russian Lit."

"Yeah, but I needed another Literature class to fulfill my gen-ed requirement. And this one fit my schedule."

I shrug. "Well, to each their own."

There's a brief silence and then she stops walking, smacking her forehead. "Oh my God." She turns to me, pointing. "You were the salutatorian of your high school, weren't you?"

Wow, she made that connection? "What makes you think that?"

"Because no normal person reads this stuff for fun."

"Now, I do take exception to that."

"Ethan." She shakes her head. "Why are you wasting your time with boxing?"

"What?" Where did that come from?

"If you're so smart, why are you risking concussions? Beating up people for kicks? Trying to be like those guys at the gym going nowhere in life?"

"Is that your issue with your dad talking?" I ask before thinking it through.

She blinks at me, lips parting in surprise.

Shit. I shouldn't have said that.

She doesn't run off in a huff like I expect, though, continuing to stare at me until she finally says, "Yeah, maybe it is."

Okay. Didn't expect her to own up to that so easily. Getting anywhere deep with her is usually like pulling teeth.

"Come on." I lay an arm over her shoulders and start walking again toward her building just ahead. "Don't want you to be late."

She stops outside the lecture hall doors, turning to me. "Should we meet at the dorm? Or…"

"I'll drive us. I'll pick you up here after your class lets out."

"You don't have to wait around here just for me."

Doesn't she realize I would do a hell of a lot more for her? "I'll be here. See you after class."

She nods and reaches up, briefly hugging me. I'm too caught off guard to return it before she's already gone, giving me a small smile. "In case anyone's watching," she says.

Right. I'm sure that was the only reason.

---

"Ethan, hey."

I startle, realizing I was zoned out, and glance toward the lecture hall doors, but they're still closed. Lexie's class should be letting out soon.

I focus in front of me and see none other than Lexie's favorite person there. Savannah. What does she want?

"Hey," I reply, acting like I'm interested. "It's Samantha, right?" That'll mess with her head.

Her brows narrow the slightest bit as she flips her hair over her shoulder. "Savannah."

"Right, right. Sorry, I'm terrible with names." I give her an ingratiating smile, but she doesn't pick up on my insincerity.

"That's okay. Hey, how'd you do on the test last time?"

"I got an A."

She sidles a little closer. "Wow. Brawn and brains."

She's still going to flirt with me after she saw me and Lexie together two weeks ago?

"Will you be at study group tonight?" she asks.

I stick my hands in my pockets, glancing again at the closed building doors. "Yep." If Lexie comes out here to find me talking to her, will she be mad?

"Me too. Want to ride together?"

I motion toward the lecture hall. "I'm actually waiting for Lexie. I'm already giving her a ride."

She laughs as if I said something funny. "Oh my God, are you still hanging out with her? I thought she would have moved on to the next guy by now."

She looks at me expectantly, clearly wanting me to ask her to elaborate, but I don't. That should come from Lexie.

"Hey," she says, changing the subject. "You have any plans tomorrow night?"

"Uh… not sure." Seriously, when is Lexie getting out of class?

"My sorority's co-hosting a party at Kappa Sigma house." She taps my arm playfully. "You have to come visit me."

She's closer now, looking up at me from under lowered lashes. Yeah, she's a girl who's used to getting what she wants.

The doors of the building burst open, Lexie at the front of the pack of students exiting. She pauses as she spots us, until someone pushes her from behind, and then she speeds up, determination on her face as she strides over. She gets closer, closer, until she's right there, reaching up to cup the back of my neck, tugging me down to meet her lips in a kiss so unexpected, it makes my toes curl.

She releases me, gaze apologetic, but she never has to apologize for doing something like that. Stepping to the side, she wraps her hand around the crook of my elbow and acts as if she's just noticing the other girl.

"Oh, Savannah. I didn't see you there."

It's obvious Savannah knows what she's up to by the fake smile she gives her.

"Savannah invited us to a party tomorrow night," I tell Lexie, trying to defuse the situation.

"Oh, I was really only inviting you, Ethan," Savannah says. "The people there are more your crowd." She turns to Lexie, tilting her head. "I know parties aren't your thing."

Could she get any more blatantly rude?

I'm just about to call her out on it when Lexie says, "Oh, I'd love to go. Thanks for the invite."

Man, she must hate her if she's willing to be that social—at a fraternity house of all places.

Savannah smiles again at her, malice in her gaze. "Great. Maybe the baseball team will be there too. That's more your speed."

Lexie's grip on me tightens, nails digging into my inner elbow. I look down, finding her shooting daggers at Savannah. How do I always get caught in the crossfire of whatever feud they have going on?

"We have to get to study group now," Lexie says through tight lips.

She tugs at my arm, steering me away, and I follow, listening as she mutters something barely audible under her breath.

"You okay?" I ask when we're distant enough.

"Oh, yeah. I'm just great." She's practically dripping with sarcasm. "I loved walking out of class and seeing her flirt with you."

"I wasn't—"

"I'm not saying you did anything wrong. *She's* the problem. She's going to invite you to a party—where she clearly intends to hook up with you—and then tell me I can't come? She doesn't know we're not really a couple."

"It's not like we're actually going to the party."

"Oh, no. We're going."

I blink at her vehemence. We are?

"I'm so sick of freaking Savannahs thinking they can have whoever they want. That they can do whatever they want."

Are we still talking about Savannah the person? Or people in general?

"Well, she can't have you," she declares. "You're mine."

She lets go of my arm, stopping in the middle of the sidewalk, eyes wide as she turns to me. "You know what I mean," she backtracks. "Fake mine."

I simply watch her. My first instinct is to tease her for her slip up, but I also don't want to make light of it. I like what she said. Really like it.

"I don't think you're mine, Ethan." Desperation bleeds into her voice, like she needs me to believe it.

*I'd be yours if you let me.*

I can't say that to her, though. Based on her reaction just now, she'd run as fast as she could.

148

"I know you don't think that." She's made it crystal clear.

We walk in silence toward my car, the tension between us thick. As I open the passenger door for her, she finally looks at me. "Are you mad?" she whispers.

Not mad, just… disappointed, I guess. "Why would I be mad?"

"Because I used you. Again. And I said we'd go to the party, right after I yelled at you the other week for making a decision for me."

She thinks I'm mad over that?

I reach out to her, enfolding her in my arms, glad when she complies without resistance. "I'll go anywhere you want to go. Do anything you want to do. Don't worry about me."

She grips the sides of my shirt. "It's like I become this awful, petty person whenever I'm around her."

"You're allowed to be petty. She was rude as hell to you."

Her shoulders drop, the tension in them loosening. "I'm sorry I kissed you."

I'm not. "Lexie, I understand. If you wanted to make her jealous, I'd say mission accomplished." I just wish she wanted to do it for another reason. "And honestly, it would make sense if we greeted each other like that all the time. That's what a real couple would do."

I hold my breath, curious as to how she'll respond, but she only makes a noncommittal noise. Not an agreement, but not a denial either. That's progress, right?

"We should get over to the dorms," she says, extracting herself from my hold.

I savor the feel of her in my arms for one last moment, letting her go and closing the door behind her as she gets in.

"What's this?" she asks when I get in and start the car, holding up the bag that was in her seat.

"For you. I already had my half earlier."

Her brows knit as she cautiously looks inside, pulling out half of a sub sandwich.

"They didn't say anything about ordering a pizza tonight, so I figured you'd be hungry."

"You went out and got this for me?" she asks quietly.

"I was getting one for me anyway. And I didn't know what you liked, so I played it safe. No crazy peppers or anything on there."

Her stomach lets out a rumble, as if it's excited about what's in her hand, and I smile. She can't refuse it now.

"Thank you," she says, somehow both grateful and defeated, my chest aching at the sound.

Operation Feed Lexie is back in full swing. I'd tried last night, but it seems she actually needs the food in front of her to cave.

She takes a bite as I reverse out of the space, and I give her a minute before I ask, "Are you going to tell me what went down between you and Savannah now?"

She wipes at her mouth with her hoodie sleeve, letting out a sigh. "I said I would, didn't I?" She nibbles at her food, delaying the conversation a bit longer, but I've got all night.

"Savannah was part of this popular clique," she finally says. "But she wasn't the worst one. They all took direction from the ringleader, Ashley."

She takes a massive bite, as if she's starving, and I regret now not getting a bag of chips to go with it.

"They spread this nasty rumor about me, which basically ruined high school. Everyone thought… something about me. I don't want to say what."

"Why does it matter if it's not true?"

She looks over at me, smirking the slightest bit. "Because then you'd have more questions. You always do."

"You got me there."

She fiddles with the edge of the paper sandwich wrapper, bending it back and forth. "Someone else actually started the rumor and told them to spread it. Told them to make my life hell."

"Why?" I can't resist asking. Why would someone try to ruin her life like that?

"He wanted me to do something and I wouldn't. And then I did something else I probably shouldn't have that really pissed him off."

He? There's a guy involved now? "What happened?"

She shakes a finger at me. "No questions."

"Fine."

She sighs. "Anyway, I tried denying it, but no one listened. For some reason, they only took it as confirmation that it was true. And after a while, I stopped trying. Stopped caring. What was the point when everyone thought... that way about me."

What way? "You're being awfully cryptic."

She stuffs another mouthful of sandwich in. "I know," she mumbles.

So what clues do I have? Savannah calling her sexy Lexie that first time we met, saying Lexie spent time doing something other than talking, now mentioning a baseball team today.

What does it mean?

I reach over the center console, grabbing her hand and squeezing softly. "I'm sorry."

"For what?"

"Anything you had to go through back then."

She keeps her hand in mine, half-surprising me when she returns my squeeze. "You had nothing to do with it."

"I know, but it just makes me feel... helpless." Is this why she doesn't trust anyone?

"Why would you feel helpless about me?" She sounds genuinely curious, as if she couldn't imagine a plausible reason why.

"Because I care about you."

There's a long pause as she seems to struggle with my words. "Ethan..." She lets go of my hand, my stomach sinking. I should have kept my mouth shut.

"As a friend," I add. Shit. I shouldn't have said that either. It's not the truth.

"You barely know me," she whispers.

I return my hand to the steering wheel, pulling into the lot by Chapman Hall. They said it was the building next to that one. "What are you talking about? We've known each other for weeks."

"Yeah..."

"So that's not a long time?"

One of her shoulders lifts in a half-hearted shrug. "I don't know. I mean, I just started having one-on-one conversations with my roommate's boyfriend, and I've known him for five months."

Jesus. I can't wait that long. "So, what? You don't want me to care about you?"

I pull into a space in a corner of the lot, away from everyone else, shutting off the engine. I stay right where I am, though, waiting for her answer.

"It's not that. I—" She blows out a breath, pulling at the strings of her hood. "If we're being honest with each other, I actually sort of like the idea of having someone else in my life I can trust. That I can rely on."

Good. I'm glad she finally sees me that way.

"But if you really knew me," she continues in a soft voice. "Knew every-thing about me... you'd feel differently."

No, she's not a forthcoming person, but what kind of secret could she be harboring that would change how I feel about her?

"So let me in," I reply. "How can I know you if you don't let me?"

She looks over at me, biting at her bottom lip. "That's the catch, isn't it?"

Yeah, it is.

"Come on," she says, unbuckling her seatbelt. "They're probably waiting for us."

I glance at the clock on the dashboard. She's right.

But as I follow her into the dorm, the thing I can't get out of my head is that if I want to know her completely, that means I have to submit myself to her scrutiny as well.

And based on her previous opinions, do I measure up?

# CHAPTER SIXTEEN

## LEXIE

I SHUT MY CAR DOOR, the hinges blessedly silent after Ethan worked his magic on them, and survey the endless row of cars parked on the street. Why did I think it was a good idea again to come to this frat party tonight?

A high-pitched shriek, followed by a chorus of giggles, comes from up ahead as a trio of girls teeter in sky-high heels toward Kappa Sigma house.

I check my reflection in my car window, my makeup not smudged, and smooth down my low-cut black shirt and skirt. This is what I used to wear to work before I discovered the benefits of the bustier. But there, it's a costume. I'm not truly Lexie. I'm the girl who earns tips based on how well I mix drinks and look good doing it.

And here, I'm me. Tonight, coming to this party in an attempt to one-up Savannah, I'm that girl in high school again. Sitting alone at lunch as the other girls whisper about me. Sticking my earbuds in as the boys approach me thinking I'll be an easy lay.

No, it's been over two years since I left that place. I'm not that same girl.

I follow the girls into the house, half-wishing I would have taken Ethan up on his offer to pick me up and drive together as I encounter the packed crowd, but that would have invited a whole other slew of problems. Travis and Isaac were both home tonight, and I know they would have given me a hard time if they knew I was going to a frat party. Would have embarrassed me fawning over Ethan, asking him questions about the nature of our relationship.

In this outfit, they'd assumed I'd picked up a shift at the bar, and I hadn't corrected them.

A stab of guilt pokes at me as Ethan's words from last night come back to me. *Let me in.* Just another example of how I keep others at bay. How I don't invite them into my life. Doesn't he realize it's easier that way, though?

If he knew about everything in my past, about what happened with my mom, about Cody's vile rumor and what he did to me... He'd want nothing to do with me. Who wants to be with the girl with baggage heavier than she can carry?

Oh, and let's not forget about how he said I have unresolved issues with my dad about my childhood. How I have barely any friends or money. Every day I'm scraping by. I seriously don't know why he even keeps hanging around me, Psych study or not.

Even Travis, the person I'm arguably the closest to in this world, doesn't know any of the stuff that went on with my mom. Doesn't know about all the shit she used to pull. What she put me through. Doesn't know how I found her there, dead in our living room, her beloved needle still in her hand. She'd loved her highs more than she'd ever loved me.

And the truth about what happened with me and Cody? Yep, that's between me, him, and his two teammates there with us that night, whatever their names were.

Travis was the only one who believed me when I said Cody was a liar. The only one who talked to me in school and on the bus the following year. He'd had his fair share of being bullied for being a quiet, effeminate boy in a school where jocks ruled. We were the two outcasts. And while he can look back at high school and laugh with Isaac about silly crushes, I'm not over it quite yet. Not if I'm here wanting to make Savannah jealous with what she can't have, using Ethan yet again.

He claimed he didn't mind, though. That he'd do anything I wanted to. How far does that offer extend? And how far do I want it to?

Savannah didn't even show up to study group last night. Have I scared her off? Or was she temporarily retreating to come up with a new tactic?

I scour the crowd for a tall, dark-haired man, but I'm in a sea of them, each more generic than the last in their polos, chino shorts, and boat shoes. Can't they get a new uniform?

There's a touch on my shoulder and I turn around, Ethan suddenly there, my stomach filling with butterflies.

"I was half afraid you wouldn't show," he says, grinning down at me.

"I wouldn't leave you alone with these animals."

His grin widens. "Speaking of, a certain someone's watching us. Should we give her a show?"

I nod, not exactly sure what he means until he leans down to give me a soft kiss, lingering for a moment. There's mischief in his gaze as he breaks away, and I look around, wanting to see Savannah's reaction.

"Where is she?"

"Hmm." He glances over his shoulder, then back at me. "Could've sworn she was here."

My brows pinch together. Well, I'm sure we'll see her at some point.

"You want anything to drink?" he asks, holding up a red Solo cup.

"No, I'm good."

And there's that stab of guilt again. The one that reminds me I should let him in a little more. He deserves it after everything he's done for me.

"I, um, actually don't drink at all," I tell him.

"No?"

There's no judgment in his voice, only curiosity. It spurs me on enough to say, "My mom had substance abuse issues. So I don't touch anything that could mess me up."

He stares at me for a moment, but there's no revulsion in his gaze, no disgust. No pity, either. Just understanding. "Thank you for telling me."

I let out a sigh of relief.

"This is water," he says, motioning toward his cup. "I'm not drinking either."

"I won't police what you do if you want a beer or something."

"Nah, I need to cut that stuff out anyway."

"Because of your upcoming match?"

He looks confused for a second before his face clears. "Right. The match. I have to get better about what I eat for that."

"So why do you have water in that?"

"Oh, it just makes it easier. No one will ask me if I want a drink."

As if on cue, some frat guy passes by us, trying to hand me a cup of beer. I shake my head at him. As if I'd take something from a stranger.

"You know," Ethan says, "I've hardly seen you without your hoodie. You decided to change it up tonight?"

My hands automatically tug at the hem of my skirt, pulling it down a little. "Yeah. Trying something different."

"You look good."

My face flushes hot, embarrassed by his attention for some reason. "I normally don't like guys looking at me," I blurt out. "That's why I wear the hoodie." The thing's practically become a security blanket for me now with how often I have it on.

"Is it okay if I look?"

Is that why I wore this tonight? So he'd see me in it? "You already are."

"Yeah, but do you want me to?"

This feels like a trick question. Or at least one with a hidden meaning.

A tall guy bumps into Ethan, holding the hand of a familiar looking girl, but it's not till they're past us that I realize who it is.

"Is that Heather?"

He turns to see who I'm talking about. "The girl from the study group?"

I nod, hoping he doesn't repeat his original question. I'm not sure how to answer it.

"And did you want to go say hi?" he asks drily, clearly knowing I don't.

"No, she's a little… occupied."

The guy she's with stops in front of one of the bedroom doors, knocking before going in, leading her by the hand behind him.

"Looks like Heather's getting lucky," Ethan comments.

I scoff. "In a room with a guy at a party? Yeah, right."

He gives me a quizzical look.

"There's no way she's getting what she wants in there. It'll be a quick fuck over the edge of the bed or he'll want a blow job."

His brows raise. "A wham, bam, thank you ma'am?"

I smirk at him. "Exactly."

"You can't say for sure. Maybe they're different."

My lips purse. "I'm taking a highly educated guess. I guarantee they'll be in and out of there in less than five minutes."

"You want to bet?"

I hold out a hand. "Fine."

He shakes it, grinning.

"Do you really think I'm wrong?" I ask, curious as to what he'll say.

"Actually, I think you're right. I just like playing devil's advocate."

I roll my eyes. Of course he does.

"So what would you like if you win?"

I tap my index finger against my chin. "How about another pint of mint chocolate chip ice cream?"

"Done."

"And if you win?" Not that he's going to. Girls always get the short end of the stick at parties like this.

He sticks a thumb over his shoulder. "You have to dance with me out there."

I look behind him where he's indicating, the living room packed with bodies. That's easy enough. If I can find Savannah, it would actually be the perfect thing to do in front of her. "Deal."

He leans in, whispering, "Incoming. Your seven o'clock."

I'm still trying to figure out where that is in relation to me when I hear a familiar, "Ethan. You came."

He wraps an arm around my waist, tugging me in closer to his hard body. I brace a hand against his chest, savoring the way Savannah's mouth turns down slightly at the action. "Thanks for inviting us," he says to her. "We're having a great time."

"Awesome," she replies unconvincingly, still only looking at him. "Well, if you get bored later and want to dance or something, let me know."

Seriously? I'm right here. "Good idea, Savannah," I tell her, forcing her to look at me. "We'll definitely dance in a bit."

She gives a half-smile before walking off, glancing over her shoulder at Ethan one more time once he can't see her. The audacity of that girl is unbelievable. She has her pick of guys here. Why is she still lusting after Ethan when she knows he's taken? Is it only because he's mine?

She *thinks* he's mine, I correct myself. I don't actually have any kind of claim to him.

I step out of his personal space as soon as she's out of sight, a small part of me missing the connection, as weird as that seems.

Ethan takes a sip from his cup, glancing around, then points toward the bedroom door, the handle turning. "I think we might have our answer soon."

The guy exits first with a cat who ate the canary grin on his face, Heather close behind, wiping at her mouth.

"See?" I declare triumphantly. "Tell me she didn't just give him head."

A guy passing by us stops to stare at me. Guess I should keep my voice down. "Move along," I tell him, shooing him away. "Nothing to see here."

Ethan's grinning widely as I look back at him. "The evidence certainly supports your theory." He strokes his beard thoughtfully. "I'll give you the win."

"And the ice cream?"

"Yes. I officially apologize on behalf of men everywhere." He bows low in some kind of exaggerated courtly gesture. "We are disgusting, selfish creatures."

"Stop that," I hiss, tugging at his arm to pull him back up before anyone sees him. "Come on."

I lead him toward the living room, smiling when I spot Savannah just beyond the edge of the dance floor. Perfect.

"Where are we going?" he asks, raising his voice to be heard over the music, loud now as we reach the periphery of dancers.

"To dance."

"But I lost the bet."

I turn around to face him. "Do you want to dance or not?"

"Of course I do."

He sets his cup down and takes hold of my waist, surprising me as he moves me backward into the sea of bodies, the bass of whatever song is playing thumping through me.

After carving out a spot for us, he yells over the music, "I see why you want to dance now." He jerks his head in the direction of Savannah and I shrug in response, unable to deny it. It was the whole point of coming here tonight.

"I've come to terms with my pettiness," I reply.

"You won't hear any complaints from me."

He moves to the rhythm of the song surprisingly well, and I follow his lead. I guess Mister Boxer's got moves.

"You dance well," I tell him.

He winks at me. "It's all in the hips."

I laugh, something in me light and loose being here with him like this. There's this feeling in me like anything could happen. The night is ours to make what we will of it.

His eyes dance with amusement as he watches me. "Is she looking?"

My gaze cuts to her briefly, finding her attention on us. "Yes."

He bends down a little, still dancing as he says in my ear, "You know what would really get her?"

"What?" I grin, glad he's become my co-conspirator in this, too.

"If we started making out here in the middle of the dance floor."

I laugh again, the idea ridiculous. "Oh, would it?"

I lean back, expecting to find him grinning, but he doesn't return my smile, his gaze serious. He's nearer than I expected too, especially as he uses his hands on my waist to bring me in closer to him.

My hands automatically move to his broad shoulders to steady myself, my fingers flexing against the muscle there.

"If you want to make her jealous," he says, barely audible over the music, "let's do it right."

My heart beats painfully in my chest, gaze dropping to his lips. I guess it's not a big deal, I tell myself. We've already kissed before. What's another time?

I find myself nodding, closing my eyes as his mouth meets mine, the music, the other dancers, the party itself slowly fading as he once more drags me under his spell, further than the other day in the Psych lab.

My hands move from his shoulders to intertwine around the back of his neck, stepping in closer until I'm flush against his hard chest, remembering how good he'd looked at the gym with his shirt off. My hands itch to travel down his body and under that shirt, tracing each ridge of his abdomen up to his defined pecs.

What would it be like to have the freedom to do that? To be his girlfriend in truth, with free rein to explore him however I want?

I pull back, confused by my train of thought, but he moves in again, cupping my jaw, kissing me deeper this time, my body singing with the way he focuses all his attention on me. No one has ever been this intent with me. Like they can't get enough.

Is it all part of the act? Is he doing this solely for Savannah to watch? Or is he really feeling it? Does he actually want to kiss me? To make out with me?

And do I want him to want that? To want me?

The idea is... terrifying. Like I told him yesterday, getting that close to him, having him know all of me... There's no way he'd stick around.

But for now, I let myself continue, too caught up in this moment to put a stop to it, even though I should. Even though it'll be harder later to act like everything is normal between us. Like we didn't spend who knows how long making out at a party in front of who knows how many people. Like his tongue wasn't in my mouth, making me moan, making me press even closer to him, wanting more.

"Fuck," he groans, the single word doing more to get me going than anything else I've ever experienced.

He shifts his hips, something hard coming in contact with my lower half, and I hiss in a breath, too surprised to say anything. Is he...

"Get a room," someone shouts at us, reality crashing back down.

We break apart, and while I'm peripherally aware of people looking at us, pointing and whispering at the two people crazy enough to get themselves worked up this badly while dancing, I can't seem to bring myself to care. Not when I'm staring into those vivid green eyes, unmistakable lust there for everyone to see. He can't be that good of an actor, right? Even if he did tell me yesterday he only cared about me as a friend.

"Do you want to?" he asks in a low voice, the sound of it sending another wave of longing through me.

"What?" I'm not sure what he's asking.

"Do you want to go in that room?"

I blink, some of the haze clearing. Is he serious? Even after my little speech earlier? "So I can, what? Give you a blow job?"

"No. So I can go down on you."

# CHAPTER SEVENTEEN

## LEXIE

MY JAW DROPS. Say what now?

"Let's subvert the norm," he whispers silkily in my ear. "When we leave, you'll be the one with the satisfied smile and I'll be wiping my mouth."

My knees weaken. Like physically weaken as I drop a little. He easily catches me, bringing me back up, supporting my weight with his arm around my waist.

There's no way he's for real. Yeah, I get that he's turned on right now. I am too, if I'm being honest with myself. But this would change everything. The whole dynamic of our relationship. Or, rather, non-relationship. Everything we're doing is fake.

"Ethan..." I trail off, not sure where I'm going with it.

"It'll be an apology for the history books," he says, as if he didn't hear me. "Again, on behalf of all men everywhere, let me make amends. Let the girl finally get something good in one of those rooms."

Is that his actual argument? I can't agree to that, can I?

His hands move from my waist to my ass, cupping me, a rush of warmth filling my lower belly.

"I want to make you feel good, Lexie. When was the last time anyone made you feel good?"

"Never," I find myself saying, compelled to answer him.

"So you'll come with me? Come *for* me?"

Oh my God, he wants me to... I can't do that. I've never done that with a man. The one guy I've been with, well, he wasn't that interested in making sure I had a good time too. But Cody never made my stomach flip like this. Never kissed me with such passion. Never even asked me if I liked what we were doing.

My gaze flicks over Ethan's shoulder, homing in on Savannah staring at us, her lips pursed in disapproval. "Yes," I say, being petty as hell, relishing her attention on us as he leads me through the crowd, back the way we came toward that bedroom.

Ethan knocks on the door, no sound from the other side. Is this really happening?

I glance over my shoulder, giving Savannah a little wave before shutting the door behind me, but there's no time to savor my victory because Ethan's on me, backing me up against the door, his lips on my neck, trailing kisses over the sensitive area.

I can't think, can't focus when he's doing that, my hips instinctively tilting to make contact with his, wanting to feel him again.

He flicks the lock and bends down, brushing his palms down the backs of my thighs, lifting me until I'm eye level with him, encouraging me to wrap my legs around his waist. I do so, head falling back against the door with a thud as he grinds into me, more intensely this time. The butterflies in my stomach are flapping their wings like mad, swooping and diving every which way, especially as his mouth returns to mine, kissing me rougher now, like he needs me. Like he can't help himself.

He said the kiss in the lab would be the one to make me forget any previous kisses, but it's *this* one that does the trick. There's no other thought in my mind but how he promised to make me feel good.

And let me tell you, this is more than I ever could have dreamed of.

He shifts me higher in his arms, supporting my back as he leads me to the full-sized bed in the corner of the room, laying me down on the soft comforter, his big body covering mine. I have no idea whose bed this is or what else people have done on it tonight, but I'm too far gone to care, only focused on kissing him, spreading my legs wider to accommodate him, my skirt riding up in the process.

I'm wanton, greedily taking from his mouth, bringing my fingers up to sift through his dark hair, softer than I expected. This is the first time I've really touched him, the first time I've had a chance to do all those things I've secretly imagined doing, even when I wouldn't admit to myself my attraction to him.

My hands are stroking his beard next, tracing his cheekbones with my thumbs, down his neck to his upper back, the muscles there heavy. Down, down, down the length of his back until I reach the hem of his shirt, sneaking under, his skin warm as I move my palms between us to his stomach, wanting to trace his abs like I imagined earlier.

He pulls away, his breaths harsh. "This was supposed to be for you," he says.

"It is. Take off your shirt."

I nearly clap my hand over my mouth, unable to believe I just said that, but he apparently likes my response, his gaze flaring with desire as he leans back to whip it off, that hard body on display for me.

I can't help staring at him, studying each dip and curve of his torso, following his happy trail down further until it disappears beneath his jeans, a suspiciously large bulge there.

My gaze snaps up to meet his, my cheeks warming. Of course he'd catch me looking.

"Anything else you want me to take off?" he asks with a smirk.

I should make him strip naked for that comment, but knowing him, he'd happily oblige.

And I don't think I could handle a naked Ethan right now.

I shake my head, afraid to open my mouth again.

"You ready?"

"For what?" I whisper. I still don't know what to expect. This is brand new territory for me.

His gaze travels over my body, a loving caress I never thought I'd welcome like this. "To feel good."

"What will you do?"

He leans over me, whispering in my ear, "Lick your pussy."

My thighs clench as arousal rushes through me, filling me limb from limb. Coming from anyone else, I'd laugh at such a statement, at his confident tone, at the idea that I'd let a guy so close.

But this is no laughing matter. He's actually going to do it.

"I've never—" I cut myself off, unsure how much to say.

"No one's ever gone down on you before?" he asks easily, his lips whispering over the shell of my ear, goosebumps running rampant down my neck.

"No."

He moves a hand to my hip, palm flat as it travels over my skirt to my upper thigh, resting there. "You ever don't like what I'm doing, you tell me, okay? You're in control."

His calm words ease me somewhat, until that hand drifts under my skirt, my breath catching as it moves higher and higher, heartbeat echoing loudly in my ears. His thumb passes over my panties, barely there, and my hips lift, seeking contact.

I push them back down, hating how desperate I seem. My body's on sensory overload, though, craving what it's never had.

He does it again, featherlight, getting me used to it before he deepens the pressure, lifting my skirt to reveal his actions, the sight of it unbearably erotic as he strokes me over the fabric.

I bite my lip to contain my moan as he slips beneath my panties, his middle finger pushing in easily with how wet I am.

"Christ, you're ready for me, aren't you?" he murmurs, my face heating once again.

He kisses me once before traveling down my body, settling in at the end of the bed and removing my shoes first, and then my panties, dragging them down my thighs, leaving me bare, spread open for him.

He takes a moment to study me, lust and appreciation in his gaze, before bending down and pressing a gentle kiss to my pussy.

I buck, a bolt of pleasure chasing up my spine as he does it again, resting a palm on my lower abdomen, keeping me in place.

"You like that?"

I nod, squeezing my eyes shut, still not sure this isn't all some crazy dream. Ethan isn't actually kissing me down there right now. There's no way we went from me telling him I'm not interested to this in under a month.

But I don't seem to be waking up anytime soon, focused now on the slow, torturous circles he's drawing with his tongue over me, building me up, need curling through my belly.

He uses his other hand to spread my thighs wider, picking up the pace, and grips my ass as he flicks his tongue faster, teasing my clit.

My hands grip the comforter, holding on for dear life, and I make the mistake of looking down, the sight of him between my legs the hottest thing I've ever seen. He looks so into it, like he's enjoying himself, but there's no way that can be right. Guys don't actually like doing this stuff, do they?

He said tonight's about me, though. Only getting what *I* want. I assume then it's not a precursor to more? Am I ready for more?

I push that thought aside, focusing on what's happening right now, my thighs trembling with unchecked lust, one of his hands snaking up my body to squeeze my breast, the action making me release a breathy moan.

He looks up at me, meeting my gaze, the intensity there overwhelming.

"You like watching?" he asks, tenderly nuzzling me.

I swallow heavily, unable to help answering him. "Yes."

Outside the bedroom door, the party rages on, but here we're in our own private bubble. A moment outside time. That has to be it. Some kind of blip in the time continuum. How else can I explain what's going on? His face is in my most private area. A place I swore no one would get near again. And here I am telling him I like it. That I want more.

And I do want more. I want him to take me further than I've ever been.

An electric thrill races through me as he finds my clit with his tongue, sucking. I jerk, groaning out his name, and a devilish smile crosses his face before he does it again, the pressure in me rising higher, higher.

I teeter on the edge, gaze glued to what he's doing, and reach out a hand to slide through his hair, needing that extra contact to send me over, my back bowing as my orgasm overtakes me. Warmth races through my veins, leaving full-body tingles in its wake, my thighs twitching as he continues to lap at me, wringing every last bit of pleasure from me that he can.

I stare at him, panting harshly, unable to believe that actually happened. That we just did that.

He winces and I realize I'm still gripping his hair, tugging at the strands, and I let go, dropping my hand to the mattress. "Sorry."

"You're fine," he murmurs, sliding his shoulders out from under my thighs. "Did you like that?"

"I loved it," I reply. There's no other answer I can give him, not when he did all that for me.

There's a pounding on the door, making me jump, and a booming voice from outside shouts, "Who the hell's in my room?"

My eyes widen, just as Ethan says, "Oh, shit."

He springs into motion, grabbing my panties from the floor to slide them up my legs, and hands me my shoes as he flips his shirt right side out to put back on.

I scoot off the bed and tug my skirt down before slipping my shoes on, attempting to smooth my hair into place before Ethan grabs my hand and leads me to the door, keeping himself between me and the guy directly outside glowering at us.

"Sorry," Ethan tells him. "We saw other people in here, so we figured it was the place to use." He rubs a thumb over his bottom lip. "Perfection takes time, you know?" He claps the guy on the back and moves off, my cheeks burning as I keep my head down and follow him.

"I can't believe you said that," I whisper when we're out of earshot.

He shrugs. "What was he going to do? Fight me?"

He has a point. Ethan could have easily taken him.

"Besides, it was worth it." He pulls me over to the side, out of the pathway of others, and cups my jaw, kissing me deeply. I can taste myself on his lips, something I never thought I'd experience.

Now that we're out of that room, now that the madness within me has subsided, doubt creeps in. What have we done?

His phone vibrates, ringing faintly, and he lets go of me to fish it out of his pocket. He silences the ringer, muttering, "Damn."

"Everything okay?"

He glances up at me. "Yeah. It was just an alarm I have set. I, uh, have to run out to my car real quick. I'll be back in five, ten minutes."

And leave me alone? Yeah, no. "I'll probably get going. I think we accomplished our mission here."

Behind him, I spot Savannah chatting with a dark-haired guy eerily similar to Ethan. Guess she gave up, then.

We make our way out of the party, Ethan easily creating a path for us with his big body, and we walk in silence toward the street.

"Where are you parked?" he asks. "I'm up this way." He points in the opposite direction of where my car is.

"I'm over here."

He starts toward where I motioned and I lay a hand on his arm. "You don't have to walk me to my car."

He slings an arm over my shoulders. "You think I'm letting you walk out here alone at night?"

Even as his words make something inside me go a little gooey, I still resist. "I can take care of myself."

"I know. But humor me."

We head down the sidewalk, his arm heavy over me. He seems at ease, but the bundle of nerves in my belly steadily grows until I actually have to hold a hand over my stomach to settle it. If I was unsure how to act around him after kissing him in the lab, I definitely don't know what to say now.

"You work tomorrow night?" he asks casually, as if we just didn't share the most intimate experience of my life.

"No."

"Want to come over? My roommate and his girlfriend are doing a horror movie marathon."

He's inviting me over to watch a movie?

"Um, sure," I say as we reach my car, my wits still addled.

"Be there around eight? I'll text you my address."

"Okay." I'm so confused right now. I need time to process everything that just happened.

"See you tomorrow." He leans down, giving me a quick kiss on the lips, and waits as I fish my keys out.

He stands at the curb, holding a hand in farewell as I pull away. It's not until I'm a mile down the road that I realize what I agreed to. We've never done anything together not directly related to the study or class. Even tonight was a way to be seen as a couple, to legitimize our fake relationship.

Sort of.

He wasn't... asking me on a date, was he? No, he said his friends will be there. And it's just watching a movie. It's not like he asked me to go to a fancy restaurant with him. That's what people do when they go on dates, right? I've never actually been on one. Cody always wanted to meet up somewhere secret where no one would see us. He said it was because his ex-girlfriend would cause trouble for me if she knew we were together, but I realize now he just didn't want to be seen with me. I was never good enough to be anyone's girlfriend.

I shove away that whole train of thought, compartmentalizing it. I need to worry about what I'm doing with Ethan, not what happened years ago with Cody. Ethan's not the same as him. Not anywhere close.

Even so, what exactly is he to me?

# CHAPTER EIGHTEEN

## ETHAN

"THERE WAS a problem with your timecard this morning," my shift manager, Keith, says, standing awkwardly a few feet away from me in the aisle.

I yawn loudly and pull the next set of hedge clippers off the pallet, sliding them on the rack. "Oh, yeah?"

"You clocked in five minutes early."

I keep my eye roll at bay. The guy always thinks I'm trying to game the system because my brother is the assistant manager. "Better to be early than late, am I right?" He's lucky I came in at all. It took forever to fall asleep last night with how worked up I was.

"Make sure it doesn't happen again."

I stand up straight, giving him a salute. "Yes, sir."

His gaze narrows, but he can't prove I was mocking him.

I go back to stocking in peace after he leaves, my work easy enough that I can zone out. And my go-to daydreaming topic this morning?

Lexie.

Our bodies pressed together on the dance floor, moving in sync. Her legs wrapped around my waist as I held her against that door, grinding into her soft warmth. Her spread out for me on the bed, watching as I'd brought her to greater heights.

The sound of my name on her lips. The remembered taste of her pussy, so fucking wet for me. The way she'd surrendered to me, her body mine to do what I wanted with, for however brief a time.

Her guard finally down, letting me in. Letting me close. That's all I ever wanted from the start.

I have no illusions we're on the same page quite yet, but we're on the same chapter at least. Well, maybe more like the same book. Same shelf? Same bookstore?

We're closer than we were, is the point. We have to be for her to let me do that to her.

Will she let me do more tonight?

"Keith give you a hard time?"

I startle, nearly dropping the hammer I'm holding. Damn, that would've hurt if it had fallen on my foot. How long was I out for?

Turning, I spot my oldest brother, Scott, his brows raised at me. "Jumpy much?" he asks.

"I wouldn't be if you didn't tiptoe around." I place the hammer in its proper place, making sure it's aligned with the others. "How'd you know about Keith?"

He takes a sip of his coffee and I silently eye it. Would it be weird if I asked him for some of his? I need to wake up. "It was the first thing he told me when I walked in. And said I needed to have a talk with you about your attitude."

I grin at him. "Consider me officially warned."

He chuckles, tipping his Starbucks cup back to get the last of his drink. Damn, there's no more. "Why are you wasting your time here? You could run circles around these guys if you wanted."

I shrug, remembering how Lexie had asked me nearly the same thing about boxing. "It's easy. I don't have to think."

"Yeah, but you could make more money somewhere else. Isn't there some engineering gig you could do? You should start building up your resume."

I point a finger at him. "Did Mom put you up to this? Do you have a hidden mic on you?"

"I'm being serious," he says, wrestling my finger away. "You're already a junior. You need to start thinking about these things."

"Or, what? I'll end up like you?"

"Yeah, exactly."

He's made no secret of the fact he doesn't particularly care for this job, but he's too complacent to actually go out and look for anything else.

"Don't worry. I've got plenty of time." Graduation isn't for another two years. And my classes are hard enough. I don't need a demanding job on top of that, especially with all my training at the gym.

"That's what I thought, too," he mutters. "It goes by quicker than you think."

The bell over the shop door rings, both of us turning toward a familiar face.

Jacob approaches us, his hands in his pockets, completely out of place among the tools. He's never been mechanically-inclined.

"Taking up woodworking?" I ask him, motioning toward the chisels and hand drills on display.

"Dad needs a level," he says, ignoring my joke. "He can't find his."

What project is he up to now? And Scott wonders how he ended up working here with as many times as Dad dragged us to hardware stores growing up?

"Aisle two," I tell him, sensing he wants to be in and out as quickly as possible.

He sighs, glancing around. "Can you just get it for me? I don't even know what a level looks like."

Wow. And he calls himself a Hudson?

"I'll grab it," Scott says. "Ethan's working."

He leaves to head to the other side of the store as Jacob kicks at a stray nail on the floor.

I go back to unloading my pallet, the rubber mallets next. "I'm surprised you offered to come here for Dad."

He shrugs. "It was either that or listen to Jordan go on and on about some girl he met. I couldn't do it anymore."

Why is Jordan even over at the house this early on a Saturday morning?

"He mentioned you, too."

"Me?" I haven't talked to him since that family dinner last week. Oh, shit. I said I'd call Mom more, didn't I? I make a mental note to do that on my break today.

"Said he saw you on campus with some girl. He was asking us if you'd mentioned anything about getting a girlfriend."

And he couldn't have texted me a heads up he was going to tell the whole family about it? Or, you know, asked me himself?

"He must mean Lexie," I say, turning away to readjust the hand saws. "She's a friend. Maybe more than a friend. I don't know." Maybe tonight will clarify things better. She at least agreed to come over. That's promising.

"Okay." He doesn't press the issue, unconcerned with the dilemmas of my love life, but he's not the guy I'd go to if I wanted girl advice. Actually... Scott is.

He returns with the cheapest level we have, ushering Jacob up to the front where he rings him up with an employee discount before Keith notices.

Scott joins me again, but before he can start in on lecturing me to quit here and find a better job, I ask him, "So you have experience with women, right?"

"What?" He blinks, thrown off by my extreme change of subject.

"I mean, you were married. You must have a pretty good idea how women think."

His brows knit, nose scrunching. "I'm pretty sure I don't. If I did, I'd still be married."

Fair point. "Well, let's say you were with a girl who was kind of a commitment-phobe. How would you get her to be more interested in you?"

"I wouldn't," he says bluntly. "I'm not chasing after anyone."

Would he be the type to end up with a Savannah? Because she's right there, offering herself? But isn't that how he ended up here at this job so long? Because it was easy? Because it doesn't offer any challenge? And then he complains about it.

Now, I'm not knocking the easy road. Sometimes you take it when you need to focus your attention on other areas of your life.

But with your partner? That's different. While the confidence Savannah first displayed might have been attractive, the way she keeps flirting with me when she knows I have a girlfriend isn't.

But am I only interested in Lexie because of the chase? Because I've had to work so hard at chipping away at her walls?

It's something to consider, but I don't think that's the case. When she finally let me in last night, sharing details about her mother, physically getting closer, yielding to me in bed… It had only made me want her more. Want to discover all her secrets. And that could take a lifetime.

Am I up for the challenge?

"Thanks, man," I tell Scott. "That was helpful."

He stares at me, confused. "I didn't answer your question."

"I know. I realized I need to do the opposite of you. No offense."

He sighs but doesn't seem too offended by my insult. "So you have a girlfriend now or something?"

"No."

But maybe soon I will.

I'm the first one at the door as the doorbell rings, Tyler looking at me as if I have two heads as I sprint out of the kitchen.

"What's your deal?" he shouts after me. "It's Mia."

Yeah, but it could be Lexie. I mean, she's thirty minutes early, but still.

Opening the front door, my smile drops. It's Mia.

She blinks up at me, her curly brown hair a halo around her head. "Can I come in?"

"Oh, yeah. Sorry." I step out of the way as she passes by, looking out at the darkening rain clouds. I hope it doesn't pour before Lexie gets here. Would she use it as an excuse to not come at all?

Returning to the kitchen, I find Mia pulling ingredients out of a tote bag, placing them on the island in the center of the room.

"What are you making?"

"Cookies," she replies. "I thought it'd be nice for the movie and to make the house smell good."

Right. A kitchen full of warm, gooey chocolate chip cookies won't be at all hard to resist. I already took an insulin shot before dinner a couple hours ago. And I'm not taking my last one of the day until ten-thirty. Can I get away with dessert? I'm sick of testing my blood sugar.

Okay, just one. That'll be fine.

"Oh, look what I have," she says to Tyler, excitement in her voice as she pulls out what looks like a magazine.

"You actually bought this?" he asks, taking it from her.

I peek at the title, *Clinical Psychology Review* on the front.

"What is it?" I ask.

"Our study we worked on earlier in the year. The paper we wrote was finally published."

"Oh, congratulations." Tyler never mentioned anything about that. I guess it's not the kind of thing we normally talk about, though. "How'd it turn out?"

"Do you want to read it?" Mia takes it back from Tyler, flipping through to the dog-eared page.

I take it from her, skimming through, but I don't know enough about psychology to fully understand it all. "So biofeedback and physical activity were the most effective?"

"Yeah. That's what we figured it would be."

"Is this a big deal? To be in something like this?"

Tyler shrugs, but Mia says, "It's a huge deal. We're only undergraduates. Dr. Price's name is first, but still."

I take a closer look at the page. "Surprised you let Mia have more credit than you," I tell Tyler, seeing his name listed third.

"It's alphabetical," he says. "Clemons comes before Jenkins." He steps in behind her, circling his arms around her waist. "And she deserves it."

Here they go, getting lovey-dovey again.

I turn away, thankful for the interruption as the doorbell rings. There she is.

But when I open the front door, it's only an Amazon package for one of my other roommates. Damn.

At least Tom and Sean are out of the house tonight at some party. Lexie would be uncomfortable with even more strangers around.

I set the package inside the entrance and walk out toward the street, peering down both directions, but her crappy car is nowhere in sight. She's not lost, is she?

I pull out my phone, discovering less than ten minutes have passed. Why is this day taking forever?

I head back inside, laying on the couch listening to Tyler and Mia idly chat in the kitchen, my arm over my eyes. I let out a loud yawn, my jaw cracking. Sleep had been a long time coming last night when all I could think of was what it would be like if Lexie were in bed with me. Would she cuddle herself around me, using me as a pillow? Be the small spoon to my bigger one? Probably neither, but a guy can hope.

I drift, the faint sounds in the kitchen lulling me, and startle awake as something pinches my leg, a yelp escaping me.

Lexie looks down at me, lips pursed in disapproval. "You invite me over and I find you asleep?"

Ah, shit.

I rub my eyes, sitting up. What time is it?

She sits down next to me, whispering, "I had to make small talk. You know I hate that."

"Mia's good to talk to." Tyler, not so much. I yawn again, willing the drowsiness to leave my body. Is it too late for coffee? "Sorry, babe."

Her spine straightens. "Babe?"

Damn. I need to get it together. I rake a hand through my hair, making sure it's not sticking up in weird spikes. "Sorry. I'm still half asleep."

"Why are you taking naps this late, anyway?"

"I didn't mean to. But I didn't get much sleep last night."

"Why? We left that party at like ten-thirty."

"I was thinking about you," I tell her, not really considering what I'm saying.

"Me?" She sticks her hands in her hoodie pocket, the thing back on after a one-night break. "What about me?"

"If you'd be a cuddler."

Her brows lift, and she shakes her head next. "I swear, I never know what's going to come out of your mouth."

"I've got fresh-baked cookies," Mia announces, bringing in a platter to set in front of us on the coffee table.

I inhale, taking in all the deliciousness, already mourning the memory of when I used to gorge myself with the desserts she made.

"Have as many as you want," she says. "I've got a second batch in the oven."

I must have been asleep for a while if she had time to do all that.

"Try one," I tell Lexie, holding the plate out to her. "Mia makes the best stuff."

"What about you, Mister Stuff-My-Face-Full-Of-Junk?" She smiles, her gentle teasing making my heart lift. She must not be too mad at me.

I take a cookie, nibbling at it. I have to make this one cookie last. "See? Delicious."

She takes a bite of hers, eyes closing in an expression of bliss, the same as when she ate that mint chocolate chip ice cream. Oh, crap. I need to get that for her next time I see her.

"Wow, you were right."

I brush off my shoulders theatrically. "No big deal, but I usually am."

She bites her bottom lip, unsuccessfully hiding her amusement.

Tyler joins us, sprawling out on the loveseat, and turns on the TV, navigating to the on-demand movies.

"You like horror?" I ask Lexie. "You didn't mention it in your likes and dislikes at the diner."

She takes another cookie from the plate. Good. Even though it's late, should I offer her dinner, too?

"I haven't watched many horror movies." She glances at Tyler, but he isn't paying any attention to us as he searches for the movie. "We didn't have cable growing up. Or sometimes a TV," she adds in a lower voice.

That sounds... awful. But as bad as it is, I can't help the small glow in my chest that comes from her opening up and sharing that with me.

"We'll get you caught up. Tonight's a classic." At least, that's what Tyler told me. I haven't seen it myself.

Stifling another yawn, I settle into the couch cushions, cursing their pillowy softness for further relaxing me.

Mia joins us, bringing in a second batch of cookies along with her, Tyler immediately making grabby hands at it. She holds it out of his reach, offering it to Lexie. "Guests first."

Lexie grabs two fresh-out-of-the oven ones, handing one to me, but I decline, as delicious as it smells. "Nah. One's my limit."

"You don't like my baking anymore?" Mia asks good-naturedly. "You're usually worse than Tyler at clearing the plate."

Yeah, that's true. But I can't inhale carbs and sugar the way I used to anymore. "I, uh…" Crap. They're all staring at me. "I've got an upcoming match I'm training for. Have to eat clean." Wow, that excuse is coming in handy.

"That's right. Tyler mentioned that. Sorry for the temptation, then."

"No problem." Besides, I have bigger temptations to deal with.

Namely, Lexie.

# CHAPTER NINETEEN

## ETHAN

TYLER PRESSES PLAY on the remote and pulls Mia in close to him, the two of them settling in on the loveseat together.

Next to me, Lexie is stiff, crossing her arms over her chest as the movie begins.

I lean in to whisper in her ear, "You can relax a little, you know."

"I know."

Ten minutes later, she's still not much better. Unfortunately for me, I can barely keep my eyes open. Damn my sleepless night.

I have to stay awake. It's a miracle I got Lexie to agree to come tonight at all. If I fall asleep, she'll be pissed.

I just have to get into the movie. Something about a brutal murder in the house thirty years ago and now with a new family moving in, evil spirits are arising. I don't know if it's unoriginal, or too many things have been done like it since, but it can't hold my attention, my body continually sinking deeper and deeper into the cushions. My eyelids are heavy, sand slowly filling them, and I eventually stretch out, unable to resist any longer.

"I'm not in your way, am I?" Lexie asks drily as I bump into her for the third time.

"I'm trying to get comfortable," I whisper back, not wanting to disturb Tyler and Mia. "Here, if you just move..." I reposition her leg slightly, but it doesn't make a difference. "Just come down here with me."

I tug her until she's horizontal on the couch, half-surprised she willingly complies, and situate myself behind her so I'm spooning her, my arm slung over her waist. "There, perfect."

She turns slightly, looking at me over her shoulder, her eyes wide in a *what the hell are you doing* expression.

"I'm comfortable now," I tell her before she can protest.

"Your friends are right there," she whispers.

With the positioning of the couches and the movie turned up this loud, at least they can't see or hear us. "We're not doing anything wrong. We're just laying here."

"They're going to think we're doing... stuff."

I yawn, turning my head into her hair, and breathe in her tropical-scented shampoo. "I'd at least take you in the bedroom for that."

"Oh my God," she mutters, turning back around, but doesn't resist the position.

I happily settle in, watching a few more minutes of the movie before that heaviness steals over me again, stronger this time with Lexie warm against me, her body finally relaxed. After fighting the good fight as long as I can, I succumb to the lure of sleep, knowing Lexie can't see me to know I'm asleep behind her.

I stir once as she stiffens against me, the score indicating something scary is happening on screen, but as I tighten my hold around her middle, she eases, and I relax again, my head so far down, I can't see the screen.

The next time I wake, I skim the edge of consciousness, something that sounds like my name pulling me out of the abyss. It's not until a hand settles on my arm that I surface a bit more, but not enough to open my eyes. The hand travels slowly over my forearm to my bicep, lingering before it glides over my shirt sleeve to my shoulder and then my chest.

It's Lexie. As brief as it may have been last night, my body remembers her touch, committing it to memory.

"Ethan," she whispers, and though I recognize her voice, I'm too comfortable to move, to fully wake, instead enjoying her exploration of my torso.

Her hand moves up, tracing the features of my face, barely-there caresses that have me letting out a sleepy sigh. She pauses, and I want to tell her to continue, to keep touching me, but I can't muster the energy.

She continues again after a moment, over the bridge of my nose, my brow, then sifts her fingers gently through my hair, a tingle washing over my scalp.

Down past the column of my neck, my chest, my stomach, until she flirts with the hem of my shirt, teasing the exposed sliver of my lower abs. Oh, fuck, that's good. If only she'd go a little lower.

She moves higher instead, under my shirt now, her palm warm as it slides over my skin, a gentle exploration I'm not sure she would do if she knew I was awake. It seems the only way I can get her to seriously touch me is if I'm asleep or she's insanely turned on like last night.

It's not long before sleep is the last thing on my mind, completely focused on where she travels next, how she makes shivers race across my body. I never want her to stop.

But like all good things, it comes to an end as the front door opens, Tom loud as usual entering, Sean close behind him.

Lexie retreats, her hand slipping out from under my shirt, and I silently mourn the loss of her. Shifting, I open my eyes, finding her sitting up next to me, her gaze on the entryway. My roommates don't look our way, instead heading to the other side of the house where their respective bedrooms are.

"What time is it?" I ask, my voice scratchy.

"Almost midnight," she whispers.

Shit. I really was out for a while. How did she not wake me before? "What happened at the end of the movie? Did the ghosts get them?"

"I actually drifted off before it ended," she admits. "The last I remember, they tried exorcising them and failed."

I sit up, scrubbing a hand over my face. "Sorry I fell asleep on you again. I wasted my chance to see you."

"You see me all the time."

"Yeah, but I was still looking forward to it."

She looks down at her hands, the moonlight coming in from the sliding glass door illuminating her. "I was wondering if you thought tonight was us just hanging out or a… date."

I can't tell from her tone which one she favors. After last night, she has to be okay with the idea of the latter, right? "It's whichever you want it to be."

She twists her hands together in her lap. "I'm still a little blindsided by last night."

I swallow heavily. While I'm glad she's bringing it up rather than pretending it didn't happen, a part of me is afraid I pushed for too much too fast. "Are you upset?"

"No, not upset. More… overwhelmed? I don't know." She blows out a breath. "I don't know what to think about any of this."

"Hey." I take her hands, enfolding them in mine. "There's nothing to stress about. I wanted you to feel good. Did you?"

She nods, almost reluctantly. Like she didn't want to feel good? Or doesn't want to admit it?

"Then that's all that matters," I tell her. "Don't worry about anything else."

"That's easy for you to say."

"Why?"

"Because you don't worry about anything."

I stare at her for a moment. "I worry about things."

"Like what?"

About how she feels about me. About how much my diabetes is going to affect my future. About how I'm bound to get torn to shreds in my upcoming boxing match.

I don't mention the first two things, though. That will either have her on her guard or invite questions I'm unsure how to answer.

"That match your dad set up for me."

She makes a noncommittal noise. "I won't say I pretend to understand now, but I could once. You'll do fine."

Even though it's probably only an empty platitude, it still warms my heart regardless.

"Most of the guys in the ring are dumb as a box of rocks," she says. "But you're so much smarter than them. You can figure out how to win."

"Will you come?" I ask before thinking about it. "To the fight? I know it's not your thing, but it would mean a lot to me if you were there."

Her fingers flex, and it's a moment before she answers, "I'll be there."

I let out a sigh of relief, unaware it meant that much to me until now.

"You can be my cheerleader," I joke.

In the darkness, I can barely see her answering smirk. "Don't push it. I'm not a ring girl."

Those girls in the tiny bikinis between rounds? "Oh, no. I didn't mean—"

"I know you didn't."

There's a sound from the other side of the house, probably Tom or Sean going to the bathroom, and she shifts, standing. "It's late. I should head home."

"Yeah, okay."

I walk her to the front door and out to her car, the street silent this late. "I'm glad you came over. Even if I fell asleep for pretty much the whole time."

"You were really that tired?"

I bring a hand up, tucking a lock of hair back behind her ear. "I couldn't fall asleep last night. I kept thinking about you." My fingers trail down the length of her neck, her eyes closing as she leans into me. "I really liked what we did."

189

"I did too," she whispers.

"If you want to get together again before Tuesday, let me know."

She opens her eyes, looking at me for a moment. "Okay."

I lean forward, taking a chance, and kiss her, waiting for her to tell me there's no reason to be doing this. That there's no one around to see, no one to pretend for.

But she kisses me back instead, briefer than I'd like, but her willingness is still there.

"Goodnight, Ethan," she says, pulling away.

"Text me when you get home."

She pauses while opening her car door. "What?"

"So I know you made it home okay. It's late."

She stares at me for a beat longer. "I've driven home this time of night from the bar a million times."

"Lexie, I just want to know you're safe."

Hesitantly, she says, "Sorry, I've never had anyone ask me that before."

There's a dull ache in my chest, but I push it aside. "Well, if you're going to be hanging around me, you should get used to it."

"I'm starting to see that," she murmurs before getting in her car.

I watch as she backs out of the driveway, staying there until she's out of sight down the street, then return inside. Damn, I never took my nighttime insulin shot, did I? I set that alarm on my phone last night since I knew I'd be out of the house, but I didn't bother tonight. I figured I could just excuse myself to the bathroom at some point. Maybe I should start setting an alarm every night to remind me.

I gather my things and finally give myself my shot and brush my teeth, stripping off my shirt and shorts once I'm back in my room. I slide under the covers, the tiredness from before gone after such a long nap.

God, what a missed opportunity tonight. I'd had her right there, laying on the couch with me, her backside pressed snugly against my front, and all I could do was fall asleep. What must have Tyler thought seeing us both sleeping after the movie was over?

Well, considering he never questioned why I invited her over to begin with, he probably didn't think much of it at all. As far as he knows, she's still my fake girlfriend at school.

I guess that part is the same, though. We're not actually anything more.

Even if I want to be.

If I'd responded to her touch before Tom and Sean came home and interrupted, would she have let me touch her, too?

I barely got to explore her body last night. I'm still dying to fully undress her, to take my time learning every curve with my hands, my lips, my tongue. To peel off that hoodie she always wears, slipping off her clothes to squeeze her, taste her, make her moan for me.

I groan at the thought, my dick rising, confined within my boxers. I reach in, gripping myself tight, and stroke up and down as I imagine what I could have done to her on the couch tonight.

Sinking into her from behind as I play with her clit. Positioning her atop me so she rides me enthusiastically. Rolling over to pump madly into her. Sitting her up, legs spread so I could feast on her again, drinking her down.

My strokes speed up, picturing her in all those ways, the remembered scent of her still in my nose, the feel of her lips under mine. Does she have any idea how much I want her?

And not only her body, but her thoughts, her secrets, everything about her. I want to know her inside and out, more than anyone else. I want to be the one she trusts, the one she confides in, the one she turns to. I want her to be mine, just like I'm already hers. I'm gone for her.

A tingle races down my spine, imagining the way it'll be between us the first time, moving inside her, her body wrapped around mine.

I whip off the covers, overheated, pumping my fist over my cock, wishing it was her doing it. Wishing she was here with me.

I groan into the pillow as I come, the sound muffled, not wanting anyone in the house to hear how desperate I am at the thought of being hers.

Grabbing a tissue off the nightstand to clean up, I nearly knock off the extra syringe and glucose pills I keep there, making sure it's all back in place before I relax against the pillows, eager for it to be Tuesday already when I see her in class.

Will she text me before then to meet up? What are the chances she'll reach out? I can't chase her forever. At some point, she has to show me she wants more with me, too.

But is that realistic to expect? Or just another fantasy?

# CHAPTER TWENTY

## LEXIE

THERE'S a knock on my bedroom door, Travis poking his head in when I tell him to come in.

"I still can't get over how crazy you look." He grins at me, taking in my bartending bustier and heavy makeup. "The clothes, the hair, the makeup. It's like you're a different person."

That's true. He's used to seeing me as the brunette, makeup-free girl trying to hide herself in baggy clothes. And while I'm still the latter most of the time, I've had to adapt.

I continue applying my eyeliner, the heavier the better. Customers seem to respond to the no-nonsense punk rocker persona I put on there. "I am a different person when I'm at work. I need their tips."

"Your new bar going any better?"

"No," I reply glumly, using a Q-Tip to smudge away the mistake I made. "The girl that does the scheduling still has it out for me. I managed to get a second shift tomorrow, but only because someone else quit last week."

"Talk to her. Explain you need more shifts."

He thinks I haven't tried that? It's like banging my head against a brick wall with Sarah.

"Thanks, Travis." There's no use getting into it with him, too. "I'll do that."

He beams, as if he made a difference. "Well, I'm headed out. I should be home around ten."

"Okay, see you."

He leaves the apartment, and I take my time applying mascara. This tube is way overdue to be replaced. One more thing to add to the list to buy once I get the Psych study money. We should be getting half the study payment this week.

Heating up the leftover ramen I made last night, I linger on the couch eating, wishing I had another one of Mia's cookies. I can't remember having a cookie so good. I'd have to go back over to Ethan's to get one, but the idea doesn't seem so daunting now. His friends were totally fine. Tyler wasn't one for conversation, which was fine by me, and Mia seemed genuinely interested in talking to me. Maybe she's around guys so much there, she was desperate for another girl to talk to.

My fork clatters against the bowl as a thought occurs to me. Does Ethan bring girls home? He has to. There's no way he was that good with his tongue without practice.

I push down the sour feeling in my stomach, reminding myself that if he does, it's none of my business. Despite keeping up appearances for the study, I don't have a claim on him. And even if I did, he's allowed to have past partners and experiences, the same as I do.

But the reminder doesn't do all that much to satisfy me.

I get up and rinse out my bowl, needing a distraction, and decide to go ahead and drive to work, even though I'll be early. Fat chance Sarah will let me clock in before my shift starts, but at least I can prep and be ready to hit the ground running.

I head out to my car and throw my bag in the passenger seat, checking my makeup one last time in the rearview mirror. Good enough.

But upon sticking my key in the ignition, it turns out things are not good. They're awful, actually. The car won't start.

"No, no," I mutter to myself, trying to get it to work. This can't happen now. If I miss today, Sarah will probably use it as an excuse to the general manager to fire me for being unreliable. Or, at the very least, take away my shift for tomorrow too.

Now I wish I'd taken Dad up on his offer a year or so ago to teach me more about my car, but at the time, I was so determined to push him away, to prove I didn't need him. He'd moved back here, asking to be a part of my life, but I felt like it was too little, too late. Things have gotten better since then, but we're still not as close as we could be. Why do I do this to myself?

I pull out my phone, about to call him to come out and see what's wrong. I could even call Travis to turn around and give me a jump.

But I don't call either of them. I call the one person I already know bone deep I can count on. Who would drop whatever he's doing to help me. Who has continually shown me he's there for me.

"Lexie," Ethan says, a smile in his voice. "What's up?"

"I need help."

His tone instantly switches to serious. "Of course. What is it? Are you okay?"

Relief floods through me. He agreed without even knowing what's wrong. "My car won't start, and I have to get to work."

"You're not on the side of the road or anything, are you?"

"No, I'm at my apartment."

"Good. I'll be there as soon as I can."

After telling him my address, I head back inside to wait, throwing on a sweater before he sees me in this outfit. I'm thankful now I left early. I might still get to work on time.

I pace the living room, wondering if Ethan's annoyed I only called him when I needed something. I picked up my phone so many times yesterday, debating whether to text him, to see if he wanted to hang out like he suggested, but I'm so unsure about what this is, what we're doing, where all this is headed. What am I to him? And what is he to me?

I'd asked him Saturday if he meant for it to be a date, but he only said it was whatever I wanted it to be. I guess the ball's in my court, then. But what should I do with it?

His SUV pulls up outside, the tension in me easing now that he's here. I swear I don't normally need rescuing, but he seems to be making a habit of it. And honestly, he's pretty good at it too.

"You doing okay?" he asks as I join him in the parking lot, enfolding me in his arms.

I breathe him in, drawing comfort as I hug him back, the heavy yoke of responsibility around my shoulders lifting temporarily.

"I'm fine. Just worried my boss will be mad if I'm late."

"You want me to try and figure out what's wrong with the car or just take you to work?"

"I'll worry about fixing it later. I'd rather get a ride for now if that's okay with you."

"Hop in."

He leads me to his passenger side, opening the door for me. No one's ever opened a car door for me besides him.

He rounds the front of his SUV, getting in and buckling up. "All right, where am I going?"

"Element. It's on—"

"Oh, yeah. I know where it is."

He reverses out, tapping his thumb against the steering wheel as he turns onto the main road.

"You've been there before?" I ask. Now that I know him, it doesn't seem like his type of spot.

"A couple of times. A guy at the gym had his bachelor party there earlier this year. I stopped by for a bit."

"You have fun?"

He shrugs. "It was okay."

"Did you dance with anyone?" That's mostly why anyone goes. To get drunk and dance.

He hesitates for a moment before answering. "Yeah."

I stick my hands under my thighs, unsure why I'm asking all this to begin with. Like I reminded myself earlier, he's allowed to have done whatever he wanted in the past.

But that still doesn't stop me from asking, "Do you... dance with girls a lot?"

He opens and shuts his mouth a few times. This might be the first time I've ever caught him off guard.

"Not excessively," he finally says. "But every so often, yeah. Not since I met you, though."

I nod, unsure what I even wanted his answer to be.

"I know you sort of not really said before that you don't date," he says, "but do you ever... dance with guys? Or girls. You know, whatever."

A small smile escapes me, despite the serious topic. "There was a guy, back in high school." I take in a breath, releasing it slowly. "He was the one who started that rumor."

"Oh, shit," he mutters, pausing to make a right-hand turn. "That actually makes a lot of sense."

The blood pumping through my veins goes icy. "What?" He doesn't know about Cody, does he? About the rumor?

He glances over at me, reaching out to take my hand. "I just meant for someone to hurt you that way, after you had let them in close... I get why it must be hard to trust guys. To think they might do something like that again."

I swallow, my palm turning sweaty, but he doesn't let go of my hand. "I thought for a second you might know what happened. That maybe Savannah had told you."

He squeezes my hand reassuringly. "No. I'm pretty sure she wanted to that day I was waiting for you outside your class, but I wouldn't take her bait. I figured if you wanted me to know, you would have told me."

I drop my head back against the headrest, shutting my eyes. I should just tell him. Get it over with already. The longer I don't, the more it'll weigh on me. "His name was Cody," I blurt out. "And he told everyone I slept with the entire baseball team. That they passed me around, that I gave great head, that I'd let any guy do whatever they wanted to me. The nastier the better."

I keep my eyes shut, not wanting to see his reaction. For a kernel of doubt to wedge its way in his mind, the same as it did everyone else. *Well, everyone knows her mom's a druggie. This isn't too far off the mark.*

"What the actual fuck?" he finally says. "Why would he do that?"

"Because I punched him and broke his nose."

There's silence in the car for a solid twenty seconds. I count them, each passing second weighing me down further. Has any length of silence ever felt longer?

"Lexie… You have to give me more than that. You can't stop the story there."

I sigh heavily. He's right.

Letting go of his hand, I cross my arms over my chest, pulling my sweater tighter around me. "I was a freshman in high school and pretty much left to my own devices at home. Mom didn't care at all what I did, and Dad was off somewhere on the other side of the country." I think I only saw him twice that entire year.

"I went to some party one weekend someone was throwing, and Cody noticed me. He was captain of the baseball team, which was a big deal for a junior, and everybody knew him. Big man on campus, you know?"

Ethan is silent next to me, not that my question needed an answer.

"Anyway, I… I slept with him at that party. It hurt like hell, but he didn't seem to notice, so I thought that's how it was for girls. And I liked the attention. The idea that this popular guy singled me out. Noticed something special about me. I'd never been special to anyone else. I was the girl with the thrift store clothes. The one who got free lunch. The one who never had any of the basic school supplies until some teacher took pity on me and gave me a notebook and pencil."

"You don't have to tell me this," Ethan interrupts, his voice tight with tension. "I'm sorry I said you had to."

"No, I do have to." It's past time he understands who he's getting involved with. "And I kept sleeping with Cody, on and off for a couple of months. He didn't talk to me at school. He said we should keep it a secret because his ex would've given me a hard time. That she was still in love with him. Ashley."

"That's the girl you said was Savannah's friend?"

"Yeah. And he was right. She did slander me afterward. But looking back, he obviously didn't think I was good enough to be seen with. I wasn't on his level. We would hook up in darkened rooms at parties. The way Heather and that guy went in that room at the frat party. Entering separately. Anonymously. And to me, at the time, it was a thrill. Even if I didn't like the actual act of what we were doing, I liked that he was seeking me out, that it was a secret no one else knew."

He stops at a red light, the car idling, everything quiet as the words pour out of me, confessing what I've never told anyone else.

"Until one night he invited me over to his house. I was so excited. I thought this was it. That he was introducing me to his family, that maybe we'd finally go public, that I could be his girlfriend. But it turns out his parents were out of town. And two of his friends were there. Other guys on the base-ball team."

He makes a noise of displeasure, like he can sense where this is going.

"He said he wanted to try something new," I continue, the way I'm telling it almost like I'm talking about a different girl. I haven't been that naive in a long time. "He'd told his friends about me. And they all wanted to share me. They'd never shared a girl before."

I glance over at Ethan, his hands clenched around the steering wheel, knuckles white, but he doesn't interrupt me.

"I was frozen. I didn't know what to say. Couldn't believe what he was suggesting. But it made me realize he had never seen me as a person. I was a thing. A living doll. Something for them to play with. I finally found my voice and told him no way."

He breathes out a sigh, but that's not the end of the story.

"He said okay, just him and one other guy, then. As if that was any kind of compromise. I said no and tried to leave, but he blocked my way. Said if I didn't do it, he'd tell everyone at school they all had me anyway, so I might as well do it. They'd keep quiet if I did."

I pause for a moment as a wave of emotion passes over me, but I will it away. I can't mess up my eye makeup right before work.

"I told him to fuck off. If he wanted to be with his friends so badly, they could have a threesome together and I'd watch."

Ethan lets out a choked laugh, a hint of desperation in it. Looking back, it was a good line. But in the moment, it only made things worse.

"He grabbed me and shoved me up against the closest wall, holding my throat. Told me I'd do whatever he said and kissed me. That's why I freaked out about that day we had to kiss. I kept remembering him."

"Shit, I'm so sorry, Lexie." There's genuine remorse in his voice, but I don't blame him at all. "I pushed for more—"

"No. There was no way you could have known."

"Did he…" He audibly swallows. "Did he force…"

"No," I whisper. "I kind of saw red after that. I bit his lip as hard as I could to get him off me. Then I threw a right hook and broke his nose. All that training for boxing as a kid was good for something, because instinct took over. He was screaming and holding his face. There was blood everywhere and his friends started freaking out. I told him if he ever got near me again, I'd cut off his dick. I guess I was crazy enough that they believed me and let me leave."

"Holy shit."

"Yeah. But then he started that rumor, and told everyone a foul ball busted his face up at practice. Like it was some glory injury."

"None of the guys on the team contradicted him?"

"No. Probably some dumb bro-code thing. They did this thing where if someone outright asked one of them about it, they'd act all coy and say what happened in the locker room stayed in the locker room. So not technically confirming it with their words, but with the way they said it. And once Ashley got wind of it, she made sure to spread it. To let everyone know what a filthy slut I was. And as her best friend, Savannah followed suit. I don't get why they even cared, but maybe like Cody said, she was jealous."

"Did you tell people it wasn't true?"

I wipe the back of my hand under my nose. "No one believed me. It was like the more I protested it, the more they took it as proof it happened. So, I stopped caring after a certain point. Stopped trying to talk to anyone. I just… kept to myself."

I'd met Travis the next year on the school bus. Being a year younger, he hadn't been around for the worst of it, though the rumor still lingered for the remainder of high school, even after Cody had graduated.

Ethan pulls into Element's parking lot, surprising me. I completely lost track of time. I glance at the clock on the dashboard, discovering I have three minutes left to make it inside and clock in.

"I'm sorry to unload all that on you and then leave, but I have to get in." I unbuckle my seatbelt, grabbing my bag from the floor. "I'll ask someone if I can get a ride—"

"I'll come pick you up. Just text me when you need me."

"You don't have to. It's out of your way." Element's in the opposite direction of his house from mine.

"I'm picking you up." His tone leaves no room for argument. "If you leave me your keys, I'll try to fix your car."

"You don't have—"

"Lexie…" he warns.

I fish my car keys out and drop them into his waiting palm. If he could fix it, that'd be amazing. One less thing I have to deal with.

I open the car door, but he stops me with a light touch on my arm. I turn back, surprised at the intensity on his face.

"You mentioned last week that if I knew everything about you, I'd feel differently. I just want you to know that this doesn't change at all how I feel about you. I'm so sorry you had to go through all that."

My bottom lip trembles the slightest bit before I firm it, releasing a shaky sigh. This isn't all of it. There's still all the stuff with my mom. That's an issue for another time, though.

"Text me when you're done here," he says.

I nod, agreeing to his request. "If it's not too busy, I'm usually cut around nine-thirty." And Mondays are never busy.

"I'll be here."

My stomach makes a funny flip-flopping motion as I exit, looking back once when I'm halfway across the parking lot, his gaze trained on me.

What are the chances he goes home and thinks about everything I told him, then decides he doesn't want to take this on after all? There are plenty of people I went to high school with on campus. It's the closest university. And every time they see me, they'll remember what I did in high school. Ethan will be tainted by association.

And though there's a part of me that considers doing the honorable thing and cutting ties with him now so I won't tarnish his reputation, the truth is… I'm selfish. I want his gaze on me. I want him to keep looking at me like that. Now more than ever if he says it doesn't change anything for him.

*You still have to tell him about Mom. He deserves to know.*

Later. I'll do that later.

For now, I just need to make it through my shift at work.

# CHAPTER TWENTY-ONE

## LEXIE

I CLOCK IN, only one minute late, and it's only by the grace of God that the other bartender on duty tonight is here after me. Sarah can't yell at me without yelling at both of us, but I can tell she wants to from the way her lips thin.

There's hardly anyone in here with how early it is, but I still make myself busy prepping garnishes, cutting lemons and limes, and cleaning the long, wooden counter. Sarah eyes me disapprovingly but can't find fault with anything I'm doing. Why does she put herself on the same shift as me if I annoy her?

Halfway through my time here tonight, I'm still largely bored, mentally calculating how much I need to make this week to pay my bills. At this rate, I won't break forty dollars for the night. If I'm not getting any weekend shifts and only making seventy-five a week from Marty for doing his accounting work, it's still not enough, even with the money from the Psych study. I need to find another job.

Maybe I should try something new. Something that'll have a better chance of availability. What about that diner Ethan and I tried a few weeks ago? Places like that are always hiring, right?

"Hey, doll," an older guy says, leaning on the counter. "Get me a Bud Light, would you?" He makes the request to my cleavage rather than my face, but as long as he tips, that's the only thing I care about. Like I told Travis, I'm not really Lexie here. I'm just trying to make money.

Thankfully, another customer approaches after I give the guy his beer, saving me from the supremely awkward ordeal of fending off advances without offense. It's so much easier outside the bar where I can tell them to fuck off.

I make two tequila sunrises for the woman waiting, watching as she carries them over to a booth on the other side of the room, and then head in the back supply closet to get more grenadine.

I have to unfold the step ladder to reach the bottles on the top shelf, grabbing an extra too so no one has to come back here for it any time soon. I move to exit, pausing as I hear Sarah say, "No. No one calls her that here. Maybe I should start it up again." What's she talking about?

She laughs, and I peek around the edge of the doorframe, spotting her on her cell in the manager's office, her feet up on the desk. So that's where she disappeared to earlier. Not that I'm complaining. I hate her breathing down my neck out on the floor.

"I still can't believe the owner hired her. She probably slept with him to get the job. Sexy Lexie strikes again."

My insides freeze. She knows about that nickname? I thought I'd left it behind in high school.

Wait, she didn't go there too, did she? Sarah's a few years older, so I guess it's possible she could have been a junior or senior I don't remember. Is that why she hasn't liked me this whole time?

"All right, I've got to get back out there," she says, taking her feet down from the desk. "Bye, Ash."

I step out of view as she returns to the front, my heartbeat pulsing in my ears. She didn't mean Ashley, did she? The same Ashley that helped make my life hell?

Well, getting another job is definitely on the table now. I'll never get the shifts I want here. If anything, it's only a matter of time before she tries to have me fired. Why'd I have to pick the one place to work where someone has it out for me?

I wait until my pulse is back to normal before I return to the front, placing the bottles of grenadine underneath the counter.

"Where have you been?" Sarah asks me in a snotty voice, hands on her hips.

Really? After she just made a personal phone call? "Restocking," I reply calmly. I shouldn't give her a reason to let me go before I have another job lined up.

"Well, don't take so long next time. We could have a rush at any moment."

I survey the nearly empty bar. Mister Bud Light is sitting near the other end watching the game on the one TV we have and a few other customers in the booths on the other side are occupying themselves.

"Won't happen again," I tell her, pushing down the sarcastic reply that wants to let loose.

The front door opens, a tall, dark-haired man with familiar green eyes approaching. What's he doing here?

"I've got this one," Sarah says, practically pushing me out of the way. "Hey, what can I get you?" She smiles, leaning on her elbows over the counter in a practiced technique I have to give her props for. "We've got a special on well drinks tonight."

Joke's on her. Ethan's not even old enough to order one. If I remember right from our speed getting-to-know-you conversation at the diner, he doesn't turn twenty-one for another two months.

He takes a seat at the end of the bar. "Actually, Lexie's my favorite bartender," he says, pointing at me. "I'd rather order from her."

Sarah gives him a tight smile, her interest quickly fading. "Of course."

She steps back, making a sweeping motion for me to enter the space she was just occupying, and leaves to go terrorize the other bartender.

Ethan glances around, clearly noticing the lack of patrons. "No dancing? I could've sworn there was dancing here before."

"That's Thursday through Sunday. Monday through Wednesday it's a regular bar with no cover charge."

"Ah." He eyes me speculatively, and I look down at myself. Oh, crap. The bustier. "Were you wearing that earlier?" he asks.

"I had a sweater on in the car." Purposely.

"You look good."

That's the idea. "I get better tips in it."

He smirks. "And do you lean over the counter like that other girl did when you give people their drinks?"

I pick up a bar rag, scrubbing at a random spot on the bar. "Sometimes." If I think it'll help. "Do you have a problem with that?"

"Not at all. You do what you have to do."

"So you wouldn't care if I did that to a customer in front of you?" Why am I asking him this? It's like I want to invite trouble.

"No. Because I know I'm the one going home with you tonight."

My belly swoops down low near my toes. "Technically," I remind him.

He grins. "Technically," he agrees.

I fiddle with the rag, compelled to explain myself better. "Some of the other girls are good at flirting. They collect regulars that way. But I hate being fake with people."

"You don't say."

I bite my bottom lip, hiding my smile. "So this"—I point to my chest—"usually makes up for that. But I don't lead guys on or anything."

"I never thought you did."

"I just—" I glance behind me, making sure no one is within earshot. "I want you to know I'm not like that."

"Lexie." He reaches forward, brushing his fingers over mine. "I know you aren't. I wasn't criticizing your outfit. I meant I actually like it. You look beautiful."

"You mean sexy," I blurt out.

His brows pinch together. "What?"

"Nothing. Forget it." I go back to scrubbing the counter, even though it's spotless.

"You can be both," he says. "I think you're both."

I blow out a breath. "That's nice of you to say."

"But you don't believe me."

I look up at him, weighing my words. "I've had a lot of people tell me otherwise. I can't switch that off overnight."

His mouth twists downward. "Are you talking about how Savannah called you sexy Lexie?"

Fuck. He remembers that? Of course he does. His mind is like a steel trap. "Yes," I admit. "I'm not... I wasn't..."

He waits patiently for me to finish my thought, though I'm unsure where I'm even going with it.

I glance behind me again, Sarah closer than I'd like, though she's still out of range. "Can we talk about this another time?"

"Yeah, of course."

There are footsteps and then Sarah's snotty voice. "You haven't gotten him a drink yet? If you're just going to flirt with the customers, you might as well go home."

I grit my teeth, setting down my bar rag. "Yeah, it's pretty dead here. Good call cutting me early." Seriously, I won't make much more here tonight, and I shouldn't make Ethan wait if I don't have to.

She blinks at me, not expecting for me to have called her bluff like that, but doesn't make any more snide remarks as I clock out and grab my bag out of the back. I savor her confused expression as I return up front and take Ethan's hand, looking back at her as he holds the door open for me.

Seriously, how petty have I been lately with all these girls from high school? Ethan must be sick of me using him, despite never complaining.

207

I let go of his hand in the parking lot to put on my sweater, thanking him when he holds open the passenger door.

"I got your car working," he says as he gets in his seat, buckling his seatbelt. "I put a new battery in."

He actually fixed it? Holy crap.

"I think the alternator needs work too," he continues, "but that's beyond my expertise. My brother Scott's good with cars, though. I could have him take a look."

He'd do that for me? "How much do I owe you?"

"Don't worry about it."

"Ethan—"

"I'm serious. I've got it covered."

I press a hand to my chest, the hard thump inside a reminder of how much this man affects me. "I'm going to look for another job soon," I tell him, "and then I can pay you back."

He makes a noncommittal noise, ignoring my promise. "Where are you thinking of applying?"

"Maybe that diner we went to? Places like that usually hire quick."

"Oh, another customer service job? That's your specialty."

I playfully smack his arm. "I can behave when I need to."

He grins, reaching over to grab my hand, and brings it up to his lips, kissing my knuckles. "I know. I'm just teasing."

He stops at a red light, his fingers warmly encasing mine, and I make a split-second decision and lean over the center console, using my other hand to cup his jaw to turn toward me. His gaze is questioning but interested as he silently watches to see what I'll do.

I move closer, giving him time to back away if he wants, but he stays where he is, meeting my lips in a gentle kiss.

"Thank you," I whisper.

"For what?"

"For knowing me well enough to tease me. For always helping me." I swallow past the lump in my throat. "For not giving up on me."

"Lexie," he murmurs in a low voice, my stomach making that swooping sensation. "I'm always here for you."

He kisses me again, the action so much more natural than it was a week ago, our mouths fitting together perfectly, no hesitation.

A blaring honk from behind us has us breaking apart, a sheepish grin crossing Ethan's face as he realizes the light is green.

I sit back in my seat, my heart still pounding. Did I really initiate that kiss? It felt so right, though.

We're both quiet during the ride to my apartment, his thumb stroking my palm, a growing sense of restlessness ping-ponging around inside me. What does this mean? Where do we go from here?

As he turns into my complex, parking next to my car, one thing becomes clear to me. I don't want this night to be over.

"Do you want to come inside?" I whisper.

His hand tightens on mine for the briefest moment. "Yes."

He's uncharacteristically quiet as he follows me in, handing me back my keys so I can unlock the door, and as we step in, I look at the place through his eyes as I flick on the lights.

There's no trace I live here, everything out in the common area Travis's. The furniture, the decor, even most of the food in the kitchen. "This is all my roommate's stuff," I tell him, feeling like I need to explain.

"Where's your stuff?"

"In my room."

The statement hangs heavy in the air. Did he take that as an invitation? Did I mean it as one?

"Did you want to go in there?" he asks, his voice carefully neutral. "Or stay out here?"

He's putting the ball in my court again. Last time, I didn't know what to do. But this time... "We can go in my room."

He follows me in, but I keep the overhead light off, the streetlamp outside my window providing enough to see. I don't want him to get a good view of everything in here. Or rather, the hardly anything in here.

"So... this is my room." I hold up my hands, motioning to the surrounding space, but he doesn't look.

He doesn't comment on the bare walls, the thin sheet hanging over the window, the mattress on the floor. His gaze is fully focused on me. Like I'm the only thing that matters. And tonight, I want that. I want to be important to him. Because I'm coming to realize he's one of the most important people in my life. If not... the most.

He's silent as I walk toward him, my steps hesitant. I've never made the first move on a guy. Never wanted to. But with him, I do.

I come in close, brushing my palms up his hard chest, over those broad shoulders, up to the back of his neck, tugging his head down to meet my lips in a hot kiss, desire flaring between us.

He makes a rough noise of need as his hands grip my waist, pulling me flush against him, and my stomach pleasantly bottoms out, excited for what's to come.

If he could make me feel that good the other night when I wasn't even ready, how amazing will it be now that I am? Where will the night take us?

And where will it lead to tomorrow?

# CHAPTER TWENTY-TWO

## ETHAN

FINALLY, Lexie and I are on the same page. Same paragraph, same sentence, same word.

I deepen the kiss, her tongue enthusiastically meeting mine, her eagerness an incredible turn-on.

Her hands tangle in my hair, my fingers flexing on her waist, need rising within me. It's been days since I last touched her.

I snake a hand between us, up over her stomach to her breast, squeezing softly.

Her kiss falters for a moment, and she whispers against my lips, "Do that again."

Oh, fuck, yes.

I bring my other hand up, dipping my thumbs down into her low-cut top, beneath her bra, to tease her nipples, rubbing soft circles over them.

She makes a strangled sound, kissing me harder, and I revel in the way she responds to me, her lower half meeting mine, seeking contact.

One of my hands leaves her to search for a zipper, buttons, anything to remove her top, needing to touch her bare skin.

"There's a hidden zipper on the side," she murmurs, breaking away for a moment. She lifts her left arm to give me easier access, and I make quick work of it, her bra coming off next until she stands topless in front of me, her nipples puckering the longer I stare at her.

I reach out to cup her, groaning as I shape her weight, her skin agonizingly soft. "You're perfect," I tell her, leading her over to the mattress, laying her across its length. "Everything I've ever wanted."

I settle on top of her, taking a nipple in my mouth to suck, loving the way she curls herself around me in response, one leg hitching over my hip, the other shifting to let our lower halves nestle together, my dick rubbing against her core.

I switch breasts after a minute, lapping at her, pressing kisses to the sensitive area, the sounds of enjoyment she makes revving me up.

She moves her hips, grinding against me, and I return the movement, wishing our clothes were gone so I can feel her for real.

Will she let me in all the way tonight?

I keep traveling down, unbuttoning her jeans, looking up at her to make sure it's okay as I tug at her zipper.

She's panting heavily, attention rapt on me as I press a kiss over her underwear.

"Are you..." She clears her throat, some of the huskiness still there as she asks, "Are you going to go down on me again?"

A punch of arousal shoots through me at the anticipation in her voice. So she liked it that much?

I nuzzle against her, pressing another long kiss to the same spot, enjoying the full body twitch she makes. "I'd like to. If you want that."

She nods, sighing as I do it again. "I want that."

I strip the remainder of her clothes off, taking a moment to savor her nude body, incredibly beautiful as she lounges against the dark sheets.

She spreads her legs wide for me, arms moving above her head to clutch at her pillow as I move into place. I lick her long and slow, watching as her eyes squeeze shut, head dropping back as she arches off the bed, humming a wordless approval. I do it again, my dick straining at the fly of my jeans.

"You taste so fucking good," I tell her, drinking her down. The more I do it, though, the more turned on I get, until I'm grinding into the mattress, needing relief.

I unzip my jeans, palming myself, a groan releasing from me at the first stroke.

Her eyes open, head tilting to look at me, jaw dropping as she spies what I'm doing. "Are you... touching yourself?"

"Uh huh." I move to play with her clit, flicking my tongue over her. "You want to watch?"

I look up at her, her eyes widening comically. Damn, I love catching her off guard.

But it seems she has her own tricks up her sleeve, my grin slipping as she replies, "Yes."

And I thought I was on fire before?

I lean back, still stroking myself, noting how her attention shifts south, studying my every movement. I tug my jeans and boxers down, peeling off my shirt too until I'm bare for her, relishing the way her gaze eats me up. I'll gladly do this every night if it has her looking at me like that.

"You get me so hot." My fist flies over my cock, worked up now. "Touch yourself for me, too."

Her mouth opens and closes, once, twice, noticeably out of her element for a moment before she does as I say, hesitantly sliding her hand down her stomach, pussy on display for me as she rubs herself softly.

"That's it, baby," I murmur. "I make you wet, don't I?"

She nods, brows pinching together as her hand moves faster. "So wet."

God, has there ever been a hotter sight than this woman stroking herself?

"Let me see how wet you are." I move closer, using my index and middle finger to slowly enter her, pushing in and out.

Her head falls to the side, breaths harsh as she lets out a gasp. "Fuck, Ethan."

"You want more?"

She nods frantically. "Give me more."

I up my speed till it matches my hand that's still on my cock, racing toward the finish line. I'm so fucking close, but I need to get her there, too.

Her inner thighs tremble, shaking as I keep going, her feet seeking leverage on my thighs as she moans low, her arm coming up to cover her eyes. Her pussy milks my fingers as she comes, the action setting me off too, and I angle my cock so I jet on my stomach, away from her.

Her body goes limp against the mattress, pride suffusing me at the strength of her orgasm, how badly she wanted it asking for more.

I glance around the room, noticing my surroundings for the first time, and spot an open doorway toward what looks like a bathroom. I leave her for a moment, grabbing a wad of toilet paper to clean myself off with, and rejoin her on the mattress, kissing my way up her body.

She stirs, a satisfied smile on her face as I reach her lips. "That was amazing," she whispers.

I grin, in total agreement with her. "Give me a bit and we can go for round two."

She makes a soft noise of pleasure. "I love you."

I go still, hope blooming in my chest. So these feelings aren't one-sided?

But just as I'm debating how best to respond, an expression of dawning horror crosses her face. "I didn't mean that," she says, jerking to the other side of the bed, a gulf forming between us. "I don't know why I said it."

Oh.

My stomach drops, a distinctly unpleasant sensation this time, and I wince, her denial stabbing me.

"Shit," she mutters, scrambling off the mattress. "Fuck." She grabs at the nearest article of clothing, which turns out to be my shirt, and pulls it on over her. She crosses to the bedroom door, flinging it open, and escapes to the living room.

I sit up, half worried she'll race out of the apartment, but there's no sound of the front door opening. I scour the floor for my boxers, slipping them on as soon as I find them, and join her out there, finding her pacing the length of the room, biting at her thumbnail.

She looks up as she notices me, her face crumpling, and I rush to her without a thought, hugging her tightly to my chest.

"I'm sorry," she mumbles between sniffles. "I fucked everything up again."

"You didn't fuck anything up," I assure her, stroking her hair, trying to come up with some kind of reasonable explanation. "It was the heat of the moment. You were vulnerable. Everyone says things they don't necessarily mean."

"You didn't say anything."

Yeah, but I was half thinking it.

"Lexie, I'm not mad." Maybe a little disappointed, if I'm being honest with myself.

She steps back, wiping at her eyes. "What are we even doing?"

"What do you mean?"

"I mean with…" She motions with one hand between us. "With us."

I release my hold on her, lacing my hands behind my neck, not knowing how she wants me to answer. Maybe we weren't on the same page after all. Same book, but different chapters. "That depends on what you want."

"What do *you* want?" she whispers, her eyes wide, almost like she's afraid of what I'll say.

I'm tired of beating around the bush, though. At some point, I have to lay my cards out. "I want you to be my girlfriend. For real."

She's silent, frozen in place a foot away from me, her bottom lip quivering.

"I'm just being honest," I tell her, needing to fill the deafening silence. "We can take things slow. As slow as you want. No labels."

Please don't let her shut down over this.

"Ethan…" She crosses her arms over her stomach, hunching into herself. "I didn't think we were there. Like anywhere near there. I was just coming around to the idea that there was something between us." She sniffs again, running a hand under her nose. "I'm so messed up. You deserve someone better. Someone who knows how to be a girlfriend. Someone who isn't so… scared."

I force myself to stay where I am, to not reach for her if she doesn't want it. "Do I scare you?"

She takes a shuddering breath. "Not you as a person. More as an… idea. I trust you. More than I think I've ever trusted anyone. And that scares the hell out of me."

"Why?"

She takes a moment to answer, the words seeming ripped from her. "You could hurt me."

She must see the offense on my face because she reaches out herself, grabbing my hands.

"I know you wouldn't mean to," she says. "It's that you could. That you mean enough to me that it would matter."

There's a sound from outside the front door, keys jangling, and then a man enters, about our age, looking at the two of us confusedly.

What the fuck?

Lexie retreats from me and toward the door. "Travis…" she says apologetically, like she was caught doing something wrong.

There's a sucker punch to my stomach. She has another guy in her life?

His gaze darts between us and he steps back out of the doorway. "How about I spend the night at Isaac's?" he asks, not waiting for a response. Before he shuts the door, his gaze lands on me, raking me up and down. That's right. I only have boxers on. "Nice to meet you, Ethan."

He sounds genuinely friendly, confusing me even more. He knows me? What the hell is going on?

I stare at Lexie expectantly after he leaves, waiting for her to give an explanation, but she just rubs at her forehead.

"You going to tell me who that was?" I finally ask, unable to wait any longer.

She blinks at me, startled. I guess my voice is a little harder than usual. "That's Travis."

Yeah, I got that. "And he is…"

"My friend. Like, my only friend. And my roommate. This is his place. I moved in a while ago."

It's on the tip of my tongue to ask her how I was supposed to magically know that. Why she hadn't mentioned him before. I vaguely recall her dad mentioning something about a roommate, but I'd assumed it had been a girl. If I've learned anything about Lexie by now, though, it's that I can't make any assumptions.

And that talking about herself doesn't come naturally to her.

"I'm sorry I didn't say anything before," she says. "I wasn't purposely hiding it. I—I've been trying to share more with you."

"I know you have." I cross the room, wrapping my arms around her. I don't want to be at odds. "And I appreciate it. But I want to know everything about you."

She blows out a breath, returning my hug, her arms circling my waist, forehead pressed to my chest. "Can you be patient with me?" She chuckles to herself. "Even more than you've already been? I'm in completely unfamiliar territory here."

I cup the back of her neck, massaging out the tension there. "I'll work with you however you need me to. I'm not asking you to be anyone other than who you are."

She nods, looking up at me, her hazel eyes more brown than green in the dim living room lighting. "No one has ever seen me as… girlfriend material. The way I grew up with my mom, the way people treated me in school, I can't just turn it off and act like it didn't affect me." She sighs as I release a knot from her upper back, her shoulders dropping. "But I want to get past that stuff. I want more with you. And I'll probably mess up again some-where along the way, but I'll do my best to get back on track. I never expected someone like you."

"I wasn't expecting you either. But I've been gone for you since that first day at the gym."

She smiles, a full-fledged one I can't get enough of. "When I told you I wasn't interested?"

"Yeah, since then." I bend down, kissing her softly. "Can I spend the night? Just to sleep. To be next to you. I meant it when I said we could take things slow."

She bites at her lip, nodding. "I'd like that."

She leads me back to her room, the two of us lying on her bed facing each other as she tells me about Travis and his boyfriend, Isaac. About her classes and her plans to become a CPA after graduation. About how she can't wait to quit the bar she's working at. About anything and everything, the most I've ever heard her speak.

I soak it all in, enjoying how she absentmindedly runs her hands over my arms as she talks, allowing myself to finally touch her the way I want to, running my fingers through her hair, intertwining our legs. I can't get enough of this closeness, wanting to consume her any way I can.

Her voice is hoarse by the time she drifts off, her face relaxed in sleep. I smooth her hair back, lingering over the softness of her cheek, memorizing her features. Now we're on the same page, right? She's willingly sharing with me, said she wants more, that I should be patient with her.

I can do that. I've been doing it this whole time. And now that I know she's interested in pursuing this, that's all I care about. Everything will work out.

My eyes grow heavy, nearly joining her in sleep when a faint ringing wakes me.

Oh, shit. My nighttime insulin reminder.

I extract myself from the bed as carefully as I can, shutting off the alarm on my phone, and slip on my shorts. I eye my shirt that's still on her. God, I love seeing her in my clothes.

I head out to my car, glad I grabbed my go-kit before I left my house, and give myself my shot, stowing everything away again in the back seat before I return to her.

I lock up the apartment, pulling her sheet and blanket over us as I join her in bed, loving how she instinctively curls into me in her sleep. Yeah, I could get used to this.

And though I promised we'd go slow, I'm already dreaming of the day when we'll be like this every night, her in my arms as we drift off.

Things are only going up from here.

# CHAPTER TWENTY-THREE

## LEXIE

"SO THIS IS YOUR DASHBOARD." I point to the top of Marty's screen from over his shoulder. "It's an overview of everything going on in the business."

"Like a car dashboard," he says.

"Um, right." If that's how he needs to relate to it. "Over here is where you track your income and expenses. That's what we're mainly using the software for. But it also has a lot of cool features. We can create reports on cash flow or profit and loss, generate financial statements with the press of a button, and organize everything into different tax categories."

"How much are all these bells and whistles costing me?" he asks suspiciously, crossing his arms over his barrel chest.

I return his hard stare, not intimidated by him. "You think I'd choose a software that's going to cost you an arm and a leg? Trust me, I'm the queen of saving money." It was a necessary skill with hardly any money coming into the house growing up. Mom could never hold down a job for long. "The basic accounting software is free. The company only makes money if you set up payroll with them or by charging a percentage if customers pay an invoice generated through the software."

"Hmm." He leans back in his chair, swiveling toward me. "You did good, kid. I like it."

Though I knew I didn't technically have anything to worry about when he asked me to show him my progress, it's still nice to hear praise. I get the sense he doesn't give it out often.

"Thanks. I've been coming in on Wednesdays lately to work on everything, but I'm looking for a second job, too." Kate's Kitchen had a help-wanted sign in the window when I passed by earlier. I'm going to go there tomorrow and apply. "So I might be in here on a different night. I'm not sure what my schedule will be yet."

He nods, considering me. "As long as you get it done sometime during the week, I don't care what day it is. Now that you showed me this dashboard thing, I can check up on what you're doing whenever I want."

Right. He doesn't seem like the micro-managing type, but we'll see how it goes.

I wander over to the office window, looking out at the ring in the corner of the room. Ethan's in there with my dad, dodging blows and practicing his footwork.

"I heard my dad put together some fights for the guys," I comment. "How do you think it'll go?"

"They're all good kids," he says, joining me. At what age do you start referring to everyone younger than you as kids? "We've got some real contenders. My nephew there, for one."

He points to the hulking guy Ethan was practicing with last week, in the other ring with Steve, his blond hair wet with sweat around the temples.

"What about Ethan?" I ask, unable to help myself. I'm not sure what I even hope the answer will be. I want him to do well in whatever he tries if it's important to him, but there's also a part of me that wishes he would focus his interest elsewhere. I don't want him ending up like Dad.

"Great work ethic. Quick on his feet. Good at adapting to the situation and understands the sport. But he doesn't have the fire."

I look over at him questioningly.

"That soul-deep burning in his gut to prove himself," he explains. "To win. He doesn't need it the way some of the other guys do."

"So you think he won't win?"

"Oh, he still could. He's improved a lot in the last year. We'll see how next week goes."

He returns to his desk but I stay at the window, watching Ethan, admiring his intensity.

The past two days have been amazing, his arm around me all throughout class on Tuesday, kissing me goodbye deliciously outside my Russian Lit class before we parted ways for the day. And then today in our study, it was the first time I didn't have to pretend anything. I'd wanted to be close to him.

This week's test had been the perfect day for it, designed to examine how touch stimulates heart rate. I wasn't ashamed at all for him to see how he affects me, how the way he'd trailed his fingers down my neck in the lab had made my pulse rocket on the screen. I'd wanted him to make my heart race.

Everything I've avoided for so long is suddenly a possibility, cautious optimism coursing through me. The feeling is strange but welcome, like something's finally been unlocked inside me.

I mean, he said he wanted me to be his girlfriend. His GIRLFRIEND. I know it doesn't mean to him what it does to me, but for someone to want me like that... I can't even describe it. The way I'd woken yesterday morning, wrapped in his arms, listening to his soft breaths, had filled me with a sense of peace I wasn't aware was possible. And though he said he'd go slow, I think I might be ready for... more.

"I'll see you next week," I tell Marty, grabbing my backpack. It's already late and I've done everything I can for the night.

He waves me off and I head over to the ring, watching Dad and Ethan spar. I've spent the last however many years turned off by boxing, but I have to admit, I like seeing Ethan move. How serious he gets, the physicality he displays, a kind of primal vibe emanating from him. Outside the ring, he's sweet and smart and goofy. But in here...

A shudder runs through me, calling to mind the way he'd been with me in bed too. Confident. Skilled. In control. But it hadn't veered into domineering territory. He'd also been giving. Patient. Supportive.

My heart thumps painfully in my chest. What would it be like to be his girlfriend for real?

"Lex," Dad calls out, finally noticing me. "Ethan tell you he has a fight coming up?"

Why would he think Ethan and I talk? Did Ethan tell him about us? *I* don't even know what our relationship is. I never actually answered Ethan about the girlfriend thing.

Oh, wait. Dad caught us talking out in the parking lot last week and knows we have a class together. Crisis averted.

"Yeah, super exciting," I call back, laying the sarcasm on thick.

Dad grins at Ethan. "She's just jealous because she gave up on boxing years ago. She could have a title under her belt by now if she had kept with it."

My lips thin. So that's what he thinks? That I quit on a whim? Not because it had anything to do with him, obviously. Why would it possibly be his fault?

Ethan moves out of his ready position, brows knitting as he looks at me.

I rearrange my expression, knowing Dad won't catch anything out of the ordinary. Only Ethan picks up on my moods so easily.

"I'll see you later," I tell Ethan, ignoring everyone else as I cross the room and exit the gym. I take a fresh breath as I climb up the basement level stairs to the parking lot, glad to be out of the sweaty funk that's always lingering there. At least Marty's office doesn't have the same smell.

"Lexie, wait."

I turn around, Ethan at the bottom of the steps, his gym bag over one shoulder.

"You didn't have to stop because of me," I mumble.

"I was about done anyway," he says, taking the stairs two at a time to reach me. "You should talk to him, you know."

"Oh, should I?" I don't mean for it to come out as bitterly as it does, but I can't take it back now.

"Tell him why you started boxing," he urges. "That it was to be close to him. And why you quit too. He obviously doesn't know."

I blow out a breath, continuing on to my car on the other side of the lot. "There's no use in bringing up the past. We can't change it."

"Yeah, but it still upsets you."

"Who said I'm upset?"

I reach my car, turning around to face him. He gives me a deadpan look, calling bullshit without actually having to say the word.

Damn it.

"I'm fine," I tell him. "It's not a big deal."

"Do you want me to talk to him?"

"No," I blurt out, way too quickly to pass as casual. "Don't worry about it." I avoid his eye, knowing he has a point, but not wanting to admit it. "Did you say anything to him about... us?"

He shakes his head. "I figured it should come from you."

I bite my lip, nodding. "Did he think we left together just now?"

He studies me for a moment. "Would it bother you if he did?"

"No." God, he doesn't think I'm ashamed of him or something, does he? If anything, it should be the other way around. "I just want to be prepared in case he asks."

"He sort of asked about it last week but I said we were friends."

Right. But that was then. Things are different now.

"You know," he continues, "he asked me how you were doing in school too. He's proud of how smart you are."

I roll my eyes. "Stop trying to force some kind of sappy reconciliation. We're fine how we are. This isn't a Hallmark movie. Real life isn't like that."

He grins, his eyes crinkling at the corners. "It happened for us. Fake relationship turns into real feelings." He steps closer, taking my hands in his. "At least, they're real on my part."

My annoyance melts at his words, my heart softening. "They're real for me, too," I whisper. "And I'll talk to my dad. At some point."

"I only want you to be happy."

The butterflies start up their flapping again in my belly. "I am happy. Since Monday night, whenever I see you, whenever I think about you…" I squeeze his hands tighter, drawing strength. It's okay to unguard myself around him. "I'm kind of the happiest I've ever been."

I look up at him, the green of his eyes darkening as he leans in to kiss me, my arms wrapping around his shoulders to draw him down to me.

This is what I wanted. To feel close to him, that connection between us alive and kicking.

His hands settle on my waist, backing me up against my car, his big body pressing into mine as his kiss turns hungry. God, I love that I affect him like this. That he affects me so much too. He's opened a whole world of possibility within me.

He backs away abruptly, longing still on his face as he says, "I'm sorry. I said we'd go slow."

I swallow, getting my breathing under control, noticing his breathing is heavy too. If both of us are into it, is there any real reason to stop?

"I don't want to go slow," I tell him.

Lust burns bright in his gaze as he moves in again, putting his palms on my car, caging me in between his arms. "Are you saying you want to come home with me?" he asks in a low voice.

Oh, fuck. How in the world can I say no now when all I can think of is us together… In his bed… Getting naked… Getting sweaty…

"Yes," I breathe, tugging at the hem of his shirt, slipping my hands underneath to caress his abs.

"Just so we're clear, I want to go in my bedroom, undress you, and make you come. Several times. Are you good with that?"

I nod silently, my mouth dry. Oh God, I want that.

He kisses me briefly, the amount of passion in his kiss nearly overwhelming. "I'll see you at my place?"

"Okay."

He backs off, my body on autopilot as I unlock my car and get in, hardly able to process what's about to happen. We're going to his house and we're...

A shiver runs over me, goosebumps breaking out along my arms.

We've done stuff before. Tonight doesn't have to be any different.

But a part of me wants tonight to be different, to go further with him. I trust him to work with me, to be patient. He's more than I ever could have asked for.

Exhilaration pumps through me on the ride over to his house, not letting myself give in to any fear, any worry that it will be like all those years ago.

I *know* Ethan.

I park on the street, not wanting to block any of the other cars in the driveway, Ethan cruising in behind me less than a minute later. I meet him at his car, letting him take my hand as we walk up to his porch, the security light turning on as we pause at the front door for him to unlock it.

Inside, Tyler and Mia are on the couch again, the living room blanketed in darkness save for the TV screen where a man with a knife is chasing a screaming woman around some abandoned building.

Ethan doesn't stop to greet them, tugging me instead down a hallway, passing two closed doors before he stops at a third and opens it.

He flicks on the light, but I don't have time to look around before he's on me, pressing me against the door.

I reach up, cupping his jaw, tangling my fingers through the soft, wiry hair of his beard, enjoying the sound of pleasure he makes in response. How many other sounds can I wring out of him tonight?

He braces his arms on either side of me, once again caging me in, but instead of it terrifying me like it did with Cody, I revel in it, safe and cocooned in his embrace.

"I want you," he murmurs, brushing his lower half against me, the friction making my toes curl.

"I want you, too."

# CHAPTER TWENTY-FOUR

## LEXIE

MY VOICE IS all breathless wonder, completely unlike myself. But so much of what's happening is surreal, it's like it's not happening to me. It's an alternate universe Lexie. One who grew up in a loving household, who's never known any kind of trauma in her life, who can readily accept a man's touch without a freak-out.

There's a faint ringing coming from Ethan's pocket, and he pulls away from me, drawing his phone out. "Shit," he mutters, looking at the display, then at me, some of the haze clearing from his eyes. "Give me one minute. I'll be right back."

"Um, okay." I move aside so he can leave the room, another door down the hall opening and shutting a moment later. What was that about?

I press my hand against my chest, willing my heart to slow, but what I see next has it stopping completely, icy dread spreading through my veins.

There's a syringe on his nightstand. A used syringe from the looks of it. And next to it, two tablet pills.

Is he... using?

My mind unwillingly flashes back to that last moment with Mom, a syringe resting beyond her blue fingertips. Searching for a pulse on her, creepy crawlies running over my skin as I realized I was touching a dead body.

That awful call to 911 to report her death, barely able to get the words out. The white sheet they'd placed over her lifeless form when they'd come.

Will that happen to Ethan too?

Nausea rises within me, quick and strong, and I gag, barely holding it together as I make a split-second decision and leave, racing out of the room, back down the hallway, past Tyler and Mia still watching their movie, fumbling with the lock on the front door, and then I'm outside, the night air cool on my face as I rush toward the end of the drive. I lean over a bush and puke on their lawn, praying no one can see from inside the house, but I can't hold it in.

Everything comes up—my newfound trust, my faith, my absolute certainty that I knew Ethan inside and out. Maybe not all the details, but the core of him. His heart. His values.

But it turns out he's using? Why else would he have drugs and paraphernalia in his room? That's something you mention. You don't hide that from someone who's supposed to be important to you.

I told him my mom had substance abuse issues. That I don't go near any of that stuff. Is that why he wasn't disgusted when I said that? Because he has familiarity with it? Did he think I'd be more accepting then? Because I'm not.

"Lexie?"

I squeeze my eyes shut for a moment, glad at least it's a woman's voice and not Ethan's deep baritone.

"Are you okay?" Mia asks from the doorway, concern dripping off her.

I give her a wave, hoping she doesn't come any closer, and walk backward to my car. "I'm not feeling great. Tell—" Another wave of nausea passes over me and I swallow heavily, stuffing it down. "Tell Ethan I had to leave."

I turn around, not waiting for a response, and open my car with shaking hands, peeling out of there as fast as I can. I rinse my mouth out with the half-full water bottle in my cup holder, spitting it out at the first stoplight, my stomach finally settling.

How in the hell could Ethan have hidden this from me? Is that why he's always so happy? Why he has so much energy? What is it he's shooting up? Heroin, like Mom? No, that would make him drowsy. Maybe cocaine. Mom had flirted with that a few times.

And what were those pills? Something to bring him down from his high? Or something he takes when he can't inject?

I should've gone over and inspected, but there's no way I could've gotten that close. I would've retched all over his bed if I had.

I just... I can't believe this. How fooled I was. How deceived. He said I could trust him.

There's a cracking sensation in my chest, tears stinging my eyes, and I grip the steering wheel tighter, focusing on anything but what's going on inside.

I got in too deep. This is why I keep my distance from others. Because they inevitably disappoint you. They let you down. You want them to be one way, but it turns out they're not. And that's on me for believing otherwise.

I won't get involved with anyone doing drugs. Not after what happened with Mom. I can't go through that again. Especially not with someone I actually care about.

I shake my head, blowing out a long breath, the tears receding. I have to protect myself. That's rule number one. I can't get dragged into whatever mess he has going on. It's only a one-way ticket downhill. I saw it happen firsthand.

My bag vibrates from the passenger seat, my stomach dropping. My car is too old to have a bluetooth connection that tells me who it is on the phone, but I know soul-deep who it is. Who else would call me after I unexpectedly ran out of his house? As far as he knows, we were about to fuck. Now he's left with a hard-on and no girl.

Serves him right.

Still, I can't ghost him. I see him all the time. In class, at the Psych lab, at the boxing gym. I have to finish the study with him. We'd gotten paid today for completing over half—a nice chunk of change I'd immediately taken to the bank to deposit. Added with the paycheck I got from Marty tonight, that's enough to cover rent.

The phone stops vibrating but picks up again a few seconds later. I ignore it, waiting till I'm parked in front of my apartment to look at it.

Two missed calls and two texts. At least there's no voicemail to listen to. Hearing his voice right now… I don't think I could handle it.

I open the first text, taking a shuddering breath.

**Ethan**: *Are you okay? Mia said you were sick.*

The second has me sniffling, though.

**Ethan**: *Please just let me know you're okay.*

How am I supposed to reconcile the sweet, caring guy I know with a drug user? With someone who lies to me, even if it is by omission?

I type out a reply, my fingers fumbling on the screen.

**Me**: *I'll be okay. Felt ill suddenly. See you in class.*

It's all technically the truth. I did feel ill. I will see him in class. And eventually, I'll be okay.

It'll just hurt a while until I get to that point.

I stuff my phone back in my bag and head inside, dropping my backpack on the floor as soon as I enter. There's no way I'm finishing up the homework I still need to do before my classes tomorrow.

"Hey, girl," Travis says from the couch. "You're home late."

I make a noncommittal noise, focusing on getting to my room so I can collapse on the bed.

"Were you at Ethan's?" he asks in a sing-song voice. He's teasing me, the kind of thing friends do. He'd been delighted to discover us half-dressed in the living room Monday night. That I'm finally showing interest in someone.

I'd told him this morning how great things are, how I'm on cloud nine, how close I feel to Ethan.

Well, not so much anymore.

I stop in my tracks, his question paralyzing me.

"Lexie?" he asks, a frown on his face as he gets up from his spot. "You okay?"

The same as Mia asked. As Ethan asked.

No, actually. I'm not okay. Maybe someday. But not right now.

I try to hide the fat tears that let loose, rolling down my cheeks, but I can't stop, especially when Travis comes over, hugging me, asking me again if I'm okay, if I'm hurt. It's like Ethan unlocked this vulnerability within me. This awful urge to depend on others, to lean on them for support. I was doing fine taking care of myself for so long.

I rest my forehead against Travis's chest, soaking his shirt, letting the tears come. I've never cried like this in my life. Not after realizing Dad would never take me to live with him. Not after escaping Cody. Not after finding Mom overdosed on the couch.

This was the one that broke me.

"I'm okay," I finally tell Travis when I find my voice again. "I'm just... sad."

Wow, what an understatement.

He leans back, his brows knit together. "What the hell happened? I've never seen you cry."

I scrub my cheeks with my palms, wiping them on my jeans after. "Things aren't going to work out with me and Ethan." God, I sound so pathetic.

"Oh, honey." He hugs me again. "I'm so sorry. What happened?"

I don't want to get into that. Then I'd have to talk about my mom, which I'm absolutely not doing. "We have some... fundamental differences I can't get past. It's over."

Saying the words aloud is the final nail in the coffin, my chest so incredibly tight it's hard to draw a breath. But I do it anyway, forcing past the knives in my throat, making it through.

"I'm going to lie down," I tell him, extracting myself from his hold.

"Are you sure? We can talk if you want."

I give him a weak smile, holding it together. "Thanks, but I just want to be alone."

He nods, his worried gaze following me as I stumble to my room, wrapping my arms over my stomach.

I curl up on my mattress, not bothering to pull the covers over me, and stare into the darkness, letting the tears leak out, wishing I could suppress everything that wants to come up. Wishing I could shove it all down deep into that hollow void inside me like I've done for so long.

But now I'm filled with... feelings. This is exactly what I didn't want to happen.

I continue lying there, the intrusive thoughts eventually quieting, sleep overtaking me into a restless night filled with dreams I can't quite remember in the morning but leave me with a vague sense of dread in the pit of my stomach.

I can't concentrate on anything all day, going through the motions, but my mind is far away, that dread growing the closer it gets to two o'clock when our Psychology class meets.

I should skip it. Not put myself through the stress of seeing Ethan so soon.

But I have to see him at some point, and the longer I put it off, the harder it'll be. He's already texted me twice today, asking if I'm feeling better and if I wanted to get together for lunch. I had to make up some bullshit excuse about how I didn't have time, how I had to cram for some made-up test in Russian Lit later. In truth, I skipped the required reading for today. Every time I opened my book, my vision blurred.

My steps are heavy as I walk from my Macroeconomics class to the Psychology lecture hall, veering off the path before I get there. I should wait until a minute after class starts to show up. That way, he can't talk to me.

God, I'm such a coward.

I waste time doing a lot of nothing until two on the dot, then finish the trek there, doing the walk of shame up the room's steps as everyone stares at me.

Ethan is in his normal seat next to Christian and Amber and I quickly file past the other people in the row, keeping my head down, mostly so I don't have to meet Ethan's eye.

What do I say to him? Do I explain what I found last night? Tell him he needs to get help?

Just the thought of doing that makes my stomach lurch again. I'll figure it out another time, when the sting of it isn't so fresh.

I settle in my seat, leaning forward to get my things out of my bag.

"You okay?" Ethan whispers as I open my notebook, ready to take notes.

I nod, staring ahead at Dr. Clark at the front of the room.

He drapes his arm over my shoulders, the same way he did in class Tuesday. That time it was a welcome weight. Reassuring. Comforting. Today, it's a yoke around my neck, dragging me down. If I shrug him off, he'll want to know why. He'll want to talk about it. He always wants to talk about things I'm not ready to.

I sit there, internally vibrating with tension, but he doesn't seem to notice, finally taking his arm off me when Dr. Clark dismisses us an hour and a half later.

"You have plans tonight?" he asks, slinging his backpack over his shoulder. Why does he even carry that thing around when he doesn't take any notes?

"I'm going to apply for a job at the diner," I tell him, meticulously packing up my stuff.

"That's right. I hope you get it."

I'm silent, watching as Christian and Amber leave hand in hand. No problems in paradise for them, at least.

"You sure you're okay?" He squints at me, his skepticism obvious. I've never been a great actress.

"Just worried about this test in Russian Lit," I lie. "It's worth a big part of our grade."

What a load of crock. Papers make up our grade, not tests.

"You'll ace it," he says easily. "But I meant from last night. If I was too forward—"

"I'm fine," I interrupt, staring down at my shoes. "I have to get to class."

"Right. Yeah."

He sounds taken aback, and rightly so. This is how I acted with him a month ago, not now.

He moves in to kiss me goodbye, and I turn at the last second so he kisses my cheek instead. I can't share anything as intimate as a real kiss with him.

"Bye." I book it out of there, my feet on fire as I speed toward the Humanities building. All in all, that could have gone worse. I barely had to talk to him and he doesn't suspect too much.

Even so, I'm not out of the woods. Nowhere near. I can't string him along forever. At some point, I'll have to tell him I don't want to be together. Don't want to be around him even. It's only a reminder of my misplaced trust, how others will always let you down.

I take a seat in my normal spot in Dr. Kroft's class, not bothering to pull anything out of my bag yet, instead laying my head down on the desk, the wood cool against my cheek.

I'm startled what seems like a moment later as the professor calls class to begin, a sticky trail of drool on my cheek as I sit up. Oh God, that's disgusting. I guess my restless night finally caught up with me.

I surreptitiously wipe at my face, praying no one saw that, and pull my notebook and pen out of my bag, taking notes as Dr. Kroft soliloquizes about last week's read of *Eugene Onegin* and its themes of society and superficiality.

After a certain point, though, he fades out as he heads into today's topic. Crap. It's the stuff I didn't read.

"Tell me about Russian formalism," he says to the room at large, his unnaturally blue eyes staring out at us dispassionately.

236

The lecture hall is quiet in response, no one taking the bait.

"No one?" he asks, cocking a blond brow. He reaches on his desk, holding up the class roster. Oh, no. Someone's about to get their ass handed to them.

"Alexandra Adams," he says in a clear voice, my stomach sinking. The one time I'm unprepared when he calls on me.

I slowly raise my hand, holding back my wince when his gaze meets mine.

"Tell me about fabula and syuzhet and how they relate to formalism."

I swallow, my mouth like cotton after drooling everywhere, and answer, "I don't know."

His gaze sharpens, a predator latching onto its prey. "Tell me anything about formalism, then. What it is, when it started, which scholars were involved."

"I don't know," I repeat, my voice tight.

Everyone is staring at me now, worse than in Intro to Psych today.

He sets down the roster, leaning back against his desk, feet crossed at the ankle. "Did you do the assigned reading?"

"No." There's no use in lying. I obviously didn't or I'd have some clue about what he's talking about.

Somehow, his face hardens even more. It's difficult to look menacing when wearing a bowtie, but he manages it with aplomb. "You may leave, then. This class is for students who want to be here."

My bottom lip trembles for a moment before I firm it. "Look," I blurt out, "I'm having a hard time because I just found out the guy I'm seeing isn't who I thought he was."

The previous silence of the room sharpens even more. After an agonizingly long five seconds, Dr. Kroft clears his throat, the sound echoing off the walls.

Two rows down from me, a guy asks, "Like, he catfished you?"

I clench my fists then spring into action, gathering my notebook and pen to stuff them into my backpack.

"Sit down, Miss Adams," the professor says as I stand. "I won't call on you again."

I cautiously sit, surprised he's being lenient with me. For God's sake, he locks students out of the room who are a minute late.

"But I expect you to have caught up on the reading by next class."

I nod, sinking down in my seat, thankful when he calls on the boy who asked about catfishing.

I've got to get this under control. I can't let Ethan affect every aspect of my life.

He's my Psych study partner now. His fake girlfriend in the lab. And that's it.

That's all that can be between us.

# CHAPTER TWENTY-FIVE

## ETHAN

SOMETHING IS UP.

I feel it in my gut. My bones. A soul-deep knowledge that something is wrong with Lexie.

She blew me off all weekend, claiming she had to study or help Travis or start working at the new job she got at Kate's Kitchen as a server. Anything but hang out with me.

I don't want to be that clingy, needy guy, but this is kind of ridiculous. She can't spare an hour or two for me?

Maybe I freaked her out taking things too far, too fast last week. Maybe we should take things at a slower pace and ease our way into a relationship. But this isn't slow. This is a standstill.

I thought we were past this. I thought last Monday brought us closer. We were on the same page. But it's like she set the book down and decided to browse a different shelf without telling me. What the hell happened between us making out against my bedroom door and me leaving to go take my insulin shot?

All throughout Environmental Engineering, my class before Psych on Tuesdays, my mind is on Lexie. What I can do, what I can say to get her to talk to me. To get her to share what's going on with her. How can I fix things if I don't know what's wrong?

She doesn't arrive to class until the last minute again, just like last week. I keep my distance this time, waiting to see if she kisses me hello after days apart, if she greets me, if she even freaking acknowledges my presence, but nothing. It's like I'm a ghost next to her, the Patrick Swayze to her Demi Moore, forever doomed to walk beside her unseen.

Okay, so maybe I'm getting a little melodramatic.

I cross my arms over my chest, stewing, unable to focus on what Dr. Clark's saying as the class goes on, my heart sinking further and further the longer there's silence between us. Not that Lexie and I normally speak during class, but it's a comfortable silence, at least. Not this awkward tension that makes my skin crawl.

Maybe it's just me feeling it, though.

After the longest hour and a half of my life, Dr. Clark calls class to an end and Lexie packs up her stuff at lightning speed.

I move with her as she tries to shoot past me, Amber and Christian blocking her from the other side.

"I'll walk you to Russian Lit," I tell her, not giving her any room for argument.

She still does, though. "It's fine. You don't have to."

Is it my imagination or is her voice strained, like she's gritting out the words?

"Well, I'm going to."

She finally looks up at my hard tone, defiance flashing in her eyes. What's going on with her?

She sweeps past me, being careful not to touch my body, confirming my suspicion that something's wrong.

I follow her down the aisle and out the lecture hall doors, waiting till we're away from the building to ask, "You going to tell me why you're mad at me?"

She stuffs her hands in her hoodie pocket, jaw firming, but stays silent, continuing to walk along the sidewalk.

I move to take her arm, wanting her to stop and talk to me, and she flinches, angling away.

What the fuck?

She finally stops walking, moving onto the grass so people can pass by us, and stares down at her scuffed shoes. "I don't want to do this anymore," she mumbles.

My stomach drops, a hollowed-out pit with no bottom. "What?"

"We should keep things simpler," she says. "Just finish out the study together and get our money. We don't have to do anything else."

I blink at her, unable to believe what I'm hearing, even after suspecting something was going on with her. "What the hell are you talking about?" I thought this was a minor blip, not a complete roadblock. "Did I go too fast? Freak you out? We can go slower."

She shakes her head. "We're not a good fit. We're too... different."

Different? Yeah, there are some minor things, but no couple is completely the same. There's nothing we can't work past. "What are the differences? Tell me so I can fix it. I want this to work."

She's silent again, pushing at a fallen leaf on the ground with the toe of her shoe.

"I can't read your mind, Lexie. You have to give me something here."

"We're not compatible." She looks up at me, her expression pleading, like she needs me to understand.

But I don't. Not compatible in what? All this started when...

When we were making out in my bedroom.

Does she mean we're not compatible there? In bed?

Well, fuck.

"You need help," she whispers. "And I can't give it to you. I can't deal with it."

Heat crawls up my neck, my face flushing with embarrassment. It takes a hell of a lot to embarrass me, and yet she managed to do it with a few words.

"I have to go," she says, turning around and continuing down the path.

I rake my fingers through my beard, tugging at it, trying to make sense of all this. How could I have completely misread her? I swear she'd been enjoying herself. She'd come twice for me so far. I'd *felt* her come. On my fingers. On my tongue. She couldn't have faked that.

She said before what we've done is amazing. That she's happier than she's ever been. Why would she say that if she didn't mean it? She's not the type to stroke a guy's ego. If anything, she'd say nothing at all.

I need to talk to her again about this, to figure out what I did wrong. I've never had a complaint before.

And if she wasn't referring to us in the bedroom... then what did she mean?

---

"There you go," Austin says as he ducks my blow. "You're getting it now."

I took his advice, moving past my hesitancy, going straight for the jugular as I advance on him again, keeping him in the defensive position.

My mood tonight makes it easy, though, pouring all my frustration, my anger, my hurt over Lexie's rejection into my fists. Aggression runs through my veins, a part of me fearing that if I hit Austin in this state, it might do actual damage, despite his quickness on his feet.

But the primal side of me? It wants to see what will happen.

"Whoa," he mutters, moving out of the way in time to avoid my glove.

"Easy," Lawrence calls from the sidelines. "Your fight's in less than a week. You shouldn't go so hard."

Tonight wasn't supposed to be an official training night, but I couldn't sit at home and twiddle my thumbs. Not with that hollow pit still in my stomach.

In my heart.

I dial back my intensity, pushing the growing numbness out of my mind for the moment, focusing on training, on being the best I can be for Saturday's tournament.

But when Lawrence calls us out of the ring twenty minutes later so the next pair of guys can use it, I can't resist it any longer, immediately heading over to my gym bag to type out a text to Lexie.

**Me**: *I'd like to talk tonight. You working?*

I stare at my phone, not truly expecting an answer right away, but a guy can hope.

"You're improving."

I drop my phone back in my bag, glancing up at Austin. "You too." Wait, that was a dumb answer. He's always good. "Lawrence said earlier he added you to the roster for Saturday, too? I thought you were looking to turn pro."

He nods. "I still need some amateur fights under my belt first."

"How many have you been in?"

He scratches at his chin, looking up at the ceiling. "Close to twenty, I think?"

I blink at him. "How long have you been fighting?" Tournaments don't come around all that often. Not unless you do some extensive traveling.

Shrugging, he answers, "Pretty much my whole life. It's kind of a family tradition." He points to Marty's office. "You know Marty's my uncle, right?"

No, I didn't. No wonder he's so knowledgeable about everything.

"So what would you say I still need to work on?" I've only got four days left to prepare for this bout.

He claps me on the back, hard enough to make me wince. "It's too late to stress about that stuff now. I can tell you've taken Lawrence's comments to heart. You've done as much as you can to prepare."

Yeah, that's not exactly what I want to hear. If I have nothing to improve on, that means my mind is free to ruminate on Lexie. Especially on that moment

243

after class talking to her. How could she want to end things between us before they even really began? She never gave us a chance.

And if she thinks I'm going to roll over and accept her suggestion of only getting together on Wednesdays for the study, she must be out of her mind. After tomorrow, there's only one week left. And then what? We never speak again?

That's not happening.

If the thought of sex is what freaked her out so badly, we can dial back on that. I'm willing to wait her out as long as she needs. But what I'm not doing is having her keep avoiding me, giving me half-answers that only raise more questions.

I'm getting to the bottom of this.

Tonight.

"Thanks, man," I tell him. "And good luck on Saturday."

He nods, but for some reason, doesn't seem too excited by the prospect. "You too."

I clean up in the showers, putting on a fresh change of clothes after, and weigh my options. Texting and calling aren't getting me anywhere. If I want to speak to her, I'll have to force it. And the two most likely places she'd be are home or work. If I showed up at her workplace, where she can't escape me… Yeah, that'd probably piss her off.

Her apartment it is, then. Even if she's not there now, she has to come home eventually. And if I'm lucky, I can catch Travis—the one other person she seems to talk to regularly. Maybe he can shed some light on what's going on with her.

I make the drive over, keeping an eye out for Lexie's car in the complex's parking lot, but there are no rusted Corollas here. Guess I'll be waiting, then.

I park in the corner, away from everyone else, not wanting her to recognize my SUV right off the bat when she comes home, and jog over to her apartment door, knocking. Please let her roommate be home. If he lets me in, she'll have a harder time kicking me out.

Wow, stalker much?

The door opens, the same guy from before there, once again staring at me confusedly. "Ethan?"

"Hey, it's Travis, right?"

He nods. "Lexie isn't here."

"I know. Could I talk to you, though?"

He makes a pointing motion toward himself, brows raised. "Uh, sure." He steps back, letting me in, and I sigh in relief. I'm making progress.

"Would you like something to drink?" he asks hesitantly, pausing by the kitchen. Is this as awkward for him as it is for me?

"No, I'm fine."

He moves into the living room, perching on one end of the couch. "What did you want to talk about?"

I take a seat near the other end, wiping my palms on my shorts. "I just want to know what's going on with Lexie. She won't talk to me."

His brows pinch together. "I thought you guys broke up."

Did we? I never even confirmed we were dating. "Did she say that?"

"She came home crying that one night. She said you two weren't going to work out."

The dull ache in my chest that's been my constant companion lately flares to life. "She was crying?" I thought her stomach had hurt or something.

"Like, sobbing. I've never seen her cry before. It was crazy."

I can't imagine whatever we did would make her sob. Being bad in bed wouldn't provoke that kind of reaction. So why was she crying? "Did she say anything else?"

"She said... Oh God, how did she put it?" He looks up at the ceiling, blowing out a breath. "You had some fundamental differences she couldn't get past. But that's it. I've tried asking her about it since then, but she clams up."

Yeah, that part sounds like her.

I lean forward, resting my elbows on my knees. "I'm going to be honest. I have no idea why she said that. And I really want to find out why. Can I stay here until she gets home? I just want to talk to her."

He studies me, but I can't tell what he sees. Desperation? Someone at the end of their rope?

"Yeah, but I'm going to stick around. To make sure she's safe."

I nod, relief flooding through me. "I respect that. I'm glad she has someone looking out for her."

He gets more comfortable on the couch, crossing his legs. "She doesn't really have anyone else. She's not close to her family. Doesn't have any other friends. That's why I asked her to move in here after my last roommate moved out. I think she was in a rough spot before that, but she wouldn't talk about it."

"Her dad told me she pushes people away. I guess she's been like that for a long time."

He stares at me for a moment. "You know her dad?"

"Yeah. He's a trainer at the gym I box at."

He opens his mouth, then shuts it, finally saying, "She *never* talks about him. Or her mom. I'm starting to wonder if I know her at all."

Shit. I didn't mean to cause problems with her relationship with Travis, too.

The front door unlocks, both of us turning toward it.

It's showtime.

# CHAPTER TWENTY-SIX

## ETHAN

THE DOOR SWINGS OPEN, Lexie's eyes widening as she spots me on the couch.

Surprise.

Her lips press together tightly but she enters, locking the door behind her. "I should have known you wouldn't give up," she mutters as she sets her bag down on the kitchen counter. She turns to Travis next. "And you let him in?"

"He wants to talk," he replies weakly.

"I already told you I'm done," she says, breezing past us on the way to her room.

Oh, hell no. "Actually, you didn't." I stand, rounding the couch. "You said a few cryptic things I don't get, but I need more than that. I'm not leaving here until I understand what's going on. After all we've been through, after all I've done for you, you owe me that."

Her nostrils flare. "I told you I can't deal with it."

"Deal with what?"

Her gaze flicks between me and Travis. "I don't want to have this conversation."

"Well, I do."

She retreats, heading toward her room again, and I yell after her, "Were you saying I need help in the bedroom?"

She stops and whips around, shock radiating from her, an identical expression on Travis's face as he gapes at me too.

"What?" she asks.

"When you said we weren't compatible. That I needed help. Did you mean we're not a good fit sexually?"

She blinks at me, a tic forming in her jaw. "You think I've been avoiding you because you're bad in bed? Ethan, you're amazing in bed."

Travis covers his mouth, hiding a wide smile, despite the seriousness of the conversation.

She sighs, comprehension dawning over as she seems to realize what she said, resignation soon following. "Fine. If you want to talk, let's do it in my room."

Travis sits up, solemn once more. "Do you need—"

"I'll be fine," she says. "It won't be a long conversation."

Great. Glad we're both going into this with an open mind.

She shuts the door behind us, leaning against it, and silently picks at her thumbnail.

I cross over to the chair by her desk, the seat hard and unforgiving. Kind of like her right now.

I try to wait her out but patience has never been my strong suit. "So you admit you've been avoiding me," I say into the silence of the room, hoping it'll spark something.

"Yeah," she says, leaving it at that.

"Why?"

She rolls her eyes, crossing her arms over her chest. "I don't want to play stupid games. I saw what was in your room."

248

My room? What in the world could she have seen in there to make her this mad? To make her cry? What am I missing here? "I have no idea what you're talking about."

Her brows narrow. "Don't play dumb with me. On your nightstand. You're using."

What? "Using what?"

"You think this is funny?" she shouts, uncrossing her arms to clench her fists at her sides.

"No?" I'm seriously lost.

"I saw the syringe. The pills. What are you doing? Cocaine? Ecstasy?"

I finally make the connection. She saw my emergency diabetic supplies. "No, you don't understand."

"Oh, I understand perfectly." She's worked up now, pushing off the door to pace the short length of the room. "My mom ruined her life doing that stuff and dragged me down with her. I'm not going down that same path with you."

"No, Lexie—"

"No, you listen to me," she screams, voice louder than I've ever heard, her face reddening. I've never seen her like this. "Nobody listens to me. Dad didn't listen when I told him I hated living with her. No one at school listened when I said I didn't sleep with the baseball team. And you don't listen when I tell you I want to be left alone."

My heart thumps in my chest, excruciatingly heavy. "I'm listening," I tell her quietly, afraid to set her off more. If she's finally opening up to me, I have to listen.

She stares at me, calming a bit. "I ended up doing everything for my mom," she explains, urgency in her voice. "But it still wasn't enough. She wrecked everything she touched. Every job. Every relationship. Every dollar bill that crossed her path. It all got sucked up by heroin. She'd dabble in other things, but it always came back to that one."

She sniffs, running a hand under her nose. "And meanwhile, it was me cold at night because there was no money to fix the heater. Me hungry having to wait for school the next day to get something to eat there. And once I was old enough to work, you think that would solve the problem, right? But she was a thief, too. Anything to get her next fix."

She paces again, talking like I'm not even in the room anymore. "What was the alternative, though? Dad didn't want me. And if I reported her, I'd go into foster care. Who knows what kind of abuser I'd end up with there? Or, you know, I could run away from home. Nothing bad would possibly happen on the streets."

My stomach turns at the thought of the choices she faced, a second wave of dread stealing over me as I realize she's been referring to her mother in the past tense this whole time. "What happened to her?" I whisper, half afraid to hear the answer.

She gives me a feral smile, all teeth and no warmth. "She died, Ethan. I came home one day and she had overdosed. And you know what the worst part is?" A tear slips down her cheek but she doesn't seem to notice, letting the droplet sit there by her chin. "After the shock of it was over, I didn't care. If anything, I was happy." She wraps her arms around herself in the middle of the room. "I'm a monster because I was happy my mother died."

She starts sobbing then, hunching over, and I get up, catching her before she falls, holding her tight. She clings to me, a wet spot forming on my chest where her tears soak into my shirt. That's fine, though. Whatever she needs from me right now, I'll give.

"I can't watch that happen to you," she chokes out. "It would be so much worse with you. I actually care about you. I can't be there when you ruin your life."

"Shh." I stroke a palm down her hair, cradling her to me. "That's not happening."

"I meant it when I said you could hurt me," she continues, as if she didn't hear me. "It would destroy me."

"Lexie." I pull back, taking in her tear-stained face and puffy eyes. "I'm not on drugs. What you saw were diabetic supplies. I have diabetes."

She blinks at me, some of the wildness in her gaze retreating, only to be replaced with anger. "Don't bullshit me. I know what I saw."

Yeah, I goof around a lot with her, but I try to convey every ounce of seriousness I can muster when I tell her, "It's the truth. The syringe was for my insulin. And those were glucose pills. I keep them there in case I crash. I have my go-kit in my car if you want proof."

She steps away, no longer crying, and covers her mouth with a trembling hand. "Are you being for real?" she mutters behind her hand.

"I would *never* lie to you about something like that. Here." I pull out my phone, bringing up my last test results from my endocrinologist. "These are my latest fasting blood sugar numbers. And my glucose tolerance test the time before that."

She stares at the screen, but I don't know how much she comprehends, looking back up at me blankly. "But you're in such good shape. And you eat so bad."

"It's Type 1. The kind you can't prevent. And I just found out a few weeks ago. Justin was actually the one who told me I should get tested. He saw something weird in my urine sample."

"Oh my God." She moves her hand to her stomach, gripping it. "I accused you of so much. I thought the worst of you. I—"

She lurches forward, rushing into the adjoining bathroom to kneel next to the toilet. I follow her, holding her hair back as she retches until there's nothing left to come up, painfully dry heaving.

She leans back, exhausted, and I grab a wad of toilet paper, handing it to her. "To clean your mouth," I say awkwardly.

She takes it, wiping at her lips, and chucks it in the toilet, slamming the lid closed and depressing the flusher.

I search in the cabinet underneath the sink for a washcloth or hand towel, but there's nothing, so I wet the corner of her bath towel hanging on the rack and bend down to dab at her face, doing anything I can to soothe her.

"Why didn't you tell me?" she whispers, eyes wide. God, she looks so lost.

"I should have," I agree. "I'm sorry I didn't. But I'm still coming to terms with it myself. It's been a big adjustment." I fiddle with the towel, rewetting it and placing it on the back of her neck. "I had no idea those things would be a trigger for you. I'd never have left them out if I had known."

She nods. "Well, it's my fault for not telling you."

She gets up and moves to the sink, rinsing out her mouth and brushing her teeth, avoiding my eye in the mirror.

I return to her bedroom, giving her space, and sit back in the chair, my elbows on my knees, head in my hands. What a clusterfuck.

She finishes up, standing in the bathroom doorway staring at me. "I'm sorry," she says in a small voice.

I look up at her, my heart breaking at how miserable she seems. "To be fair, you did say you'd probably mess up again somewhere along the way."

She breathes out a weak laugh, wrapping her arms around herself. "I'm sorry I thought that about you. That I was avoiding you. That I yelled at you. I don't think I've ever gotten that loud in my life."

Though I hate it had to come to that, I understand how all that helplessness had to be crushing her. "Was it cathartic?"

She gives me a watery smile, wiping at her eyes. "Kind of. Sorry it had to be you it ended up coming out on."

"Maybe it was me because you know deep down you can trust me. That I'm always going to be there for you."

She shakes her head, sniffing loudly. "Why in the hell do you still want anything to do with me?"

I stand, crossing the room, and she meets me halfway, wrapping her arms tight around my waist, burrowing into my chest, and I hold her back just as tightly.

"I promised I wouldn't leave you," I murmur into her hair. "That I'd be patient with you."

"I don't deserve promises like that."

"Yes, you do. Why would you think you don't?"

"Because I'm unlovable," she mumbles into my shirt.

I go still, shocked at her statement. Is that how she sees herself? If it is... I guess it explains a lot. "People love you, Lexie. What about your dad? Travis?"

*Me.*

"They might say they do, but they don't. They don't know me. I don't... let them in."

"So let them in, then. They're still going to love you. I saw you and your dad together that first day I met you. He was proud of you. And I only really met Travis tonight, but he was so protective and wanted to make sure you were safe. They both care about you. And I care about you." I take a deep breath, deciding to just go for it. "I love you."

She pulls away, eyes wide as saucers. "Is this like last time when I accidentally said it?"

I can't help the small laugh that escapes me. "No. I mean it." I cup the back of her head, bringing her in close to me again. "When I thought you were ending things earlier... it put a lot into clarity. How much you mean to me. How much I don't want this to end."

She hugs me tighter, nestling into me.

"When you let your guard down around me," I continue, "I love how sweet and sarcastic you are. You give back as good as I give you. And I'm pushy with you because I know you can take it. You're strong. And you show these glimpses every so often of this caring, funny, beautiful girl I want in my life." I stroke a hand over her hair, relief coursing through me now that I finally have her back in my arms.

She takes a shuddering breath, fingers gripping my shirt. "It hurt so bad when I thought I couldn't trust you. You mean more than anyone else ever has. I've never felt this kind of connection. Didn't think it was possible. And I hope you can forgive—"

"I forgive you. No question. I understand where you're coming from now. What you've been through. And in the future, I want you to talk to me about it if you're having a problem. No more keeping things bottled up inside. This won't work, otherwise."

She nods, and I press a kiss to the top of her head. "That goes for me, too," I tell her. "If I'd shared my diagnosis sooner, none of this would have happened."

"There are some things that are hard to share," she whispers. "They bare a part of your soul. And you have to hope the person you show it to will keep it safe. Will protect it. You have to take a leap of faith." She looks up at me, her face tear-stained again, but she's never looked more beautiful. "I want to take that with you. I know you'll be there to catch me on the other side."

"I will," I promise her.

"From now on, no matter what happens, I will always trust you. Always give you the benefit of doubt. You've proven yourself to me so many times, and if you could see me at my worst and still love me..." Her voice breaks, and she takes a moment to continue. "I don't know what I did to deserve you, but I don't want to let this go. To let you go. I—I'm falling for you. So hard."

# CHAPTER TWENTY-SEVEN

## LEXIE

I'M TREMBLING, my heart pounding so loud I'm half-surprised Ethan can't hear it too.

I never thought I'd admit that to someone. He could laugh in my face. Could stomp all over my heart if he wanted. He holds that power now. He's breached every one of my walls, so deep within my soul it's a wonder I can even take a breath when I stop to think about it.

But like I said, I trust him. To be gentle with my heart, carrying it with two hands, no sudden movements. It's bruised and fragile and not much to look at, but it's his.

"I'm yours, Ethan. All of me. Fully. Completely. For as long as you'll have me."

He makes a desperate noise, bending down to kiss me, his mouth warm and open, the feel of it so right I nearly start crying again.

I swear, I've cried more in the last two weeks than in the past twenty years combined. That's what happens, though, when someone finally unlocks your heart.

"I love you," he whispers against my lips, the words filling me with joy. I don't think I'll ever get over him saying that to me.

He leads me to the bed, laying us down facing each other, our legs tangled together, the light circles he traces along my back like heaven. He kisses me again with drawn-out, drugging kisses that both soothe and rouse me, his body a work of art as I shape my palms over his shirt, tracing his heavy pectorals, the flat planes of his stomach, lifting the hem to run soft fingers over the dark trail of hair that leads down into his boxers.

"Are you trying to turn me on?" he asks coquettishly.

I grin against his mouth, full of lightness. "Yes."

"Good." He rolls over so he's on top of me, bracing himself on his forearms. "It's working."

Our kisses grow steadily longer, greedier, rougher the more we continue, his hips grinding into me, dick hard behind his fly. This time, there's no hesitation on my part, no one else on my mind as I tell him that I want him, that I'm ready for him, that I need him this minute.

He strips us both, pulling a condom out of his wallet to roll on. "I put this in here the other day," he says. "For us. I don't always carry one around."

"I believe you." I have no reason to doubt he's telling the truth.

He settles back over me, pressing kisses to the length of my neck as he rubs my pussy, gliding in once, twice, working me up, making sure I'm ready for him before he enters me. There's pressure, but it's never painful as he goes slowly, giving me time to adjust to him, his murmured words of encouragement in my ear doing more than he knows to relax me.

My neck arches off the pillow as he begins to move inside me, pumping, our bodies growing slick with sweat the longer we go, that feeling of rightness intensifying. It's like every sensation within me is magnified as he works my body, need winding through me, my breaths growing harsher in the quiet of the room. My nails dig into his shoulders and he groans, his Adam's apple bobbing as he swallows heavily.

I stare up at him, liking his reaction, wanting to see more. I snake a hand down to brush my thumb over his nipple, to stroke his happy trail again, to grip his ass.

"Lexie," he grunts. "I'm going to come if you keep that up."

"Isn't that the idea?"

"Yeah, but you need to get there first."

God, he's so good to me. "So make me come," I challenge.

He leans in, murmuring in my ear, "Anything you want."

He lifts one of my legs, propping my foot on his shoulder, changing the angle so he hits deeper, just as he picks up his pace.

Oh, shit. Now this is where it's at.

I bring my hands up, gripping my pillow, a growing pressure deep in my lower belly doubling, tripling, a shaky moan escaping me as he keeps hitting this one spot within me that makes my toes curl.

He brings a hand between us, brushing over my clit with light passes that leave me wanting more, my thighs quivering as it becomes too much to take.

"You're making me regret challenging you, aren't you?"

"I would never."

He's such a tease.

He presses more firmly against my clit, finally giving me what I need, rubbing me carefully as he brings his mouth to mine, kissing me with such passion it sends me over the edge, holding onto him tight, my back bowing with the force of it.

When I come down from my high, he's looking at me tenderly, his movements slowed.

"Did you come?" I ask.

"Not yet," he murmurs.

"What can I do to help?"

He lets out a choked laugh. "You don't have to do anything."

"You want me to touch myself? That got you going last time."

He falters in his rhythm for a moment, squeezing his eyes shut. "Christ."

I'll take that as a yes, then.

I reach up, palming my breasts, the action attracting his gaze like a magnet when he opens his eyes again, such lust in them it sends a fresh wave of arousal through me.

"You like that?"

He nods, his strokes speeding up within me once more.

"What about when I rub my pussy?"

"Oh, fuck." He grunts, brows knitting in concentration, and I don't even get to make good on my promise before he comes, groaning low, the sight of him in the throes of passion forever etched in my mind.

He drops down beside me, pulling out, and kisses me, cupping my cheek. I pour all my love for him into the kiss, silently expressing my joy, my pleasure, all these foreign but welcome emotions unfurling within me.

He breaks away, going to clean up in the bathroom, and I stretch out luxuriously on my bed, deliciously full. My heart, my body, my mind.

And as he returns and I drape myself comfortably over him, I let out a contented sigh, my eyes growing heavy, knowing I can relax around him. That I'm safe. The first time I've ever felt truly, one hundred percent that way.

It's a feeling I could get used to.

And one I won't be letting go of anytime soon.

---

"You've got a little something right here."

Ethan motions to the corner of my mouth, not giving me a chance to wipe away whatever it is before he leans in, kissing me.

My lips tilt up. "You could have kissed me without making up a reason."

"I like to keep things interesting."

He pokes at his salad with his fork, the two of us at one of the umbrella tables outside the student center. "This salad, however, is not interesting. It has to be the most boring salad in the history of salads."

I take a bite of my peanut butter and jelly sandwich, actually wishing I could have the salad, instead. It's too expensive to buy regularly. I'd offer to switch with him, but he needs to watch what he eats.

"Even if you weren't diabetic, you'd still need to be careful about what you eat today. Your match is tomorrow. What time is the weigh-in?"

"Nine. Lawrence said if I'm late, I can't compete."

"Then plan on being there at eight-thirty at the latest. You'll be glad for the cushion if something happens."

He takes a bite, frowning, and swallows it down. "And you'll be there, right? When my match starts?"

I reach over and take his free hand. "I'll be there all day. I'll drive you if you want."

"With your car? Yeah, right."

Okay, he's got a point. Even with the new battery, it's still not running perfectly.

"Well, maybe I should spend the night at your place so we can ride together in the morning."

He kisses me again, a smile on his lips. "You could ask to stay over without making up a reason."

I bite my lip, hiding my grin.

Our schedules have been too different the past two days to easily get together, but tonight, we're both free.

I've been insanely anticipating tonight.

An approaching couple snags my attention, not too many people on campus on Fridays compared to other days of the week, and my brain takes a minute to recognize the brunette. "Oh my god, she bagged a lookalike."

"What?" Ethan turns his head in the direction I'm looking, and lets out a soft, "Oh, shit."

"Weird, right?" The guy Savannah is with is like a lesser version of Ethan. A little younger, a little shorter, a little less muscular. Wait. Isn't that the guy I saw her talking to when we left the frat party?

"That's Jordan," Ethan says.

Jordan... Jordan... Why does that name sound so familiar? Hold on... "Your brother?"

"Yep."

The guy waves to Ethan, who holds up a hand in response.

"Are they coming over here?" I hiss under my breath.

"Yep."

"Aren't you concerned?"

He shrugs, no time to answer as they're suddenly in front of us, Jordan appearing delighted to have happened upon his brother like this, Savannah looking supremely uncomfortable.

Good. She should be.

"So this is why you're always too busy to eat with me on campus?" Jordan asks good-naturedly.

"Just spending time with my girlfriend," Ethan replies, not acknowledging the ribbing.

"Nice to meet you," he says to me. "I'm his brother, Jordan."

"Lexie," I say cautiously, sensing some kind of strange undercurrent going on.

"And this is my girlfriend, Savannah."

He looks at us expectantly, frowning when we don't seem overjoyed to meet her.

"Oh, we've met," Ethan says, dropping his fork in his salad bowl.

"Hey, guys." Savannah gives an awkward wave. "I didn't realize Jordan was your brother," she says to Ethan.

"Well, we certainly look enough alike."

"I… guess." She gives a nervous chuckle, her gaze shifting repeatedly from Ethan to Jordan and back again, as if she's just now making the connection. Seriously?

Jordan finally picks up on the awkward vibe, glancing between his brother and his new girlfriend. "How do you know each other?"

"We were in a study group for our Psychology class," Savannah says before Ethan or I can answer. "I stopped going, though."

Yeah, because I'm pretty sure I scared you off.

Ethan turns to me, raising his brows as if to ask *do you want to tell him or should I?*

I shake my head, not wanting to get into it right outside the student center.

"Well," Jordan says, clapping his hands together, "if you all already know each other, how about we go on a double date sometime?"

I nearly choke on the bite of sandwich I just took, turning away to cough.

"I don't think we're up for that," Ethan tells him diplomatically.

"Okay, but at least come to dinner tonight. Mom should have texted you already about a family dinner. It's to introduce Savannah to everyone."

It's been, what? Two weeks since that frat party? And he's already bringing her home to meet his family? The guy moves quick.

"And it'd be great if you came too, Lexie," Jordan adds. "Another girlfriend would take some of the pressure off Savannah."

Oh, yeah. I'd love to do her a favor.

Not.

"I'm not sure if we can make it," Ethan says, "but I'll let you know." There's clear dismissal in his tone, Jordan at least picking up on that as he makes his goodbyes.

Beside him, Savannah is silent, staring at Ethan until they walk away.

I wait until they're out of earshot to say, "What alternate reality did we step into?"

"I know, right?" He eats another mouthful of salad, leaving it at that, but there's something niggling at the back of my mind.

"Would you want me to meet your family?" I ask, voicing it aloud rather than keeping the question to myself. He said he wants me to share my thoughts with him more.

He looks over at me sharply. "Of course," he mumbles through a full mouth.

I peel the remaining crust off my bread, giving my hands something to do. "Well you said you didn't know if we'd go, but it sounded like you were leaning toward no."

"I wasn't going to make the decision for you. Last time, you yelled at me for doing that."

Yeah, I did, didn't I?

"And besides, I figured you wouldn't want to willingly spend another night with Savannah. She and Jordan are a match made in narcissistic heaven."

So there's tension with his brother, then? "It doesn't bother you they're seeing each other? I mean, she made her interest in you *very* clear."

He lets out a soft chuckle. "If he can't see through her act, that's on him. And if I told him she wasn't worth it, he'd probably propose to her just to spite me. He thinks he's hot shit, that he knows best. So, whatever. Doesn't affect me."

And he honestly doesn't seem bothered, calmly finishing up his salad.

But the notion of Savannah meeting Ethan's family only raises a dizzying number of what-ifs in my mind.

"What if she says something about me at dinner? Like, tries to discredit me?"

He sets down his fork, turning to me. "First of all, it'd be pretty tacky of her to bring anything like that up. Second of all, we'd tell them the truth. And third of all, I'd let everyone know how she continually hit on me knowing I had a girlfriend. After I'd repeatedly reminded her. How she did it in front of you, for Christ's sake."

He blows out a breath and studies me carefully, his gaze tenderly tracing my features, relaxing me. "If you want to go tonight, I'm fine with that. If you don't want to, I'm fine with that too. It's totally up to you. Whatever you're comfortable with."

"I want to go," I tell him slowly, deciding it as I say it. "I'd like to meet your family."

He smiles at me, reaching over to squeeze my hand. "Now before you start worrying about it, they're going to love you."

I cover my eyes with my other hand, both hating and loving that he read my mind so easily. "It's probably silly, but I want them to like me. Especially your parents. I've never met a boyfriend's parents before."

His lips curve in a wide grin, eyes crinkling at the corners. "That's the first time you've called me your boyfriend."

"It is?" I swear I've said it a million times in my head. Maybe even doodled *Lexie Hudson* in my notebook a few times during Cost Accounting this morning, just to see what it would look like. "Well, if it makes you feel better, I've referred to you as my boyfriend to Travis a bunch already. He's probably sick of hearing it."

We'd had a big heart to heart the day after Ethan and I got back together. It was pretty necessary, though. The walls of our apartment aren't soundproof, and he'd heard everything I yelled from the bedroom. But Ethan was right that I need to share more. After talking with Travis about everything that went down with my mom, I couldn't believe the amount of support he gave me in response. Maybe he really does love me.

That still leaves the talk I need to have with my dad, but that's a problem for another day.

"So, what can you tell me about your parents? What should I know before we go?"

He strokes his beard, looking up at the umbrella shading us from the midday sun. "Okay, there's a chance Dad won't be there because he works a lot of nights, but just talk about the Patriots or whatever new Black and Decker tool is on the market."

I know next to nothing about football or tools, but okay.

"Mom will definitely be there. You can't have a family dinner without her. She likes the idea of traveling to France or collecting these weird ceramic figures I was never allowed to touch."

Um, okay? That's not really helpful either.

He gets up, throwing the last scraps of his salad in the nearby trash can. "How about I pick you up around five-thirty tonight? Dinner's supposed to be at six."

"That's all the prep I get?"

"I have to go to class," he says, holding his hands out in a helpless gesture. "Linear differential equations wait for no man."

"What about a woman? Namely, me."

His mouth quirks to one side in amusement, and he bends down to press a soft kiss to my lips. "You'll knock 'em dead. Love you."

The returning words bubble to the surface, lingering, waiting, but ultimately don't come out. I told him I'm falling for him. That I'm his. Fully. Completely. So why can't I tell him I love him? I know in my heart I do.

I give him a warm smile instead. "See you tonight."

If he's disappointed with my answer, he doesn't show it at least. He hitches his backpack over his shoulders and walks toward his next class, turning back toward me about fifty feet away to cup his hands around his mouth and shout, "Love you, Pookie Bear." He waves an arm too, in case any passersby didn't get the message, my cheeks heating at his ridiculousness.

I thought he'd forgotten about that nickname. Hoped he'd forgotten, more like it. But if I know him at all, there's one thing he'll love. And it's kind of the perfect way to tell him.

I wave a hand back, yelling, "Love you, Snookums."

He pumps his fists in the air, letting out a holler, and runs back to me, cupping my face with both hands when he reaches me. "I love you. Like, seriously love you right now."

"I love you too."

He kisses me long and slow, a prelude to something more even though we both have classes to get to, desire in his eyes as he pulls away. "I can't wait till you sleep over tonight."

"Me too."

He gives me one more quick kiss, then jogs down the path toward the math building, shouting to no one in particular, "My girlfriend loves me!"

He gets a few answering claps and whoops, people looking at me too, but for once, I'm okay with the attention. If he's happy, then I am too.

Besides, I've got more pressing things to worry about.

Like getting his family to like me.

# CHAPTER TWENTY-EIGHT

## LEXIE

"EVERYTHING'S GOING TO BE FINE," Ethan says for the hundredth time, turning onto a residential street with green lawns and two-car garages. Very firmly middle-class.

"I know." But that doesn't change the fact that my armpits are sweating as if I recently ran a triathlon. "What are your parents' jobs?" I ask, wiping my palms on my jeans again.

"Dad's an assistant grocery store manager and Mom's a school administrator."

"Where were they born?"

He breathes out a sigh. "You don't have to memorize facts about them. This isn't an interview."

"I know," I repeat. Not that I'm really getting the message. Savannah is the type of girl you bring home to meet your parents, not me.

He slows near a two-story gray house with a big bay window in the front, parking behind a truck. "Looks like Scott and Jacob are here, but not Jordan," he says, unbuckling his seatbelt. "It figures he'd be late to his own dinner."

"Is there something going on between you two?"

He pauses in getting out of the car. "Hmm?"

"You seem annoyed by him."

"Yeah, because he's annoying. I mean, look at who he's interested in. That should tell you everything you need to know right there."

I hide my smile with my hand.

"I love him, but he's always been that stereotypical pesky little brother. Jacob's way better."

Maybe all families aren't as functional as sitcoms led me to believe.

He takes my hand as we enter the house, leading me down a hallway toward the kitchen where a tall woman with dark hair the same color as Ethan's is chopping a head of lettuce at a center island.

"Hey, Mom," Ethan says casually, glancing around. "Where is everyone?"

She continues chopping, focused on her task. "In the garage. Dad got a new riding lawn mower."

"Oh, cool."

She rolls her eyes, then seems to notice me, setting down her knife. "You must be Lexie," she says warmly, instantly putting me at ease. Ethan must get his charm from her.

"Yes, hi." I clear my throat, getting rid of the frog in there. "It's nice to meet you."

I'm unsure what to do, whether I should offer a handshake or hug or stay where I am. What do normal people do in situations like this?

"You want to see a lawn mower?" Ethan asks me, and I have to suppress the urge to elbow him in front of his mother.

"Not really." Why would he think I'd be interested in that?

"Ethan, you go check it out," his mom says, waving him off. "Lexie will keep me company here."

I will?

"I'll be gone two minutes," he says, leaning in to give me a quick kiss on the cheek.

I fumble for his hand, wanting him to stay, but he saunters off in the opposite direction we came from. He turns around once he's out of his mom's line of sight, pointing to her and mouthing *talk to her*.

Ugh. It's like him pushing me to be nice to Amber all over again.

"So, you go to the university too?" she asks me, picking up her knife to continue chopping the lettuce. Just what I need is a parent with a sharp weapon.

"Yes, ma'am."

"Oh, you don't have to be formal with me. You can call me Mom."

I swallow, knowing she didn't mean anything by the comment.

"Have your parents met Ethan yet?"

"My dad has. He likes him. And my mom... She passed away."

She looks up at me. "Oh, honey. I'm so sorry. When I said call me Mom, I didn't mean—"

"Oh, I know." I step closer. "I was... estranged from her anyway."

She nods, moving on to chop tomatoes next. Damn it. I shouldn't have said that.

"Your home is beautiful," I blurt out, needing to change the topic.

"Thank you. We've lived here for a long time. Bought it right before Ethan was born, actually." She looks over at me speculatively. "How long have you two been together?"

"About a month." If Savannah's connected to his family, we need to keep our story in line with what she knows. "We've been taking things slow up until now, though." I pull my sweater tighter around me, sticking my hands in the pockets. "He's pretty amazing. Probably the most caring, respectful man I've ever met. He's so patient and understanding with me and I'm really lucky to be with him."

She sets her knife down once more and holds a hand to her chest, pressing her lips tightly together. "Thank you," she whispers, holding her arms out to me. Before I know it, she's hugging me, my hands still trapped in my pockets by my side. "I needed to hear that. I've felt like he doesn't need me as much lately, but it's good to know I raised him right."

I finally get my hands free, briefly returning her hug before she lets go. Maybe we could come over here more often. Talking to her isn't too bad.

"Do you need any help with that?" I ask her, motioning to the vegetables on her cutting board.

"Oh, sure. If you want to toss the salad, that'd be great."

I work on incorporating everything into the bowl as Ethan returns, and she conscripts him into slicing the cucumbers as she turns to the stove, taking the lid off of a huge pot of simmering sauce, a boiling pot of water next to it.

"Do you like spaghetti, Lexie?"

"Yes." Who doesn't love spaghetti?

Wait, can Ethan eat that with his diabetes? Isn't it really carb heavy?

She fills the boiling pot with noodles, a clamor at the front door catching our attention.

"Here comes the happy couple," Ethan whispers.

Where normally I might tell him to behave, I'm in agreement with his sarcasm today. I wonder if Savannah will ever reveal to Jordan that she was interested in his brother first.

Jordan and Savannah enter the kitchen as three other men join us from the garage, clearly Ethan's dad, older brother, and younger brother. That must be Scott and Jacob. Ethan said Brian lives too far away to easily drive down for one night.

There's a flurry of activity as introductions are made among everyone, and I know Ethan says my name at some point, but I'm hardly able to remember who says what before Ethan and I are seated at the kitchen table along with Jordan, Savannah, and his dad, while his other brothers and mom finish up dinner and set the table.

"It's nice to see two of my boys settling down," his dad says. "A man's only as good as the woman by his side."

Scott rolls his eyes as he sets silverware in front of me but stays silent.

"I must be the greatest guy in the world, then," Ethan whispers in my ear, bringing a smile to my lips.

"Did you set up a time yet for your match?" Scott asks Ethan, a small noise of displeasure coming from his mom a few feet away.

"Yeah. It's tomorrow, actually."

Scott pauses. "Is that why you asked for this weekend off? Why didn't you tell me? I wouldn't have put myself on the schedule tomorrow if I'd known."

Ethan rubs at the back of his neck, looking embarrassed. "I don't know if I'll be any good, guys. It's my first time. You won't be missing much."

So he doesn't want his family there, but he wants me to come?

"What do you think of him boxing?" his mom asks me, setting down a pan of fresh garlic bread on the table.

It's clear from her tone she doesn't hold it in high regard, and while I want to agree with her, I can't disparage boxing in front of Ethan's family when it's important to him.

I slip my hand in his under the table, squeezing. "I think he's a great boxer, but I also worry about him getting seriously hurt. It can happen to anyone."

He squeezes my fingers back reassuringly. "Lexie will be there to doctor me up in case anything happens."

"At least someone with some common sense will," his mom mutters, taking the pasta off the burner and draining it in a colander.

Ethan grins at me, not perturbed by his mother's comments.

Ethan's dad changes the topic then, going on about how the Patriots whooped the Eagles' ass last night. "Either of you watch football?" he asks me and Savannah eagerly.

"I don't do sports," Savannah says, a hint of dismissiveness in her tone. Doesn't she realize who she's talking to?

I take a deep breath, deciding to just go for it. "That fifty-yard pass was amazing." I didn't actually watch the game, only skimmed the highlights, but I'm not telling him that.

His gaze flashes approval, but he doesn't have time to say anything else about it as his wife brings the spaghetti over to the table, instructing me and Savannah to fill our plates before the boys ravage it.

Savannah doesn't wait for me, taking the first turn, and his mom makes small talk, asking us what our majors are and what we plan to do after graduation.

Ugh. Small talk. Why does everyone insist on it?

"I'm majoring in Mass Communications," Savannah says, loading up her plate. "I'm going to be a celebrity publicist."

That sounds like my worst nightmare.

"And you, Lexie?" his mom asks, turning to me as she takes her seat.

"Accounting. I'll take my CPA exam after I graduate and apply to some firms in the area." Should I add something about France? Ethan said she dreamed about going there. "I might take a week or two after graduation and travel to Europe too. Especially France. I've always wanted to go there."

Beside me, Ethan clears his throat, probably covering a laugh, but I don't care because his mom's eyes are lighting up.

I don't get a chance to hear what she has to say, though, because Savannah butts her way into the conversation, commenting, "I did my summer semester abroad in France. Trust me, it's not worth it."

"You didn't enjoy an entire summer in France?" Ethan's mom asks, her mouth turned down at the corners.

Savannah makes a scoffing noise. "Oh, they were all so rude over there. No one would speak English."

"Well, did you make an effort to speak their language?"

"No, but they should know English. They teach it over there."

"They also teach French here," I comment, helping myself to the spaghetti.

Jordan frowns at her, and she glances around the table, her face dropping. Finally realized the hole she dug herself in, huh? If she keeps this up, she'll have hung her own noose by the end of the night. For someone going into PR, she doesn't have the best grasp on what should come out of her mouth.

The rest of dinner plays out in a similar fashion, with awkward moments galore. My personal favorite is when it comes up that Savannah didn't realize Jordan was a freshman and younger than her. What'd she think earlier today when she found out Ethan was his brother? That Jordan was the older one?

I offer to collect the plates when dinner is over, placing them near the sink as Ethan's mom retrieves a delectable looking chocolate cake from the fridge and a container of vanilla bean ice cream from the freezer.

"Who's hungry for dessert?" she asks, grabbing a set of dishes from the cabinet and serving up massive slices topped with two scoops of ice cream.

I return to my seat, thanking her as she sets a plate in front of me. There's no way I can eat all this after that huge meal.

She hands a bigger portion to Ethan, who eyes it warily.

"You sure you should eat that?" I ask him. He already had a ton of garlic bread with his spaghetti, and hardly any salad.

"What, because of his boxing match tomorrow?" his mom asks, bringing another two plates over for Jordan and Savannah, now awkwardly avoiding each other's eye. Hmm. Maybe their relationship won't be lasting much longer.

"Well, yeah, that. And because he's diabetic."

Everyone at the table goes still, Scott and his dad's side conversation going silent as all eyes turn to me.

What did I say?

I glance at Ethan, whose face has gone pale.

Oh, God. I messed up, didn't I?

"He's what?" Ethan's dad asks in a low voice.

His mom shakes the ice cream scoop she's holding, white droplets flinging on the table. "That's why you were going to see a specialist."

"Wait," Jordan says, shaking his head. "You have diabetes? And you told her before us?"

Scott's brows pinch together as he looks at Ethan like he's a stranger. On his other side, Savannah appears delighted that I started drama.

Jacob's the only one who doesn't particularly seem to mind, scooping a bite of cake and ice cream in his mouth.

Everyone starts talking over each other then, a chaotic cacophony asking questions, demanding answers, growing louder until Ethan shouts, "Enough!"

He looks around the table, his face no longer pale but flushed. With anger? Embarrassment?

I'd give anything to rewind the last few minutes.

"I just got diagnosed and was going to tell you, but I hadn't done it yet. Lexie found out by accident. I wasn't telling her over you all. Let's talk about it another time when we don't have guests."

It's silent for a beat, until Jordan says, "We can't *not* talk about it."

Ethan's hands clench at his sides. "Fine. Then I'll leave."

He grabs my hand, and I scramble out of my chair to follow him, mumbling, "It was nice to meet you," to the room at large before we're past the kitchen, down the hallway, and out the front door, heading toward his SUV.

Agitation pours off him as he holds the passenger door open for me, but I don't dare say anything, shame and regret waging a war inside me. There goes making a good impression in front of his family.

He gets in on the driver's side, violence under his skin as he grips the steering wheel tight for a moment, knuckles white.

Oh, God. It's going to be a long night.

# CHAPTER TWENTY-NINE

## ETHAN

I SHOULD HAVE TOLD THEM.

The phrase keeps repeating in my head ad nauseam on the drive back to my place, my stomach churning.

If I had, it wouldn't have come to this. Wouldn't have blown up in my face the same way it did with Lexie. Mom had outright asked me what those insurance claims were about, and I wouldn't tell her. It's like I want to sabotage myself.

Beside me, Lexie is silent, probably wondering what else I keep secret. I don't blame her. If I didn't tell my own family about something like this, what else could I be hiding from her?

After an agonizingly long five minutes, she whispers, "I understand if you don't want me to spend the night."

My mouth opens to respond, but nothing comes out. What is she talking about?

"I'm sorry I messed everything up with your family," she continues. "I—"

"Whoa, whoa," I interrupt her. "You didn't mess anything up. I did. This is on me."

"But I—"

"Uh uh." I reach over the center console, intertwining my fingers with hers. "Don't think about blaming yourself for that back there. I should have already told them. Or at least given you a heads up I hadn't. Of course you'd assume I told my family. It's just—" I let out a sigh, not sure how to explain it. If it'll even make sense. "It's weird to tell people about it. I don't want them to look at me differently."

"It's not your fault, though." She brings her other hand over mine, tracing my knuckles. "Things like this happen."

"You saw how they all reacted. I've always been the smart Hudson boy. Or the funny one. And lately, the boxer. But I don't want to be the one who has a disease. I don't want that to be what defines me."

"It doesn't," she insists. "But it is a part of you. And if they love you, they'll accept it along with the rest."

I nod, knowing she's right. "I'll go back over there Sunday. Talk to them more about it. I couldn't do it with Savannah there, though. Did you see her face when you said I was diabetic? It was like she'd won a free lifetime supply of candy."

"She's the *worst*. I don't think her and Jordan will last much longer, though. When she found out he's only eighteen, I thought she was going to have an aneurysm."

I laugh, some of the tension draining from me, but my shoulders are still tight as we get to my house. Thankfully, no one is in the common areas as I lead her to my room.

"I put everything away," I tell her as I shut the door behind her, "so you don't accidentally see anything." I'm not having her freak out again over the sight of a needle.

"Thank you," she murmurs, hugging me. Her arms wrap around the back of my neck, and she quickly pulls away. "You're still so tense. Come here."

She pats the edge of the bed for me to sit down, kneeling behind me as she massages my shoulders, her hands working magic across my stiff muscles until the stress melts from them.

"If you ever want to quit accounting, you could make a career shift to masseuse."

She hums a sound of contentment behind me, kneading away a knot in my trapezius muscle. "I wouldn't want to touch anyone other than you."

"Yeah?" I can't help the pleasure that suffuses me hearing her say that. "Anywhere else on me you want to touch?"

"You're incorrigible." Though the words are prudish, she can't hide the smile in her voice.

"Don't act like you offering this massage wasn't a ploy for seduction."

She bends low, nipping at the shell of my ear. "I would never," she murmurs in a husky voice.

My dick jumps in excitement at her playfulness, and I groan low as her mouth moves to the column of my neck, her kisses branding me, marking me for her own.

"Keep doing that," I murmur, her hands moving down the front of my chest, exploring my torso, turning me on.

After another minute, I can't take much more, turning around to kiss her for real, wanting to press her back into the bed and cover her with my body, but she places a hand against my chest, staying me.

"Tonight's about you," she murmurs.

"Hmm?"

She trails a finger down my sternum to the hem of my shirt, pulling it up. I raise my arms so she can lift it off me, her heated gaze making my breaths pick up.

"That night at the party, you said it was all about me. Well, I want tonight to be about you."

My heart pounds, my tongue darting out to wet my lips as she situates me again on the end of the bed, coming around to face me, kneeling on the ground.

Is she…

She strips her shirt off slowly, giving me a fantastic view of her cleavage, and looks up at me with sultry eyes. Where the hell did this vixen come from?

And how can I get her to stick around?

"Let me take care of you," she murmurs, tugging at the button of my jeans. "The way you always take care of me."

I'm dumbstruck as she unzips me, my brain functioning enough at least to toe off my shoes and help her take my pants off. My dick strains at my boxers, wanting to be let out, to feel her touch, and I don't have to wait long before she hooks her thumbs in the waistband, dragging them down my thighs until my dick pops out, ready for her.

She stares at it hungrily, and I bite my lip to hold back my moan, the anticipation rising within me.

But before she starts, I need one thing.

"Lexie."

It takes her a moment to shift her attention upward, her gaze hazy, and I place my hands on her shoulders, guiding her up. "Will you strip for me? I want to see all of you."

She nods, keeping eye contact with me as she toys with the button on her jeans, spinning around as she unzips them, presenting her backside to me as she pulls them down, her bare ass glorious.

Oh, fuck. I didn't know what I was asking for, did I?

My hands grasp at my comforter, wanting to reach out to her, unsure if it will break the spell. How in the world did I get so lucky to land this girl?

She removes her jeans and panties, stepping closer to me, between my legs, and lets the straps of her bra drop from her shoulders as she reaches behind her, unhooking the clasp.

I can't help myself anymore, taking off her bra and leaning in, giving one nipple a strong suck, then the other.

"Ethan," she moans, tangling her hands in my hair as I worship her breasts, greedy for the taste of her.

278

She lets me play with her for a minute, but when my hand snakes down to tease her pussy, she releases me, sinking to her knees again.

"You first," she murmurs, grazing her palms up my thighs, taking my cock in one hand and gently stroking.

My hips arch up, giving her better access as my hands fall behind me, propping me up, unable to look away at the sight of her hand gripping me.

"Where did this seductress come from?" I ask, my eyes closing as a tingle races its way down my spine.

"She was waiting for you. I would only ever do this with you."

A groan escapes me as she reaches out, licking the head of my cock lightly.

"I love hearing you make that sound," she whispers, doing it again.

I drop back to my elbows, watching her take me in, my cock disappearing inside that beautiful mouth, an expression of pleasure on her face.

I wasn't expecting this at all tonight, but the detour is fully welcome as desire pools low in my belly, her tongue soft and warm as she explores me enthusiastically over long minutes, building me up. And as she uses her hand to stroke the base of my dick while she sucks the head, I'm done for, groaning again, reaching down to pull her up.

"I need you," I mumble, kissing her desperately. "Let me come inside you."

She nods eagerly, and I move to my nightstand drawer, rolling on a condom. She pushes me back with gentle fingertips toward the head of the bed, and I lie down, waiting with bated breath as she straddles me, taking my dick and guiding it inside her.

She lets out a soft moan when I'm all the way in, moving her hips, riding me, her breasts gently bouncing as she works herself on me.

I reach out and palm her, shaping her, enjoying the breathy sighs she makes, the way she says my name like it's a benediction. She leans forward, changing the angle of her hips, and I pump into her from below, each of us getting more turned on.

"I didn't know it could be like this," she says, resting her hands on my chest. "That it could be this good."

"It's you and me. It wouldn't be anything but good."

She gives me a shaky smile. "I love you."

Her words send me over the edge, still worked up from when her mouth was on me, and I grip her waist, coming hard, the force of it like nothing I've ever experienced.

"God, I love you too," I choke out, reaching up to bring her down to me, kissing the ever-loving hell out of her.

She responds greedily, sliding her tongue in my mouth, this bold, brave Lexie someone I hope she shows a lot more often.

Especially in bed.

I roll over so she's underneath me and pull out of her, replacing my cock with two fingers, sliding in easily with how aroused she is.

Bending my head, I capture a nipple with my mouth, sucking on her, loving how she clutches at my shoulders, how her thighs drop open, how her toes scramble for purchase against the crumpled comforter.

I stroke her faster, harder, until she comes for me, the unintelligible sounds she makes spurring me on, keeping at it until she can't take any more, her body exhausted as she rolls on her side, curling herself around me.

"I've never felt so close to anyone," she whispers. "It's like... Never mind."

I run a hand down her arm. "No, what is it?"

She looks up at me, the green in her hazel eyes more prominent than ever before. "It's like there's a part of me inside you. And the idea makes me feel safe. That you'll protect that little piece of me I've given you."

Warmth blossoms in my chest, as if that part of her she's referring to is glowing inside me. "Babe, you're turning into a romantic."

Her lips tilt up at the corners in amusement. "I know, it's awful. You've given me..." She pauses for dramatic effect. "Feelings."

"I'm a monster."

"You are." She grins, leaning in to kiss me deliciously, my mind at peace knowing that no matter what tomorrow brings, I'll still have her by my side.

She's mine. Forever.

# CHAPTER THIRTY

## LEXIE

THE DIN of the crowd is unbearably loud, nearly to the point where I want to cover my ears with my hands. But I don't because that would be weird to do here in the middle of this random high school gym, surrounded by others waiting to watch two people beat each other up for fun.

Really, of all places for them to host this boxing tournament, did they have to pick the one place I'd never want to revisit in a million years?

At least it's not my old high school. If that was the case, I might not be here, even for Ethan. I'm willing to put myself in some uncomfortable situations for him, today being one of them, but that one might cross the line.

I check my phone again for the time, shifting uneasily on the metal folding chair. Ethan's match should start any minute now. At least he isn't scheduled for later in the day. I've already been here two hours, barely getting to see him as he registered, weighed in, and started prepping.

Dad seemed surprised to see me show up with him, but thankfully didn't make a big deal of it. I still haven't told him about us with how new everything is.

Over in the blue corner of the ring, Dad is talking to Ethan, both of their faces serious as he gives last minute advice. In the other corner, his opponent bounces on the balls of his feet, throwing jabs at the air, warming up. This guy is no joke, about the same height and build as Ethan, but with an aggressive air about him I don't like. He even has custom boxing shorts with his name, *Sokolov*, printed on the front. He must be serious.

The announcer comes over the loudspeaker then, announcing Ethan Hudson in the blue corner and Dominic Sokolov in the red. Dad puts Ethan's mouthguard in for him, since his hands are already wrapped and gloved, and exits the ring. Ethan turns to the crowd, searching, his brows pinched. I wave, his face clearing when he spots me, holding up a gloved hand in return.

I'd shout *go get 'em, Snookums*, but I won't ruin his man cred here.

The referee brings them both to the center of the ring, gesturing as he says something, but it's too loud in here to make out what it is, despite being in the front row. The two boxers touch gloves in a show of good sportsmanship before returning to their respective corners, and the ref holds his arms out wide between them, a bell dinging loudly to signal the first round has begun.

Sokolov comes at him right away, not letting Ethan get to the center of the ring, but he luckily isn't pushed against the ropes right off the bat. The two feel each other out, circling one another, throwing jabs, not looking to do damage yet but fishing for reactions.

The guy fakes a punch, Ethan holding his right hand up to block, and I recognize the tactic for what it is—a way to see how his opponent instinctively defends. Now, he can use that knowledge to force an opening.

Uh oh. This guy is smart.

The ref stands back as Sokolov grows bolder with his jabs, Ethan continuing to defend. To the untrained eye, it looks like Ethan's only reacting, but I know he's biding his time, waiting for the other boxer to slip up, waiting for the right moment to counterpunch.

After another minute of a lot of posturing, Sokolov tires of Ethan's inactivity, closing the gap between them, forcing something to happen. He tries a jab but doesn't get the reaction he wants, then throws his hands up in a defensive position in front of his face, inching forward, wanting to get in and do damage. He dips down, like he's going to spring for an attack, but it's actually a feint, Ethan coming up to guard his face, leaving his torso exposed for Sokolov to hit.

Damn. I know that hurt.

Instead of retreating, Ethan goes in for a body shot in a one-two combo, and Sokolov brings his arms down to cover, leaving his head free for Ethan to hit his face, but he pulls back in time, escaping it. It would have been a good combo for Ethan if the other guy didn't have such quick reflexes.

Ethan manages to get in a few more blows, but the guy easily shrugs them off, like he's the Terminator or something and Ethan's merely a pesky fly. Sokolov comes in again aggressively, maneuvering Ethan around the ring until he's backed in a corner, leaving nowhere to retreat to.

The bell announcing the end of the round sounds, my fists unclenching, and I shake out my hands, realizing my nails left little divots in my palms. Has it only been three minutes? It feels like a lifetime.

Dad tends to him during the minute break, my leg jiggling up and down as my stomach sinks, watching Sokolov stare him down from across the ring. He's a terrible opponent for a first match, sure to scare Ethan off boxing forever.

Maybe that's a good thing, though?

Ethan's got two more rounds to figure out how to get the upper hand on this guy, but as the second round starts, it's only more of the same as Sokolov comes at him hard, and now that he's discovered some of Ethan's tells, he's more assertive. Instead of jabbing and backing away like before, he stays with him, landing two punches, slipping to the side, and giving three more in quick succession.

Ethan looks like he's panicking, his game plan to wait for the perfect strike falling apart, throwing wild punches with no form.

Dad yells, "Calm down," from his spot on the sidelines, but Ethan doesn't seem to hear him.

Sokolov backs him into a corner again, coming at him with a flurry of blows, forcing Ethan to protect his head. I stand, knowing exactly what the guy will do now, yelling, "Watch out," even as he punches lower at Ethan's unprotected midsection, landing a strike to his exposed ribs on his right side.

It takes a moment for Ethan to react, his arm coming down to cover his ribcage before he falls to his knees, wincing. That was a liver shot. Not a move that looks particularly flashy but can easily end a fight with the amount of damage it does.

The ref sends Sokolov to his corner and starts the count, my heart in my throat as Ethan struggles to get back up, making it to his feet by the count of six, the ref counting one more to make sure he stays on his feet.

He grabs Ethan's gloves, pulling, testing if Ethan's still in control of himself and able to fight, and Ethan pulls back. He says something, Ethan nodding in response, and he backs away, signaling for the fight to continue.

Sokolov goes right back on the attack, on him with a barrage of blows Ethan can't defend against, his reflexes slowed after the hit that almost took him out. Sokolov lands a surprise body hit to his exposed sternum, sending him back to his knees.

I clasp my hands in front of my mouth, silently praying he'll get back up, but it must be too difficult this time, my heart breaking as he's unable to get fully upright before the final count.

The ref waves off the fight and Ethan slumps down again, exhaustion and defeat pouring off him.

Dad slips through the ropes to come to Ethan's side, looping an arm around his waist in support as he half-carries him to his corner.

Ethan rests against the ropes, his head hung down low, Sokolov's loud cheers in the opposite corner rubbing salt in the wound as he celebrates his victory.

I hurry to Ethan's corner, but he won't look at me, staring down at his shoes instead.

"You did the best you could," Dad says. "It was your first match, and that boy obviously has a lot more experience than you."

Ethan nods silently, not responding.

"I'm going to talk to the ref," Dad says, excusing himself.

Ethan undoes his gloves and takes off his hand wraps, still avoiding my eye.

"I'm proud of you," I tell him.

He removes his mouthguard, glancing at me with a *yeah, right* expression, before taking off his headgear too.

"I mean it. It's scary to try something new, but you did it."

"I just lost in front of a whole crowd of people."

"You got your liver punched. You have a good excuse."

He gives me a half-smile, his heart not really in it. "I wanted to look cool in front of you," he admits.

I climb up the ring, staying on the outside of the ropes. "You're the coolest person I know. And that guy you fought? With a last name like that, he was probably trained by KGB spies. It wasn't even fair."

His smile this time is more genuine. "Thanks, Pookie Bear." He leans in, kissing me softly.

"Anytime, Snookums."

Someone clears his throat from behind Ethan, and I realize Dad is standing there. How much of that did he hear? Or see?

"They're ready to call it," he says, though there's not much of a decision to make.

I jump down from the ring, Dad joining me as the ref asks the cornermen to clear out.

Ethan joins Sokolov in the center, both of them standing on either side of the ref.

"And your winner is," the announcer calls over the loudspeaker, "Dominic Sokolov."

The ref raises Sokolov's arm, and afterward, Ethan shakes his hand, the two of them clapping each other on the back. My heart fills with pride watching him be such a good sport about it.

"So, you and Ethan?" Dad asks beside me.

"Um, yeah." I guess he saw, then.

I go to stick my hands in my hoodie pocket, then remember I'm not wearing it today. Damn it.

"If you stay with him tonight, keep an eye on him. I don't think Sokolov knocked him hard enough in the head for a concussion, but you never know. And that hit on his side will need some attention."

"I'll take care of him," I promise. "But shouldn't you, I don't know, not encourage me to spend the night with a guy?"

He gives me a sheepish grin, rubbing at the back of his neck. "I've seen the way he looks at you. And he's a good guy. You could do a lot worse than him."

I watch Ethan, still in the ring posing for pictures the tournament photographer wants. "I love him. And he said he loves me, too."

Dad whistles low. "Well, shit. I didn't know it was serious."

My hackles rise. "You don't think anyone could be serious about me?"

"Hey, now. There you go getting defensive again." He crosses his arms over his chest, giving me a stern look. "I didn't say anything about that. But to be honest, I'm surprised you would get serious about anyone. I love you, but you push everyone away. You push me away."

There's hurt in his voice, enough to cause a pang in my chest.

Ugh. There go the feelings again, along with Ethan's voice in my ear saying *you should talk to him.*

"I'm sorry I push you away," I mumble, crossing my own arms. "But it's because you did the same when I was younger."

"What?" he asks, sounding genuinely confused.

"You wouldn't let me come live with you."

"The road's no place for a kid. I told you that."

Yeah, I know he did. I heard it too many times. "But I needed you."

"You were better off with your mother back home. Trust me."

I look up at the mess of rafters in the ceiling above us. "No, actually. I wasn't."

"Lexie…" he starts in a patronizing tone, but I'm sick of him not listening.

"She was a hardcore drug user," I interrupt him.

"What? No." He shakes his head, furrowing his brow. "I mean, she dabbled in a few things a long time ago, but she cleaned up her act when she got pregnant with you."

"Well, she apparently slipped back into the lifestyle once you left. It was a nightmare dealing with her."

He shuffles back a step, staring at me. "Why didn't you tell me?"

"She wouldn't let me. She monitored my phone calls to you, made me swear I wouldn't tell you or she'd take away my stuff. And you were hardly around anyway."

"I know, and I'm sorry." His chin drops to his chest. "I… I didn't like being around her either after we split. She was always asking for money, trying to get more than the child support payments I sent every month."

I didn't know he paid child support. Where'd that money go? Probably straight into her needle.

"If I'd known that was going on, though, I would have found a way to make it work having you with me. Lexie… I'm so sorry."

He wraps an arm around my shoulders, tugging me into his side, and I allow myself to accept his comfort, his apology, inhaling a shaky breath. I won't cry, though. I've done that way too much lately.

"Why didn't you tell me sooner?" he asks.

"Because I was still mad at you."

"How was I supposed to know you were mad if you never told me?"

"Fair point," I whisper.

"Is that how she… died?" he asks carefully. "Drugs? You were so adamant about not talking about it when it happened."

"Yes." I swallow compulsively, forcing the words out. "If I didn't talk about it, didn't think about it, I wouldn't have to relive it."

"Lexie." He pulls me into a bone-crushing hug, murmuring nonsensical apologies, and I cautiously loop my arms around his middle in return, squeezing my eyes shut.

Maybe I should have confided in him sooner. Leaned on him for support. I'm discovering more and more lately that it's okay to do that.

"Everything good?"

I open my eyes, finding Ethan there, finished with his stuff in the ring. God, he looks exhausted. "I told him about Mom."

Ethan nods in understanding, wincing as he holds a hand to his side.

"How is it?" I ask him. "Tender?"

He gives me a resigned half-smile. "Hurts like a motherfucker."

I need to get him home, then. "Dad, how about we talk about this more another time? You still offering that dinner at your place?"

I have no illusions that things are magically resolved between us. Not by a long shot. But it's a start. Maybe we can build on this to become actually close, the way I wanted us to be when I was a kid.

He lets go of me and nods, apologizing again for everything that happened, but I don't want him to get too caught up in that right now. He still has other boxers to coach today.

I walk Ethan out, taking his car keys from him when he keeps grimacing with each step, and drive us back to his house, drawing a warm bath for him when we get there.

"I don't do baths," he says skeptically, leaning heavily on the doorframe of the bathroom.

"Trust me. It'll help. And I stopped at the store yesterday before you picked me up and got these." I pull out the bag of Epsom salts I placed underneath the sink cabinet late last night and pour them into the tub. "The magnesium and sulfate will relax your muscles. I figured you'd need it, win or lose."

"Okay, I'll take a bath. If you join me."

I glance at the small tub. "First of all, you alone are barely going to fit in there. And secondly, you're in no shape for any kind of funny business tonight."

He shrugs, wincing again as he does so. "Thought I'd at least give it a shot."

"Come here." I step over to him, carefully removing his shirt, trying to cause the least amount of upset to his side. There's already a bruise forming over his ribcage, the area pinkish-red. By tomorrow, it'll be a nice purple.

Across his abdomen are more bruises, tiny and barely noticeable if I wasn't looking for them. "What are these?"

"I inject my insulin shots before meals during the day in my stomach. And in my thighs at night before bed."

My brain makes a quick connection. "Those alarms on your phone…"

"Were to remind me to take them. I'm never going to do it around you, so you don't have to worry."

I nod, hoping someday I can work past my trigger to needles, knowing he might need my help. What if he'd been knocked unconscious today in the ring? Who would have given him his insulin?

His phone rings, and he pulls it out of his shorts pocket, the display reading *Mom*.

"You take that," I tell him. "I'll finish drawing the bath."

He wanders to his room to answer the call, keeping the door cracked open. I catch snippets of their conversation but I try not to eavesdrop, busying myself with making sure the salts are dissolved and the water is warm enough without being scalding. I also fill up a cup from the kitchen and find two ibuprofen for him to take. He has to be sore.

He returns after a minute, shutting the door behind him, and after taking the medicine, he finishes disrobing, easing his way into the bath. I find a towel underneath the cabinet and roll it up, placing it under his head as a cushion.

"This is actually kind of… nice," he says, sinking further into the warm water. "We should light some candles next time. Put on some Yanni."

I roll my eyes, settling down beside the tub on the bath mat. "Did you make up with your mom?"

He sighs. "Yeah. She wanted to see how I'm doing and said she was sorry everyone ganged up on me yesterday. And I apologized too for not telling her sooner."

"I'm glad you were able to work things out."

He nods, resting his arm on the side of the tub, reaching for my hand and intertwining our fingers together. "She said she liked you. Invited us both to dinner next week." Wow, really? "And she won't be inviting Jordan. I guess she wasn't too impressed with Savannah."

That news shouldn't make me as happy as it does, but I can't help the wide smile that crosses my face.

He grins back, closing his eyes and relaxing in the water. "Thank you for doing this. I wouldn't have even thought to take a bath. I'd be in a fetal position on my bed without you."

"I like that I can do something for you. You do so much for me normally."

"I'm not keeping score."

"I know." I stroke my thumb over his palm. "And that's one of the things I love about you."

"Yeah?" A smug smile crosses his face. "What else do you love about me?"

I dip my fingertips in the bath, flicking water at him. "How humble you are."

"And gorgeous and athletic and charming and smart, right?"

I laugh, the sound echoing off the bathroom walls. "Did you memorize that?"

"Obviously. I've been riding high on that compliment for weeks."

He's so ridiculous. "Did what I think about you really matter that much back then?"

He brings my hand to his lips, kissing my knuckles. "Of course. You're my girl."

My smile softens, a pleasant warmth filling my chest. "I love you."

"Love you too."

I still can't believe how natural it feels to say that. And how much I mean it, too.

I never thought I'd be at this point, as comfortable and relaxed with a man as I am with him, but he makes it easy.

And I'm never letting him go.

Ever.

# EPILOGUE
## ETHAN

*Six Months Later*

"DR. PERKINS POSTED the accounting internships for the summer," Lexie says, spearing a bite of chicken and popping it in her mouth. "I'm going to apply tomorrow."

I poke at my salad, still not crazy about eating so many green things, but I've come around to the necessity of it since I need to eat better.

"Working on Marty's books for so long will give you a leg up," I say, eyeing the grilled chicken on her plate. Would she notice if I stole a piece?

"And I got an A in her Cost Accounting class last semester. There are only ten spots, but I think I have a good chance. Here." She pushes her plate toward me. "Just take some."

I grin, taking her up on her offer.

"Why do you keep ordering that when you hate it? Manuel makes good food that's healthy too." She points toward the back area of Kate's Kitchen, the cook visible through the open pass-through behind the long counter.

Thank God she gets an employee discount on meals here. And with regular shifts serving, she was even able to quit her bartending job at Element.

She has a point about my insistence on continuing to eat something I don't like, but there's a method to my madness. "Every time I order a salad, I think *this is the one. This is the salad that'll make me love salads.* But then, you know, it's not. It's just a boring salad."

"Stop torturing yourself. You want me to order you a piece of grilled chicken? You need to actually eat something before you train later."

I'm scheduled in an hour to go across the street and work with Lawrence, training for another tournament in three weeks. I've been doing better, even winning the last match I'd had two months ago. It'd been by the skin of my teeth, but a win is still a win. I won't be going pro anytime soon, but I'm enjoying it.

"Nah, it's fine." I shouldn't fill up too much, anyway. I can eat again later tonight. "Oh, Jordan texted me. He's got a new girlfriend. Wants us all to meet her at a family dinner on Friday."

She rolls her eyes. "What is this? The fourth one in three months? Where does he find these girls?"

He and Savannah hadn't lasted long after that fateful night he brought her home to meet the family—not that Lexie and I were too broken up about it.

"Some kind of girlfriend store?" I suggest. "Maybe on clearance? That's why they don't last long."

"Or maybe it's him," she mutters, taking another bite of chicken.

"That, too." She finally understands my general annoyance with my younger brother. He's family, though. What are you going to do?

"Oh, wait," Lexie says. "We already said we'd go to my dad's for dinner on Friday. So I guess we can't make it."

"Darn." She smiles at my blatant sarcasm. "And this one was probably *really* going to be the one."

My phone buzzes in my pocket, and I pull it out, seeing it's an email from Mia.

How does she even have my email address?

I skim her message, my brows popping up in surprise.

"What is it?" Lexie asks.

"Check it out." I hand my phone over to her across the table. "Mia found this in one of those psychology journals she subscribes to."

"*The Physiological Effects of Romantic Love*," she reads. "Wait, is this our study? The one we did last semester?"

"It must be. Dr. Clark and Justin are the two main authors of the paper."

She reads the article aloud as we finish up our food, though there are a few terms we don't understand, especially the parts related to the brain.

"So, basically, they determined that love has a significant effect on the way our bodies function?" I say when she's finished. "And they were paid how much to come up with that conclusion?"

"Well, we got paid too, so I'm not complaining. And I probably skewed the results of the first half of the study anyway."

"Nah, I know you were secretly in love with me the whole time."

Her lips tilt up at the corners. "Right."

I pick up my fork, circling it around the edge of my plate. "You know, Tyler and Mia were both accepted to Psych programs for grad school in Boston."

"Oh, wow. Good for them."

"So Tyler will be moving out soon."

"Okay."

Not exactly the response I was hoping for.

"So there's not really a reason for me to stay there anymore, and my lease with Tom is up soon, too."

She sets down her fork, seeing where I'm going with this now. "Actually, Isaac asked Travis to move in with him last week. I pushed it to the back of my mind, but Travis is planning on moving his stuff in before our lease is up in a few months."

Well, that certainly aligns with my plans.

"And what are you going to do?"

"I don't know," she whispers.

The obvious question lingers in the air, and I bite the bullet, taking a leap of faith. "Would you want to get a place together?"

She grabs her napkin, twisting it in her lap. "Are you ready for that?"

"Yes." There's no question in my mind.

Nervousness and interest play over her face. "It's a big step."

"It is," I agree. "But hear me out. We could get a dog. Skittles Junior, obviously."

She laughs, the apprehension leaving her. "No dog. I have enough trouble taking care of you."

"Fine, no dog. But yes to moving in together?"

She nods, a smile creeping over her lips. "Yes."

I let out a whoop, standing and pulling her out of the booth, and lay a long kiss on her.

"Hey, none of that."

I break away, spotting Kate, the owner of the diner, behind the counter shooing us apart. Turns out there was a Kate this whole time. And despite the frown on her face, she totally loves me.

"We have a good reason," I explain. "Lexie and I are moving in together."

The woman sighs. "Well, then. Mazel Tov."

"Congratulations," Manuel yells from the kitchen.

I pick up Lexie, spinning her around, and as I set her back down, she says, "You are so ridiculous." After this long together, she no longer tries to hide the amusement in her voice.

"I love you too, Pookie Bear."

She kisses me softly once more. "Love you, Snookums."

And as long as I have her love, that's all I need.

# ACKNOWLEDGMENTS

Thank you to my husband for always being my sounding board for every book's development. Your help with the boxing scenes in this one was crucial!

Thank you to my beta readers and editor for your support and encouragement. You help me more than you know!

Thank you to the bloggers, reviewers, bookstagrammers, and anyone spreading the word about this book. Your time and efforts are so appreciated! If you enjoyed the book (or even if you didn't!) please consider writing a review. I love to hear your thoughts.

And last (but not least) a huge thank you to my readers. I'm excited to continue writing in this world with Austin's story coming next!

# ABOUT THE AUTHOR

Allie is the author of the Suncoast University series, the Bishop Brothers series, and the Lessons Learned series. She lives in sunny Florida with her husband, daughter, and two cats. A librarian by day, she spends her nights writing happily ever afters. She enjoys reading, playing video games, and all things Disney.

Find out more on her website or follow on Instagram or Facebook.

Find Smartypants Romance online:
**Website:** www.smartypantsromance.com
**Facebook**: www.facebook.com/smartypantsromance/
**Goodreads:** www.goodreads.com/smartypantsromance
**Twitter:** @smartypantsrom
**Instagram:** @smartypantsromance
**Newsletter:** https://smartypantsromance.com/newsletter/

# ALSO BY ALLIE WINTERS

Want more Ethan and Lexie? Get a free sweet and sexy bonus epilogue featuring their engagement when you sign up here.

\*\*\*

**Set in Penny Reid's Educated Romance World, these angsty new adult romances explore human development in the heart and mind.**

### Under Pressure (Lessons Learned #1)

Mia knows stress. She's dealt with it her whole life. So when she gets an opportunity to run a psychology study to help her get into grad school, it should be no problem dealing with the prickly guy she suddenly finds herself paired with.

The one she had a secret crush on last year. The one who refuses to let anyone close. The one she's discovering by the day may have a softer side than he lets anyone else see…

Tyler knows stress. He's grappled with it for as long as he can remember. And just because he has to share credit with this girl on his new psychology study doesn't mean he has to be friends with her. Except she somehow keeps worming her way into his life. In school. In the boxing gym.

In his bed.

But everyone knows it's safer to keep to yourself. You can't hurt anyone that way. Even if it means giving up the best thing that's ever happened to him.

As things heat up in the Stress Lab, will this match be able to work together without disruption, or will this growing attraction between them eventually... combust?

Stay tuned for Austin's story coming in 2023!

\*\*\*

**The Bishop Brothers series is a contemporary romance trilogy featuring three sexy billionaire brothers who find love in Manhattan.**

### Resisting the Billionaire (Bishop Brothers #1)

- Gabriel - When I'm forced to make a deal with my father to marry the woman of his choosing for a business deal, I never expected to find someone I connect with. Someone who doesn't fawn all over me because I'm the heir to a billion dollar fortune. Someone who sees the real me. And someone I can't get enough of in turn.

There's only one problem—I can't have her. She's the wedding planner.

- Mackenzie - It's the chance of a lifetime—plan the wedding of a billionaire's son that'll put my event planning business on the map and get me out of debt. A no brainer, right?

Except the bride wants nothing to do with this arranged marriage. And as the groom and I get closer, the professional lines between us keep blurring until there's something there neither of us can deny. With my business on the line and our chemistry off the charts, I'm torn whether I should keep resisting the one person I never expected to fall for.


## Marrying the Billionaire (Bishop Brothers #2)

- Serena - Marrying the man of your dreams after crushing on him for the last decade should be cause for celebration. So why am I crying alone in the honeymoon suite on my wedding night? Because there's just one problem—it's a fake marriage. Purely for appearances as part of a business deal between our fathers' companies.

But I can't sit idly by pretending this is only a platonic relationship, especially as sparks begin to fly between us. So what will I have to do to convince my stoic Prince Charming I want him for real? And what will I risk along the way?

- Archer - The plan is simple—act like a husband in love publicly after I foolishly got myself involved in this fake marriage, and behind closed doors keep things separate. But the longer we continue this charade attending events and staging selfies, the more I'm unsure what's fake and what's not, especially when things start to heat up in private.

As the successor to my father's billion dollar company, work has been my life. Focusing on my job has never been harder, though, when there's a temptress living in my guest bedroom. What are the chances this business deal of a marriage could turn into the real thing? The last person I ever expected to fall for is… my wife.


## Seducing the Billionaire (Bishop Brothers #3)

- Connor - It's all on me now. The billion-dollar company I just inherited from my late father. The public eye waiting for me to slip up. The pressure of keeping it all together.

At least there's one bright spot in my life—my new assistant, Emma. My dream woman come to life if I didn't know better.

It's too bad the paparazzi would have a field day if they discovered something going on between us. I can't afford for anything to jeopardize my new role as CEO of Bishop Industries.

Even if she is temptation personified.

- Emma - It was supposed to be a simple assignment. Become Connor Bishop's new assistant and convince him to buy my father's company, Montague Media. So how do I do that? By any means necessary, according to my dad—including seduction. Otherwise, I lose everything.

But no one told me how hard it would be to seduce a billionaire who insists on acting like a perfect gentleman, especially when real feelings begin to emerge. At what point do I stop the charade and tell him who I really am? Before or after I fall in love with him?

\*\*\*

**Check out the Suncoast University series – Four steamy new adult romances that will have you swooning.**

### Let Go (Suncoast University #1)

- Charlotte - Putting yourself out there? Getting close to others? No, thanks, I'll pass. It's safer to keep to yourself. I've learned that lesson the hard way. So when I accidentally tell the muscled hunk I've been secretly drooling over all semester how I really feel about him, it's not like I meant for him to take an interest in me. I don't want a boyfriend. Not even when it turns out he's so much more than just brawn.

My goal for so long has been simple—get into grad school. And when I get a dream TA position at the beginning of the new semester that will help me achieve just that, I'll have to forget about him now that he's my student. Easy, right?

- Luke - I can't get her out of my head—the shy, sexy brunette that's trying so hard to keep me at a distance. I can be patient, though. Anything to break through that reserve and get under her shields. But just when I thought I've succeeded, she's off-limits. Say hello to my new TA. Even though I'm hot for teacher, there's no way she would risk this opportunity. Right?

### Watch Me (Suncoast University #2)

- Samantha - I need a place to stay ASAP when my living arrangements fall through before college starts. And I shouldn't have any trouble resisting my new roommate… despite how much I find myself connecting with him.

- Levi - I have absolutely no interest in the beautiful blonde living in the room next door. She's not my type. Not even when it turns out she's nothing like I expected.

She's only here for the summer, so it shouldn't be a big deal to act on this attraction before she leaves. It doesn't have to mean anything, right?

## No One Else (Suncoast University #3)

- Evan - I messed up. I admitted to the girl of my dreams I'm in love with her, only to have her run away. Why don't they ever warn you things like that happen?

Now that we're paired up for a class project, I have to figure out a way to keep things from being weird between us. I can't lose her again.

- Natalie - We shared a kiss the night after I broke up with my boyfriend of three years. A heart-stopping, panty-melting kiss I still dream about. But I wasn't ready then for anything more.

Now that I am, he's unavailable. What will it take to get us both on the same page - and stay there?

## First and Only (Suncoast University #4)

- Jake - When my dreams of going pro are crushed by a career-ending knee injury, I have to figure out how to use brains over brawn for the first time to graduate college. Enter Eden, my new Biology tutor. Except she doesn't want to be paid in the usual way. She wants me to give her relationship tutoring to attract a guy she likes. But this shy, awkward brainiac is turning out to be so much more than I expected. In the words of a scientist, will this equal exchange turn out to be more than the sum of its parts?

- Eden - Hot guys don't fall for nerds like me. It's just a fact of life—one I've come to accept like gravity or thermodynamics. So even though others think Jake's interested in me, I know it's just this tutoring deal we have going on. I show him the electron transport system and he shows me how to kiss. Simple as that. There's no sense in getting my hopes up, even as I realize this ex-jock and I fit together in a way I never thought possible. Rarely does an equal exchange turn out to be more than the sum of its parts. Even when I desperately want it to.

# ALSO BY SMARTYPANTS ROMANCE

*Weights of Wrath by M.E. Carter (#4)*

## Common Threads Series

*Mad About Ewe by Susannah Nix (#1)*

*Give Love a Chai by Nanxi Wen (#2)*

*Key Change by Heidi Hutchinson (#3)*

## Educated Romance
## Work For It Series

*Street Smart by Aly Stiles (#1)*

*Heart Smart by Emma Lee Jayne (#2)*

*Book Smart by Amanda Pennington (#3)*

*Smart Mouth by Emma Lee Jayne (#4)*

## Lessons Learned Series

*Under Pressure by Allie Winters (#1)*

*Not Fooling Anyone by Allie Winters (#2)*

## Out of this World
## London Ladies Embroidery Series

Neanderthal Seeks Duchess (#1)